I0628635

Objects in View

Lela Markham

Published by Breakwater Harbor Books

A Word from Lela Markham

Thank you for reading my book. If you enjoyed it, please take a moment to leave me a review at your favorite retailer. Only with your help can writers like me reach more readers. I appreciate it!

In the 18 months since I published *Life As We Knew It* in 2015, some lovely people have contacted me concerning the book, complimenting me on the themes of faith and libertarianism found in its pages. I appreciate your support. While not a work of Christian literature, I have tried to be true to my faith and the beliefs of the larger evangelical Christian body while also showing Christians who make mistakes and act badly from time to time. I will continue that effort.

Transformation Project is at root a polemic against our rigged system of elites telling all of us "lessers" what to do while failing miserably on so many levels in their attempt to centrally manage the society. I hope I present the arguments in an entertaining way.

In *Life As We Knew It*, I introduced a president who came to power through a rigged system and in *Objects in View*, I showed his appointees attempting to manipulate horrific events to their personal benefit. You might wonder where I'm headed in *A Threatening Fragility*. Things can only get worse, which means a better story for you, right?

I've called this series a "cozy apocalyptic". It doesn't focus on major events and world-stage actors. The town of Emmaus can only react to what is decided in other locations. My heroes aren't out to save the world. They just want to save their town. Yet, I also believe that the mighty mustard plant grows from a tiny seed. It is the reaction of the people of Emmaus to events beyond their control that will determine the future they live in.

Ultimately, that is the same power that you and I have. We can't affect what goes on in Washington DC. If the last few elections haven't proven that to you, you haven't been paying attention. Maybe things will be different in November, but I doubt it. The system is rigged and the elites in the two major parties always win. But, we can affect things right where we live, by educating ourselves and our children, by encouraging our neighbors to do the same. Our rescue will not come from whomever takes the White House, but it might just come from us.   Lela Markham

Thanks!

This book is dedicated to my lifelong friend and mentor Richard "Dick" Vance Underwood who went to be with the Lord in the week before the completion of the draft of this book. The character of Dick Vance is a good representation of my friend, who I will miss, but who I expect to find canoeing a heavenly river when I get there. Dick, when we draw up to the bank, we need to discuss "extensive redemption." John 3:16

This book contains short snippets of lyrics from the Eagles, Sean McDonald, Mercy Me, Keith Green, John Newton, Eliza Hewitt and Horatio Spafford. Although copyright laws allow my very incidental use, I want to thank them for writing amazing music and lyrics.

Table of Contents

"We are not to expect to be translated
from despotism to liberty in a featherbed."

Thomas Jefferson

Objects in View

Book 2

Transformation Project

Prologue

We were going along living life. There was nothing extraordinary about that day. We were drinking mochas, commuting on interstates, talking on cell phones, eating in restaurants, chatting on the Internet, making money and spending ourselves into debt. In a million parks across the nation, women tickled their babies' toes and men tossed the Frisbee for their dogs. We were all tied up in the latest reality show or political drama, downloading our personal playlist from the Internet, and ordering baubles from afar. The President was talking on television that night and a lot of us were gathered around to absorb his latest lies.

And, then, suddenly, it all ended. There was no warning. The life we knew just ended. In the days that followed we learned the details – the number of people dead, the number of cities decimated, the millions of connections that were severed, destabilizing the fragile network of our society. That devastation did not touch us because we were rural, but what followed would transform our lives in unexpected ways.

The coming days would redefine who we were. We'd stop being afraid of the paper tigers the elites used to distract us and start concentrating on the very real dangers that had been lurking all around us.

But first, we had to learn that rescue was not coming and that we needed to save ourselves.

JT Delaney

End of What We Knew

New York City, Columbus Circle
Wednesday Evening

*T*he lights of New York dazzled.

Katherine Sullivan paused for a last look around Columbus Circle before stepping into Robert, the restaurant. The sun wasn't down yet, so the lights were not at their brightest, but she wanted to eat before she went to a concert on Carnegie Hall.

I hate doing this all on my own. Joseph should be here.

As the hostess showed her to a table, she tried to remind herself that Joseph had promised ... *promised* ... to be here tomorrow night. He was doing a good fatherly thing in taking their daughter to the doctor tomorrow morning. It had been a miserable three months for Allison stuck in a brace and Joseph did not want her to have to wait longer. That they had planned this trip six months ago did not mean he was choosing their daughter over his wife. Katherine *knew*, but it was hard to reconcile her solitariness with her knowledge.

She ordered the watercress soup and duck breast with snow peas and a single glass of Pinot Grigio, feeling quite decedent to be drinking before the sun was down. She reasoned that it would be dark before she left. There was a delicious pleasure in knowing that tongues would be wagging in Emmaus if she drank wine in public before 5 o'clock.

Sirens swept by the corner. Hardly anyone in the restaurant seemed to notice at first. Katherine remembered what it had been like when she lived in a big city. The sirens were background noise, like birdsong in Emmaus. Few noticed and fewer cared.

If Joseph is here on Friday, maybe he'd agree to the Roof Garden at the Met. Oh, I do hope Ren hasn't delayed him. What does Ren care that Joseph had plans? We're all just serfs to the great Ren Sullivan.

Her phone beeped.

I'm thinking of you. Have some bomboloni. J

She had planned to finish the pasta, but Joseph was right. She deserved a treat for being a good sport. Katherine waved the waiter down and asked for a coffee to go and bomboloni.

Great idea. I did it. Miss you.

When she hit SEND, the phone spun for a few seconds and then announced "No Signal."

That's odd. Well, probably just a glitch. I'll try again in a few minutes.

Katherine thanked the waiter for the check, gave him a generous tip and gathered her things to set out for Carnegie. The lights from the sirens were still flickering over by the park. There seemed to be a lot of them.

Hopefully, it won't affect the concert.

She stepped out of the entrance. From the corner of her eye, she saw a blue uniform move abruptly in her direction. A gun barrel filled her view and a loud male voice ordered her to the pavement. Terrified, she obeyed, but apparently not quick enough because rough hands shoved her face forward into the coffee-splashed concrete.

"Don't move. Stay down." She turned her head so she could breathe and saw that people all up and down the sidewalk lay prone with uniformed cops pointing guns at their heads.

My god, what is happening?

Above her, the lights of New York were in full brightness, but Katherine no longer noticed.

Boots on the Ground

Wichita, Kansas
Wednesday Evening - Two hours later

Mike Biurrarena y Sanchez forced his fingers to release from the webbing as other soldiers began to grab their gear and file toward the back of the plane where the tail door would soon drop.

Ridiculous that flying still made him nervous. How many flights had he taken? He shouldered his pack and slung his AR-15. Warm air rushed into his face as he followed other men downward.

Men with wands waited at the bottom of the ramp. Mike didn't recognize the equipment, but the odd clicking noises reminded him of Geiger counters. There'd been rumors in the air that something "big" was happening, but the details had been sketchy when the cell phone coverage cut out.

Nuclear? Dios mio!

The day's heat still radiated off the tarmac while a huge tow truck pulled a passenger jumbo toward the far end of the terminal where the runway lights illuminated a string of passenger jets parked wingtip to wingtip in what was usually a no-man's security area.

"Sanchez, Vasquez, Carlson, with me."

Mike recognized Crispin, who was already surrounded by a dozen black-clothed men with duffels resting at their feet and various semi-auto rifles slung over their backs. Crispin had been the CO on two of his last three assignments. A competent leader, ex-Special Forces, given to ironic jokes that Mike usually didn't get until Ric laughed. He'd have to pay closer attention without Ric to be the smart one.

"Men, thank you for getting on that plane. Do you know what is going on?"

They didn't, really. They'd sat on the tarmac of a backwater airfield forever before they'd been given the scramble order, but no reason had been given for any of it. The cell phone chatter had been suppressed early in the flight. Crispin sighed then stood a little straighter.

"At precisely 7 pm Eastern Standard Time, terrorists struck an as-yet-undetermined number of US cities with low-tech nuclear weapons." He let that sink in a moment. Everyone looked stunned. "I know many of you have families and friends to be concerned about, but we have a mission to accomplish. I only know that Denver and Kansas City were hit. There are others, but the information is sketchy right now. Our job here in Wichita is to maintain order and protect the governor, who is relocating here because Topeka is considered too close to Kansas City. As soon as we can get communications channels cleared, we will let you call your families."

Mike remembered to take a breath. A memory of Ric saying "Don't be near any big cities on Wednesday" surfaced. How had he known? *Pay attention to the briefing, a voice that sounded a lot like Ric ordered.*

Someone at the front of the group asked a question Mike had been too distracted to hear.

"The techs say we're not in any danger here. Denver and Kansas City are both gone, but this sort of radiation heats up really fast and then dissipates as it goes out from the source. It doesn't get up into the atmosphere easily. We may get orders to seek shelter from time to time over the next few days depending on the weather and wind. Don't hesitate. Get underground or into concrete as soon as possible. You will be issued suits. They are not adequate for long-term exposure, but for short term they'll be fine."

A US Army truck drove by and Mike raised his hand.

"Are we working with the military here?"

"For now, we are. Someone with a uniform asks you to do something, do it. I'll let you know when that changes. These are your assignments for this evening." He began calling off names and orders. "Sanchez, process statements at the National

Guard trailer. They just brought in a couple of NGs who were shot at the Kansas-Colorado border. Could be terrorists, could be pissed off locals."

Mike sighed. He really wasn't a statement-taking sort of soldier. Eric had always been good at that and as partners they'd often been assigned to such duties, but Mike had been there to watch Ric's back, not ask questions. He worked his way to the front of the line to ask for clarification and, hopefully, a new assignment.

"I heard your buddy retired," Crispin said.

"He took a break, anyways. Good timing. While we're dodging nuclear fallout, he's lounging on a beach in Thailand. Sir, I'm much more of a walk-the-point kind of guy than the take-a-statement guy."

"I need you where I need you. Take a notebook and pen." He leaned in close. "I don't want to spread this around. There is something going on out there. I've got chatter on my radio that there's something building out that way. We need the intel."

Mike gave a semblance of a salute to show respect for a commander who could probably take him out with his thumb and forefinger and headed in the direction indicated. *Ric always said this was not brain surgery. I should have paid more attention. It's just asking questions. I can do this.*

Knight Industries had already uploaded a map of the facilities to his company phone, so he quickly pulled up the file and located his target destination and started on a surreal journey through the terminal. National Guard and Knight Industry uniforms openly carrying semi-auto rifles was not a new sight for him. He'd seen it in Miristan, but this had been a working America airport three hours before. TSA uniforms were guarding the entrances to concourses filled with stressed looking civilians intermixed with flustered airline staff. Mike exited the main entrance and crossed the parking lot, pausing to let tow trucks pass. They were clearing out the lot for something big. He presented his credentials to the National Guardsmen at the door of their trailer and stepped up into a high tech command center.

They had been expecting him in this pleasantly air-conditioned sanctum of surveillance, so he didn't have much time to marvel at the telemetry readouts. How much safer would his job be if the Knights knew what the government knew? After he surrendered his sidearm and AR to an MP, an E6 ushered him into the back of the trailer where a young soldier was sitting on a table edge, gingerly pulling on a uniform shirt over a rib girdle. The bruises radiating up from the white elastic said it all. Mike had taken a few in the vest in his career. He'd cracked a rib once. It was better than the alternative, but it was still the most painful injury he'd ever experienced, far more than the graze across his left bicep he'd taken in South America.

"Private Lawson, this is the man who will debrief you," the E6 said and slid out of the exam room, followed quickly by the medic who had been cleaning up the first aid supplies.

"Mike Sanchez."

"Kris Lawson." Lawson was maybe 20, a young guy with an earnest expression who was probably paying for college by playing soldier. He was lucky to be alive.

"Where'd this happen?"

"I70 at the state border."

"Who did it?"

"There were two guys. The first one came on his own, looking for the second. Cocky son-of-a-bitch, just headed into the cars as if we'd given permission."

"Military?"

"No. His credentials were CSA with a Homeland stamp."

"I just got thrown in here, so forgive my ignorance. CSA?"

"Central Security Agency. They're sort of a combination of the NSA and the CIA. And don't feel bad. I didn't know that until I checked his credentials and my CO explained it."

"So this guy was a spook?"

"Maybe. He was my first, so I don't really know what to say about it."

"Why were you holding cars at the Colorado-Kansas border?"

Lawson frowned, then shook his head, wincing slightly at the pull on his ribs.

"It didn't make sense, actually. Division ordered that we hold traffic coming out of Denver to screen them for radiation. Okay, that makes sense, but then we weren't given the order to start letting them through. This guy – Delaney – he said he was looking for someone in the containment zone and then he just barged right in. A little while later, they reappeared at the roadblock. The other guy got in the car. Hell of a driver. Delaney – he spoke with us – but then all of a sudden, he shot us."

Mike picked up the Kevlar vest beside Lawson, prying a slug loose with the edge of his SOG.

"Us?"

"Jordan – Rob Jordan. He was just bruised, so he stayed on duty."

"Looks like a 9," Mike observed of the flattened slug.

"Yeah."

"What's your head gear look like?"

"I'd say he aimed for our chests. It was like Rogue's Gallery. Two to the chest and then, while we were on the ground and before anyone could relieve us, he was rabbiting."

"So, he wasn't trying to kill you, just knock you down?" Lawson nodded, attempted a shrug and regretted it. Mike typed Lawson and Jordan's names into his phone. "You said his last name was Delahanty?"

"Delaney." Mike typed that.

"What did he look like?"

"Dark hair and eyes, heavy tan." He groaned, reaching into a cargo pocket. "Here. I snapped a picture to send to my CO." He opened his album and turned the screen so Mike could see the photo.

For a moment there was no air in the room. Mike thought of several things to say, then cleared his throat and asked to take the phone. The photo was paired with a snap of Delaney's ID. Mike emailed both of the photos to himself, then deleted the photos from the young soldier's phone. With luck, he'd not notice the cover-up before Mike was across camp.

"I think that just about covers it. I'll get the data guys on trying to identify him. You heal up. You ought to get some R&R for that."

"Doubt it, not with what's going on right now." As Mike had hoped, he slid the phone back into his pocket. "You got family?"

"Most people do." You couldn't trust people, so he didn't generally share with strangers, not even as thoughts of Alicia and the small swelling in her lower abdomen flowed through his mind. Kris seemed like a nice guy, but you just couldn't trust people. It was why he used his mom's maiden name for everything work-related and his real surname for everything personal. "Worried about your folks?"

"Nah, my Dad and Mom will be fine. My girlfriend and little girl, though ... they live here in Wichita, but I can't go see them."

"Wichita looks like a pretty safe place to be right now."

14

"She says she's okay, but …."

"Yeah, I get it. I'd better get back to work. Thanks for the help, Kris."

Mike headed out of the trailer, pausing in the short corridor to listen to an open radio that was broadcasting the sounds of a firefight. The E6 from earlier spotted him and directed him toward the exit.

"What's going on there?" Mike asked while retrieving his sidearm and AR.

"Can't tell you." The E-6 smelled of fear as he slammed the door in Mike's face. Mike hesitated in the warm fall evening. Should he go tell Crispin that Eric Faraday was near and going under the name of Shane Delaney or should he keep that information to himself? A true friend would keep it to himself … *or tell you that he was a secret agent.* Mike needed to work out that dilemma first.

He passed a squad of Army soldiers walking with such a purpose that one of them had the temerity to brush shoulders with Mike. He glanced over his shoulder as they leveled their rifles at the National Guardsmen before the trailer. The young weekend warriors relented quickly. Mike kept walking, hardly flinching when he heard gunfire from within the trailer a moment later. He counted three shots. One for each MP he'd seen and probably one for the E6. That should be enough to bring the rest to heel. Most of the soldiers had surrendered their weapons upon entry.

In a world gone mad, it made a great deal of sense that professional soldiers would take the place of weekend warriors. Shooting them seemed counterproductive, but he could understand needing to gain control over the situation. He hoped K. Lawson had not fought and so survived, but Mike already couldn't remember his first name, so he knew it wouldn't matter to his life in the least. What would matter more was the lesson he'd just learned. He'd never relinquish his weapons again. *This may not be Miristan, but the same rules apply now. The military is not on our side here.*

His radio crackled.

"Knight Industry, assignment update. All unassigned Knight Industry operatives report to the parking garage ground floor. If you are at an assigned post, hold. All unassigned Knight Industry operatives, report to the ground floor of the parking garage."

Mike turned around to orient himself. The parking garage was unmistakable. He thought he heard gunfire from inside the terminal. An MRAP pulled up to the main entrance and Army soldiers wearing assault gear formed up outside the doors. Two Knights settled in beside him as he walked toward the parking garage.

"What's going on?" Jacobson asked. Mike had served with him in Miristan.

"Looks like an interdepartmental battle," the other Knight said. Mike didn't know him, but his name patch read KRICZEK.

"We should probably just stay out of it," Mike said. When did he start thinking like Ric? Or had Ric been thinking like Shane Delaney?

Crispin called Mike to him. There were two others gathered around him. Other Knights went to other COs.

"Good to see you were out of the command center before the Army got there. You overhear anything about what's going on?"

"About an hour ago, there was an incident with someone from the CSA out on the Colorado border. The guardsman I interviewed had some painkillers in him. He didn't know names. I'm not sure the CSA agent was out of line. From what I overheard in the command center, the Army is scrubbing civilians coming out of Denver, the National Guard is resisting, and it appears the Army is trying to bring the National Guard under more direct control."

A moment of shocked silence ensued. Crispin's rock-solid face rippled with a subtle human emotion. He'd served for 20 years. Of course he had loyalties. And then he stiffened his spine.

"We don't care. The Army and the National Guard can fight it out. We were brought in here to protect the governor and maintain civilian order. Same rules apply here as applied in Miristan. We cooperate with the US military, but we do not work for them. In connection with the public, remember, this is the United States, not Miristan. These are Americans. So long as they are not actively shooting

17

at you, they should not be considered a threat unless they meet a certain profile. Your phones have surveillance footage of the suspects for the New York bombers. It appears we're dealing with Middle Easterners."

Mike looked at the two men in overalls hauling what looked like helium tanks across a crowded concrete plaza. Although the CCTV footage was grainy, the two men were both dark with short beards.

"The guy in the back could be Hispanic," he remarked. Being the only Hispanic in the group at the moment meant he was the only one free to point out the obvious.

"The company they were working for provided their names. Robert Noreen and Francis Xavier. Noreen's mother was from Syria. Xavier's background before a stint in prison is unknown. Yes, he could be Hispanic. Intel says there have been some huge conversions among the Hispanic prison population over the last five to 10 years. Memorize those faces. Consider what they might look like without beards or with their heads shaved. It's unlikely they are going to show up here, but we need to be on the lookout, just in case. Sanchez, head over to Level 2. We're processing the people there before releasing them. You're working with Warrant Officer Bradford. Polaski, Level 2."

Mike headed toward the terminal again. He was already in motion before he realized that he'd made his decision about Ric. He had a right to keep information to himself. He was paid for his services.

He wasn't an Army slave who couldn't use his own judgment. Besides, Ric could be here by tomorrow. It wouldn't be so bad to have him at his back in this insanity. Who cared if he moonlighted for the government?

The Rain

Emmaus Kansas, Jericho Hotel
Friday

Silence woke him. He blinked into the darkness, disoriented, tasting the staleness of the air, sensing the concrete a couple of inches from his face and the echoing chamber at his back. He remembered and rolled onto his back, listening for the patter of rain on the concrete roof. The growl of a dog-day storm had drifted off to the south while he slept and now the rain ceased to fall. Its absence deafened him in this dark prison.

Halfway there, he thought.

Could he last that long?

Shane had known sheltering would mean an uncomfortable time underground without fresh air. The alternative had never occurred to him until after he'd closed the door. Death by radiation poisoning was too slow to be attractive.

Or had been, before he shut out the light and fresh air. Contemplating the carbon dioxide levels made radiation poisoning seem almost preferable.

He'd lost track of the time, refusing to waste battery power by checking his cell, but he had slept, so he figured it was morning.

He guessed 12 hours since he had last peed. The bruises on his face were less tender. Maybe he'd slept longer than he'd thought. Or else the aspirin had been more effective than he'd supposed. Or maybe the lack of air was starting to affect him.

Did Rigby set this room up? Do I trust that Dylan was telling the truth? Am I losing my mind? Did I do it and not remember? I did smack my head.

His stomach growled. He needed light to prepare an MRE, but light held its own dangers. He had opted for darkness because it was less crazy making. Would it have been easier if he had sheltered with Alex and Keri at the farm? No, seven people in the root cellar would be much worse. They'd expect him to be civil when all he wanted was to retreat in his misery and wait it out ... which was pretty much what he was doing now. Except he was hungry and he needed to urinate.

Hunger was a good sign. Alone and trapped might have turned badly for him, but he wasn't hungry for the barrel of his gun. He was dreaming of MRE gourmet.

He unzipped the sleeping bag and fumbled around on the floor under the cot to find his cell. He'd slept 16 hours. He supposed that was possible given how little sleep he'd had over the last week – the last month – and smacking his head. His knee still hurt. His leg was stiff as he stood, using the cell phone lantern to guide him to the bucket. When he was done, he hit the lantern again to inspect the purple bruise. No permanent damage. He still chose to sit on the cot to prepare an MRE rather than kneel on the floor. The wan light of the gravity lamp hardly penetrated the darkness by the generator and day tank though he could make out his drying clothes hung on the pipes. He donned the jeans and t-shirt, but not the over-shirt. The bunker had grown warmer and moister even since he'd woke up. Warm, moist and close were the enemies of claustrophobics who needed to stay indoors.

The almost edible food relieved the mind-numbing boredom for a moment. In his initial investigation, he'd discovered his guitar and case were in the emergency shelter. He noodled with that for a little while. He'd not played much in the last year. Although he still had calluses, he couldn't play for hours anymore. He set it aside when his fingertips became tender.

Seconds multiplied like amoebas. If he'd planned this, he would have brought a book. Apparently Rigby was not a reader. What was that file folder on the table? The gravity light turned off. The advantage of sheltering with Alex would have been the entertainment value of other humans. On the other hand, he could pee in private.

His mind turned toward the terrorist attack. Human beings could be counted on to be horrible to one another, but 30 million people in a matter of minutes was beyond even his low opinion of humanity.

Who would do that? And how to coordinate a dozen separate attacks and not trigger any alarms?

He could power up the tablet and try to get some information, but recharging the batteries needed the generator and the generator smell would probably push him over the claustrophobic edge. A commitment to lasting out the radiation left him chasing his thoughts in circles around his now wide-awake brain. *Who? How? Why?*

Time ticked by. He dozed and dreamed ... of Miristan and an interpreter he'd been more than friends with, of Marnie telling him she'd married Cai, and the weighing look in the eyes of the people he'd met again for the first time since his return to town.

They'd hate me if they knew who I've become.

The air grew suffocating. He reset the gravity light and went to inspect the file folder. Land deeds in Joel Rhys' name. The attached maps showed coordinates just to the west of town. Rigby had thought of everything, as if he fully expected everyone to survive this thing.

She materialized on the edge of his vision, causing him to flinch.

"No, you don't belong here!" he snapped. Knowing she came when he was alone and unable to distract himself, he'd unloaded the guns and stripped them, but that would only slow him down, not stop him. "You are not real," he insisted. She'd come before since he'd been in the bunker, and he knew what she wanted. It was the same every time, but he'd made promises and he meant to keep them. He'd opted for darkness because she never spoke and the smothering darkness was better than her dark-robed figure and accusing eyes.

He disconnected the weight from the gravity light and vision faded. *How could the first 18 hours pass in a moment and the last hour be four days long?* He hummed softly to himself. Eventually, his heart stopped hammering and he no longer tasted gun oil. His head rolled and he snapped awake. Was the CO_2 level so high that he was being poisoned? He put the weight back on the gravity light, lit a match and watched it burn.

I'm not the canary in the coal mine. It's all in my head. God, it's hot!

Surprisingly, he had bars even within the concrete tomb – uh, generator room. He wiped sweat from his face and considered texting Rigby. No, it was supposed to be email this time. That meant the tablet. *Not yet.*

The boiler-room/bunker began to cool off. The sun must have gone down. He slept and dreamed of bands of radiation victims turning into zombie hordes. He lost count of how many he killed because his gun never ran out of bullets. When he started to recognize some of the zombies as family members, he woke up with a bellow.

Thirty-two hours! Two gallons of water. How many hours of sleep? He'd eaten two MREs for four meals. One entree had been decent. The other had good sides. Neither beat a hand-pressed burger with a cold Coke. It was cooler now, so he did 50 pushups and 100 sit-ups, then shaved, brushed his teeth and washed his underarms. Then he stared into darkness some more. *Thirty million people in the initial attacks, but how many people in the aftermath? Double that?* The first deaths were kinder perhaps than the latter ones – the people who didn't have concrete or dirt to put between them and the fallout that would slowly cook them from the inside out. Parents watching their children die, husbands watching their wives --. He powered up the tablet and immediately saw the icon that said he had a message from Rigby.

First, sorry Dylan startled you. He was supposed to make sure you knew about the boiler room, not nearly break your neck. Rigby 7:05 pm Thursday

Most of the fallout passed to the south of you. Rigby 9:16 pm Friday

Anything after 30 hours ought to be no more rads than a dental x-ray. By 40 hours, it will be no worse than a transatlantic flight. Your failure to reply is making me nervous. Rigby 4:27 am Saturday

I'm okay. No harm done. So it's safe to go out now? Shane 4:49 am Saturday

Safe enough Rigby 4:55 am Saturday

Shane trusted Rigby, but not fully. He opened the Internet through a secure government channel and logged into a NOAA website that confirmed Rigby's contention about the weather. He wondered briefly that NOAA was still operating. Silver Springs, Maryland was practically in DC. Of course NOAA's satellites didn't require headquarters to operate.

He located the wireless network at Emmaus City Hall. A teacher from the school had rigged a Geiger counter on the roof that fed into a laptop in the bomb shelter. Shane stared at the report. The rad levels had gotten to levels worth being concerned about, but not an imminently fatal dose, and they'd been down within a comfortable range for nearly five hours.

So why isn't anyone blowing the storm siren?

Shane investigated with the tablet as much as he could. He found the wireless network at the clinic. It didn't take too much to find the password – 1745MainStreet. *Yeah, no one could have figured that out!* Cai had sent a message to the science teacher an hour ago asking if the levels had dropped yet. There'd been no reply, so he'd sent another message 10 minutes ago. The lack of response didn't bode well for the people under City Hall. Maybe they were all asleep, but … eventually he'd have to risk it. Someone had to be the first one to venture out into this new world and see the aftermath of a world gone insane.

He messaged Cai, asked his situation.

Warm and close. I think I get what you feel now. There's been no reply from Marv or Bart. I don't want to panic people, but I'm not sure how much more time we've got. I think the air handling system is not doing its job. So what do we do?" Cai 5:12 a.m.

Shane knew the answer. Someone had to take the risk. He delayed. Funny how the thought of frying in your own skin could make a claustrophobic embrace a life inside concrete with no air. Of course hiding was against his basic nature.

Someone has to take the chance. If you're wrong, you fry and not quickly. It could take weeks to die at low levels. Be sure. Be very sure! And, you do not have to live with it. You can choose an easier death. Be sure. Be very sure!

It only took a quarter-hour for Shane to decide what needed to be done.

I'll be guinea pig. Source says the rad levels down. If don't hear from in 2-3 hrs, assume wrong." Shane 5:31 am

And do what? Cai 5:32 am

Shane hesitated. Good question, but ....

IDK. Use own judgment. Shane 5:37 am

He donned his shoes and shirt, reassembled and reloaded the guns, then stood at the door thinking for a long while. He finished the bits and pieces of an MRE, drank some water, peed and then stood at the door thinking for a long time. He checked the tablet again, convincing himself that this was not a foolish move, and then he strode to the door and flung it open, went to the door on the other side of the vestibule and strode out into the warm glow of a glorious September dawn.

Black Shirts

New York City, Casa Blanca Hotel
Saturday Morning

Katherine Sullivan paused just outside the door of the Casa Blanca. The bright lights of Times Square still blinked and dazzled, but the street was mostly deserted. The shelter-in-place order had been lifted this morning, but the police presence was still heavy. Mixed in with the New York City blue uniforms were men in black cargo pants with black assault rifles at the ready. She'd never expected to see anything like it on an American street.

Stanley, the doorman, smiled at her. He'd been very friendly and outgoing before the terrorist attack, but in the third day of the siege, his demeanor was wearing thin.

"Morning, Ms. Sullivan."

"You haven't gone home."

"The bridges and subways are closed and I live in Brooklyn. My relief can't get here, so ...."

"Is your family okay?"

"I've spoken to them and they're fine. Yours?"

"I don't know. They're in Kansas. I've tried to call, but the long distance is down. Ren Sullivan can afford to keep his family safe."

"Aren't you family?"

"I am, but I'm not there and he doesn't have global reach ... I think. At least my daughter and husband are safe, and really, the Casa Blanca seems safe too."

Stanley lit a cigarette, then offered her one. She was surprised at how much she wanted one. It had been years. When she turned it down, he smiled and put the pack away.

"How old's your daughter?"

"Fifteen. You have kids?"

Down the street, one of the men in black was staring at them and speaking into his headset.

"I have three ... a boy and twin girls."

"How old are they?"

His boy was 12 and the twins were eight. While he spoke, the black-suited soldier (she supposed he was some sort of soldier) was joined by a camouflage-clad one. Stanley followed her gaze.

"They're everywhere," he told her. "Supposedly they're keeping us safe."

"Do you feel safe?" She rubbed her arms, remembering the smell of gun oil as the black rifle had hovered inches above her head.

"No." They laughed without mirth. "I served in the 2nd Gulf War and this reminds me a lot of the streets of Baghdad."

"I was thinking Brussels, Madrid or Paris, but you're right. It reminds me of a warzone."

She'd feared death when she'd been prone on the sidewalk and that fear had not gone away as she'd been corralled with hundreds of others and questioned sharply. What's your name? Where are you from? Where are you staying? What's your employment? How many kids do you have? Are you married? Where were you born? Who were your parents? Why are you in New York? After that round of questioning from 5 or 6 different police officers, she had been loaded into a police van with a dozen others and dropped off at the Casa Blanca. She felt an alternate-universe shiver thinking about it three days later, but she was starting to expect such brutality.

"It does and it doesn't. The real warzones are out there, the cities that were hit, the towns near them. But here, it's like we're in the green zone. It's not at war, just adjacent to it."

"It's safer here, right?"

"Safer, but .... Outside the green zone, life is less safe, but more free. Inside the green zone ... you exist at the sufferance of the security forces."

They both gazed down the street toward the two armed men. The canyons of New York were growing warm with the afternoon sun.

"How wise would it be for me to go looking for an ATM?" she asked after a bit. She had no desire to ever have a gun pointed at her head again.

"Technically, the shelter-in-place order has been lifted, but you wouldn't want to do anything to make them nervous. Soldiers, whether Army or mercenary, are trained to treat all threats in a single way – by ending it."

"They're putting people out of the hotel starting Monday morning. I heard the manager saying they can't verify credit cards."

"You're a Sullivan. You should speak to Gillam, but I'm pretty sure your credit is good."

"But if it isn't ... I want to be prepared with cash in hand."

"You weren't born rich, were you?"

"No. That obvious?"

"To those who know what to look for. There's an ATM at the end of the block."

"Which way?"

He looked toward the security forces. Damn! Still, she had to protect herself. Regardless of what Mr. Gillam decided about the worthiness of Katherine Sullivan's credit, Kate Lansing needed cash in her bra to feel safe under these circumstances.

Her calfskin boots clicked on the pavement as she slowly strolled toward the most terrifying scene she'd ever encountered ... three men dressed in black with assault rifles at the ready. They didn't bring their guns up, but they watched her as she advanced. A block away, a man crossed the street, trying to keep his hands visible. The neon flashed. There'd been a song about that … a favorite of her mother. She continued walking past the first of the guards. He turned to watch her as she walked up to the ATM machine. There was a daily limit of $300 here. She asked for the maximum and a message came up –

This ATM has been temporarily suspended by Homeland Security. Please speak with your financial institution to make other arrangements.

She knew certainly that there was money in her Chase account. She walked slowly to the door. The guards had separated, though one still kept a close eye on her. The cool lobby immediately insulated her. There were guards here too, but they seemed much friendlier in their rent-a-cop clothing, though one wore a bullet-proof vest and all were armed. She queued up with the dozen other customers.

"It's disgraceful," the woman in front of her said to the man she was with. "Mercenaries on the streets. Where is the military?"

"Don't speak too loudly," he said in a much lower voice.

A man at a teller window began arguing, something about limits and balances.

"I've been a depositor at Chase for 25 years. How dare you tell me this! I want my money and I want it now!"

35

Two guards braced him, hands on the butts of their guns.

"Sir, please come with us." He hadn't a choice, of course, so he walked stiffly to a side office where a flustered looking manager spoke with him as he was closing the door.

Katherine soon walked up to a teller window and presented her identification.

"Thank you for your business, Mrs. Sullivan," the teller said as she began typing in her computer. Her blue eyes flickered back to Katherine and her smile grew larger. "What can I do for you today?"

"I want to take out the maximum withdrawal allowed." Katherine kept her voice low and calm. The teller's gaze flickered.

"We're only allowed to withdraw $100 per day."

"You can see on your screen that I have a great deal more money than that."

"Yes, ma'am, but Homeland Security has set the limit."

"It's not your fault. I understand. May I speak to your manager, please?"

The teller spoke into her phone. The others before her must have known about the limit, which explained why they had left so quietly. Her hotel room alone was more than $100 a night.

While the teller spoke on the phone, the angry depositor was escorted from the manager's office, his hands bound by zip-ties. He was taken out the back. Katherine suppressed a shudder. The scene tasted of doom.

"The manager can speak with you in a moment," the teller told Katherine. "Thank you for not causing a fuss," she added in a very low voice. Katherine smiled at her and walked to where the teller indicated. It seemed forever, but was only two minutes by the clock when a female manager came to shake her hand and invite her into an office.

"Mrs. Sullivan, so nice to meet you!" Carol Laurent said. "Have you been in touch with your husband at all?" she asked as she swept the door closed behind them.

"Unfortunately, the long distance lines are down." Katherine took a plush chair. "I'm sure you can understand why I want cash in this situation."

"I can. Unfortunately, Homeland Security has set the $100 limit."

"My hotel is more than that per night."

"As is everyone's. You have a credit card on file with the hotel, surely."

"They are turning guests out of the hotel starting Monday morning if they can't verify their credit cards."

"Mrs. Sullivan, your family owns one of the largest privately-held businesses in the United States. I'm sure your credit is good. If you would like, I will call the manager of your hotel and assure him of that."

"Yes, of course, I would appreciate that. But I would still like some cash on me."

"I can authorize a $100 withdrawal for you."

You stupid bitch! You know that isn't adequate.

Katherine bit down on her anger. Screaming wouldn't do any good.

"Yes, please do call my hotel. It's the Casablanca. The manager's name is Gillam."

Ms. Laurent dialed with elegant nails and spoke to Gillam in warm tones. Katherine formulated a plan while she waited.

"Your lodging and food are secure during your stay, however long that may mean. Some of the depositors who I have made these phone calls for plan to return every day for $100, just to assure they have cash on them."

"Thank you." There was nothing else to say. There was a tap on the door and Ms. Laurent rose to receive Katherine's withdrawal.

"Thank you for your understanding."

"Thank you for making the phone call." Katherine accepted the two crisp $50s. As she turned to the door, she deftly settled them into her bra under her blue silk blouse. She shook hands with Ms. Laurent, promised to return on Monday and set out to fulfill her plan.

Fresh View

Emmaus Kansas Listening Post
Saturday Morning

Grant Rigby emerged from the analyst world when Emily set a cup of coffee on the table that served as a computer work station.

"What's going on out there?" she asked.

Right. Honesty. I promised honesty. He restrained his trained inclination to dump the screen.

"Weird."

"That's not communicative," she said with a giggle. He smirked.

The rest of the shelter was quiet. They were the only two awake.

"Bear with me. Learning a new skill here." He rubbed the back of his head. "Dylan said the same thing. Maybe you can make sense of what is confounding us."

"Oh, sure, honey. I know so much about terrorism." She sipped her coffee. "Or is this espionage?"

To Grant, this was just workaday life. Terrorism and espionage ran together in his mind.

"Maybe you know more about people and that's what we need now."

"Shoot."

"We've got three different organizations taking credit for the attack seconds before it happened. What do a green organization, an anti-corporate group, and a rightwing militia have in common? The green organization was protesting oil development. The militia was convinced that a trial of Muslim terrorists was rigged. These are the AP feeds picked up by the New York Times and the Seattle newspaper."

Emily grinned like a fiend and scanned the page.

"Although no terrorist organizations have taken credit for it, the foiled double attack in New York has been tied to a Muslim terrorist cell," he added.

"How do you know that?"

"It was one of our deep operatives who tipped me off about Operation Sunset."

Emily cocked her head.

"What am I supposed to be looking for?" she asked.

"Anything that stands out as odd to you."

"You mean besides the fact that they're taking credit for a terrorist attack?"

"Right. That's a given. You are the fresh pair of eyes."

"I need more coffee for this."

He took their cups into the dimly lit living area, crept to the makeshift kitchen and poured coffee from the thermos. Dylan had taken one of the futons. His eyes opened briefly at Grant's movements, but he went back to sleep as soon as he recognized him. The rest of the family was asleep in the bunk room. Grant opened a tin of shortbread and put four of them on a plate, then returned to Emily in the work room. She thanked him for the coffee, took a shortbread, then turned the screen his way.

"They never mention nuclear bombs," she noted. Grant frowned at her, perplexed. "What?"

"I didn't see that. What do you mean?"

She looked flustered, but then pointed to the print blocks on the screen.

"The green organization – Fresh Air for All -- 'The destruction of this building'. The anti-corporate -- 'the death of these workers will serve as a warning to their neighbors'. It's almost as they thought these were limited attacks. Then the militia – 'They would do the same to us and have done more. Justice will be served by the destruction of this building ...'"

Grant reread the press releases.

"It does seem as if they didn't know these were nuclear bombs. 'We will rejoice when we see this capitalistic symbol collapse as rubble into the street' and 'at least these terrorists will not come back to us dressed in fresh uniforms.' Pays to have fresh eyes. Now I have to figure out why the terrorists in New York knew they were using nuclear bombs." He moved to boot up that press release for her to read.

"Maybe they were the planners. That guy across the bridge just came out too." She pointing to the camera screen. "Why are we watching him anyway? I thought we were on the same side."

"We are." For a minute, Grant watched as Shane stared up at something off camera and then began to lock up the old hotel.

"A lot is riding on Shane staying healthy." He turned his attention back to the matter at hand. "I still can't figure out the connections among these groups. I seriously doubt the Neharis Network was the planner and I can't see how they would have anything in common with any of these other groups."

"It doesn't seem like they would have anything in common, but it does seem awfully coincidental that they would all decide to blow something up all on the same day."

"You should have been an analyst," he complimented.

I am glad to be honest with her. It's just going to take time to learn this skill.

"It appears I have been drafted into the profession. Can we go upstairs now?"

"This evening. The levels are low enough now, but I want to be more careful with our family."

"Really? I feel so loved," she quipped.

"So am I forgiven?"

"For not warning the world about what you knew? No. There had to be a way around that. But I do appreciate you getting us to safety and keeping us safe. You'll have to be content with that."

He sighed, but he knew there was no use arguing about it. The peace of the house needed to be paramount for now or the winter would be painfully long.

"You said 30 million people died in the initial attacks. How many have died since?"

"Maybe double are either dead or the walking dead."

"And cancer?"

"We know from Chernobyl that cancer rates after the initial event are really only slightly increased. We're past the worst of it, but we'll have to keep an eye on the Geiger counters for some time to come. There may be a cloud of radiation circling the earth for a bit."

"The terrorist attacks are over, then, so why are we in hiding? Shane can go into town, but we can't. Why?"

Grant had debated how he was going to answer this. Honesty didn't make the answer any easier to provide.

"I'm not keeping anything from you, but I really don't know the answer. If my suspicions are correct, we're at risk. Nobody is really looking for Shane Delaney, but if I'm correct, it's best that people think we died in San Diego, so that means we can't risk coming up on traffic cameras."

"Who do you think might be looking for us?"

She had a right to know.

"My employers, Emily. We're hiding from the United States government, because my gut says that nobody could organize a conspiracy of this level without government resources and Dylan has credible evidence that I'm right."

Who is Shane Delaney?

Wichita Kansas

Mike stirred MRE eggs and bacon with hot sauce before spooning it into his mouth. A lot of guys complained about the freeze-dried food, but Mike didn't really care. You could make anything taste good with hot sauce. Not the Tabasco included in the MRE, but actual hot sauce he carried with him. He enjoyed every bite.

He'd spent the last two days in the outer ring of defense protecting the governor of Kansas, Harmon Lancaster. This Saturday morning, they were finally being relieved. Most of his squad had already headed back to the camp at Eisenhower Airport, but Mike had determined to call Alicia under the guise of seeing some of Wichita.

That was as good a cover as any because Ric had always wanted to see the "lay of the land". That made sense now that he knew Ric had been playing a role. He'd been scoping for whoever his bosses were. *How did I never see that before?* A lot of the guys they'd worked with before knew that he and Ric had always gone out to reconnoiter, so nobody questioned Mike when he dropped off the back of the transport about a mile out from Garvey Center.

According to his map, this was Water Walk. The fountains had been turned off on account of the emergency. He wondered if they'd ever be allowed to turn them back on. How many years had Miristan been under occupation? Seven?

His personal cell had bars. He'd sat down on a park bench to eat breakfast and now he dialed Alicia's number while he drank the faux-mocha that came with the MRE. Sugar and caffeine weren't nutritious, but they would keep you going for a long time. Alicia picked up on the second ring.

"*Dios mio*," she muttered before he could say anything. "Where are you?"

"Wichita," he told her. "We can't talk long. Communications are being monitored. Remember what you wanted to tell me before I left?"

His wife had learned throughout their relationship to not ask a lot of questions and to not divulge much information even to him on the phone.

"I'll look it up again." That was code for she'd send it via email.

"Good girl. Enough said. How are things where you are?"

"Pretty quiet. There are restrictions on travel and the grocery stores are completely cleaned out. I never thought I'd be so glad that my mother is a hoarder. How's Wichita?"

Magdela was indeed a hoarder. She had enough canned goods to feed four people for a year and she had just bought a quarter of beef before they had come to visit. One might think she'd known this was about to happen. Mike watched as a woman and her child neared where he was leaning against a building, but they didn't come too close. Even with his rifle slung, he intimidated. He'd never really thought about that image before. It had been an advantage in Miristan and South America. Was it an advantage in the United States? Did he want it to be?

"This is the provisional state capitol until they're sure Topeka is safe, so it's all about guarding the governor. I patrolled all night. I'm missing Ric."

"Mmmm," she hummed. "You wish he was with you. I wish it too, because he was very good at guarding your back."

"How's our cargo?"

"I'm fine and so is the little tag-along. I wish you were here."

"Me too, but I think this is going to go on for a while."

"I understand."

"Good. I love you, *mio*. I'll call when I can. Gotta go."

"I love you. Please … come soon."

"As soon as I'm able."

Mike hung up then, because he knew how long it would take for a bot to start recording their voices. He pulled the sim card from his cell and hailed another passing truck. There was some sort of command center at Home Depot, so he stayed on the truck until it arrived at a heavily guarded Walmart where trucks were confiscating food. He slipped around the back and put a second sim card into his phone, opening his personal email. Alicia's email was waiting for him. Of course, even here, he had taught her a simple cipher for sending information they didn't want anyone to understand.

Joel Rhys? I bet that's an alias. Good girl, you didn't send the whole email address.

He swapped the sim card again and looked in his second personal email where the rest of the email address was, but with a different name. *So Ric is Shane Delaney? Yeah, he could be a Shane. And Delaney? He's awfully dark for an Irishman, but maybe there's something else back there.*

Mike pulled the sim card and stashed everything away before hopping a supply truck to a mall within sight of the airport. The idea was to keep moving from tower to tower while the phone couldn't broadcast or be traced, then swap sim cards so any bot wouldn't recognize it was a communication. He sent a simple email to Joel Rhys alias Eric Faraday AKA Shane Delaney.

Joel? Are you playing whack-a-mole? I'm not surprised, but now I really want to know. Tico

Some idiot drunk had called him that once and Eric had dumped him in a cesspit for it. It had remained a secret code nickname ever since. He trusted Ric to be smart enough to figure out the two GPS coordinates he sent.

There wasn't an immediate answer, so Mike assumed Shane/Ric/Joel was busy or maybe whoever his real bosses were had him occupied. Mike caught a supply truck headed back to the Green Zone. He'd have to check for a reply tomorrow.

Are You Part of the Problem?

Emmaus Kansas, Factory Mall

Jazz sat beside Jacob on the cot he'd had the presence of mind to set up for himself. He'd not offered to give it up to anyone. There were advantages to being 95 years old and owning the building you were using as a bomb shelter.

The corridor before them was filled with sleeping people on a string of mattresses, but they'd turned the lantern out some time ago, so they couldn't see them. They'd both woke when the rain stopped and neither had been able to go back to sleep. He'd made up the cot and invited her to sit with him.

"I tape your radio program," she told him.

"Which one?"

"You have two? I only know about the gun education show."

"That's a good one. I do another program on Saturdays with Dell Conopher and Andrew Bennett."

"The anarchists?"

"Yes. You've heard it?"

"Tuned in once or twice. Didn't know it was you."

"I'm not there every Saturday, so you could miss me."

"So, you're an anarchist?"

"Minarchist edging toward anarchist. Voluntaryist."

He had gotten to know her well enough over the last two days to believe she knew what those terms meant. She had a vague concept.

"So you don't like government, but you were the mayor once and your son is now?"

"That's a sign that I evolved politically, right?" His tone made it a joke. She smiled in the darkness.

"So do you regret having been the mayor?"

"No. I was a good mayor. I just question the role of mayors, whether we need them as currently conceived."

It was a subject she knew a little about, since her college degree was political science. Teaching was something to pay the bills until she could write her masters ... except she actually enjoyed teaching. The subject provided them with something to talk about to keep the boredom at bay, but it was also a fascinating discussion. She'd stopped calling him Mr. Delaney. Her parents would be scandalized that she spoke so casually to a contemporary of her great-grandfather. Jacob had insisted.

"Explain that."

"Mayors should represent the people, but instead of being the servant of the people, they are become the ruler of the people. Their job is to execute city ordinances – laws – that other representatives create to make the people comply – regardless of whether the people actually think the law is a good idea. More often than not, they are implementing ordinances required by the federal government, whether people like it or not. And then there's the way they are elected?"

"What do you mean?"

"Well, back when I ran for mayor, 60% of the adult residents of the town were registered voters and about 60% of those turned out. Rob was elected with 23% of registered voters. So about 10% of the adult population of the town elected him to tell us what we should do."

"Do you object to his method of mayoring?"

"No. He's been a good enough mayor. What I object to is a small minority being able to force everyone else to do what they want. But I also object to the majority being able to force the individual to do what they want. Voting is force – coercion."

"You don't vote?"

"I haven't for about a decade now."

"Not even for Rob?"

"Not even for Rob. That was a hard one for me, but I couldn't do it and stick with my principles."

Since they were moving beyond small talk, she hoped it was okay to state her mind.

"If you do away with the ballot box aren't you left with only the bullet box?"

"No, that's a false dichotomy. There's actually four boxes of liberty – the soap box, the ballot box, the jury box and the bullet box. All four have validity."

"But how would we choose our leaders?"

"Why do we need leaders?" She didn't step in the silence he allowed. She didn't know the answer. *Because everyone does?* That didn't seem reasonable right now. "Yes, we need representatives and people who know how to do things, but we don't need 10% of the population choosing leaders. If we did away with voting, we'd be forced to get together and discuss the issues, choose representatives for time-limited specific tasks and then meet again when the next issue comes up. Maybe if that had been done, someone would not have just blown up the world."

For a moment, Jazz tried to ignore the feeling of radiation seeping through the walls and into her body. They'd regularly checked the Geiger counter and, so far, the levels had remained in the safe range within these walls, but knowing the facts did not stop her from the paranoid fear of radiation poisoning.

"So how would we organize the country under your system?"

"We wouldn't. I doubt there's going to be a country by the time we stop rolling with this mess. I'm thinking we'll be organizing on a local level."

"So Rob wouldn't be the mayor anymore?"

"Maybe. We'd still need people to represent the community and he is good at that. Or maybe you would represent us for some things. And maybe some people would prefer to go their own way and not be part of the community. It's just a different method of organizing ourselves."

"How would we choose these people?"

"Group consensus. It definitely is a less efficient way of doing things, but it focuses on the rights of the individual to choose for themselves what they want their lives to look like."

"So a little bit like a congregational church?"

"Similar."

"In a church, people have Jesus as their guide. The rest of the world doesn't have that guidance. Wouldn't it just lead to chaos?"

"It might, but chaos is fertile soil for liberty. There are folks who would call liberty chaos because people wouldn't be forced to do what the majority wanted, but eventually, they'd get used to it. Consider what just happened under the system we have currently. More than a dozen cities are now uninhabitable and we're hiding in a factory hoping the concrete protects us long enough for the radiation levels to go down. When something fails completely, it's a good time to try another way."

"What if ... what if someone wants to take control? I mean, that's what terrorism is about, right? Someone wanting to take control from someone else and feeling that democracy isn't allowing that to happen. If there's no one in control, won't it be easier for those people to take control? Isn't that counterproductive to what you want?"

"You're forgetting that we all have the ability to fight back. At least, here in Kansas we do. Not so sure how it's going to work out for people in the disarmed cities that have survived, but for us ... we can fight back."

Jazz shivered, envisioning hordes of Islamists on horseback rushing across the plains toward Kansas farmers with AR15s.

"We don't even know who did this," she reminded, more to herself than to the old man.

"Nope."

"When we were all talking about it last night, you didn't answer the question. Who do you think it was?"

"I don't think it matters. Not for us anyway. We have to concentrate on surviving going forward. Your generation is going to have to be wiser than the ones who came before you because you won't have the luxury of living in the most powerful country in the world during times of peace and prosperity."

"You think it's over then ...the United States ... just like that?"

"I think it's going to keep twitching for a while. That's the dangerous part. Because during its death spiral, we have to stay out of the way of the flailing arms so we can go about our business. We have to keep the important objects in view and not get distracted by the unimportant things."

"How do we know the difference?"

"Now there's the right question, young lady, though I'll tell you honestly that you'll know or you won't when you see it. If you don't, then you're part of the problem and not the solution."

Jazz let her head settle back against the feed sacks behind the cot and just thought about the future he suggested. At 23 years of age, she thought she knew how the world was supposed to work, but what if she was wrong? Was she part of the problem or part of the solution?

A Bid for Freedom

Leavenworth Penitentiary

Coincidence could work miracles. Daniel McAuliff had not believed that until that very week. On Tuesday, he had been taken from his cell at Florence Supermax in Colorado, loaded into a transport vehicle and brought to Leavenworth. Given that he was considered a terrorist, he hadn't expected his stay to last long. In fact, he was pretty certain he would be transferred to Terra Haute High Security by Thursday. Wednesday, terrorists had bombed Kansas City, creating a perfect set of circumstances for a man of his intelligence.

A conspiracy of events had brought him potential good fortune. There were at least 10 of his former colleagues in Leavenworth. Because the guards here didn't seem to know or care about his special status, Dan had managed to meet with eight of his old crew so far. Two had gone to the dark side and would not be included in the plan. Josh was young and therefore not in control of himself, but the kid knew the plans because he had the most freedom of any of his compatriots. The fact was, his father would probably be the best resource they could find on the outside. That didn't mean including him wasn't dangerous.

Right now, the debate was whether they should strike while the prison was on lockdown, cut off from the outside world by the radiation cloud from Kansas City or if they should wait until they could actually go somewhere.

"If we strike now," Kletti said. "There's no chance of SWAT hemming us in. They have no communications. The radiation screws with it."

"The longer we have to hold the guards, the more chance of the situation spinning out of control," Patterson advised. "If they mount a counterstrike, we'd have to kill some of them."

Five years of filing applications for general population had not done what nuclear Armageddon had accomplished. There were five of them sitting around a table, talking in low voices. The understaffed guards patrolled the gantry, but they couldn't' get close enough to hear. Dan assumed the relaxation of protocols were because these guards never worked day shift and didn't know that Special Unit prisoners were not allowed to interact face-to-face with other prisoners. A man with a clear vision could get a lot done under the cover of crisis.

"Word on the block is that the radiation levels are pretty high outside, but they're dropping now,"

Josh explained. "These guards have been on duty for days. They're worried about their families and exhausted. I don't understand why we haven't taken them yet."

"People die in those circumstances." Dan did not want a riot and a lot of deaths on their heads.

"Not so many if they have the right leader," Kowalcsky reasoned.

"I appreciate the vote of confidence, but killing guards in federal prison carries the death penalty. We need to be sure we can take them without killing them. When we're out, we want the government to consider us the least of their worries, not worth tracking down."

"Maybe there's a way," Monahan said.

"Yeah?"

Kowalcsky cleared his throat.

"I've had four years to educate some of these guys. There's about 50 who would move if you told them to and who would try not to kill anyone. We lock the guards up, we take control of communications and we prepare to make a break for it when the radiation levels drop."

"How do we control the other prisoners?"

"We lock them down. Some of the 50 will want to come with us. Others will want to head out on their own. There's about 10 prisoners – they're not part of the 50 – who if they escaped, the marshals would expend all efforts toward reacquiring them and not care that much about us."

"You mean murderers?"

"Some. One guy shot up a mall. Another killed his wife, kids and the neighbor. A third ...."

"No. You are describing people who belong behind bars ... or dead. We can't let them out."

"Okay. You seemed to want a diversion. What about the rest of the plan?"

"I think the country is going to need men like us and the totalitarian regime that will rise from these ashes is just going to bury us. So, hell, yeah, pursue the plan, but let's not forget who we are. We can't hold to the principle of non-aggression in order to break out of here, but we don't have to kill people in the process. Murder doesn't win hearts and minds."

Kowalcsky nodded. Josh frowned. *He might be a problem.*

"I'll get started." Kowalcsky rose to leave. Josh rubbed a hand across the tabletop.

"Without a diversion, they'll be looking for us."

"Will they? They certainly appear to have a situation on their hands that will keep them busy for a while. When was the last time you spoke with your father?"

"A couple of weeks ago. He visited on Labor Day."

"Can he help us?"

"Probably. The question is ... will he? He's been walking the straight path since I went in. He doesn't seem interested in going back."

Dan sighed. He and Jason Breen had known each other for some 20 years. Jason had always agreed with the anarchist cause. He'd been more willing to break the law than Dan had. It would be ironic if he had changed his mind right now.

"Has he said anything about the compound?"

"No, but your brother is part owner of the salt mine now."

"Anders? Hmm." That seemed unlikely. Anders had had a good career in Cleveland. Why would he decide to move to rural Kansas, to a town where Dan had been arrested?

"Could that work for us?" Monahan asked. "Would he supply us at the compound?"

"Doubtful. Anders is a straight shooter, more conservative than liberty-loving. He'd call the cops. Dell Conopher's property backs up to it and he might turn a blind eye while we're sneaking through. Not sure the compound is the best idea. We might want to just grab what's left there and head somewhere else. We need to move slowly, think out our plans. If the food and ammo caches are still there, we have a shot of making this work. If not … we might be better off staying here."

Josh looked stunned.

"What? You thought I was suicidal? We're no use to the world if we're dead."

"There's a guy off my dad's crew here. I'll see if I can get any information off him."

"You do that." Josh left calm and collected, but Dan could see he had purpose. Monahan watched him go, then turned back to Dan with worry in his eyes. Dan nodded. They both knew. While he desired to get out of this grave as soon as humanly possible, he knew that it had to be done right. He wanted them to be the least of the government's concerns when the time came.

"I'll keep an eye on him," Monahan assured. "What about Kowalcsky?"

"I think he's fine. This world, it makes you forget your purpose. He just needed reminding. I'm not sure Josh has ever understood."

"What do I do if he turns out to be dumb?"

"Wait. We'll decide together." Monahan left the table, leaving Dan alone to calculate the odds of pulling off a prison break in the middle of nuclear Armageddon. Sometimes coincidence handed you an opportunity that you could turn to luck with the right decisions, but this coincidence sure had some major complications.

Morning Milking

Emmaus, Lufgren Farm

Alex Lufgren shifted uncomfortably, trying not to disturb Keri. He could tell from her breathing that Poppy was awake. Deaf people could never pretend to be sleeping around him. You needed to be able to hear your own breathing to control the sound of it. The rain had stopped pounding on the bulkhead door some time ago, but no storm siren had sounded. That wouldn't bother Poppy of course, but she was probably thinking the same thing he was … why wake people who were asleep if you didn't have to. Mocha shifted on his legs and whined. The chocolate Lab had reluctantly peed in the shower pan when his bladder had become too full, but he was still holding his urine for as long as possible. Alex checked his cell, keeping it cupped in his hand so as not to awaken anyone else. It was just about dawn. *Time to milk the cows.* He rolled up off the floor. Mark moved on one of the two cots.

"Something?' he asked.

"Cows." Mark was more than willing to help with anything Alex asked of him, but the man didn't know how to milk cows by hand.

Mark's son Pete awoke as Alex stepped over him. He'd drawn the short straw for sleeping sitting up against the wall. If they were in the shelter one more night, he and Poppy would get the cots. Being young sucked for the first two nights.

At the bottom of the stairs, one of the chickens clucked under the blanket they'd thrown over the cages. He'd have to have Poppy clean those cages today before the smell overwhelmed them. When Alex's uncle had come up with the idea of storm barns, Alex' father had improved on it by providing a means to get to the barn from the storm cellar. Although the Lufgren clan had all copied one another, it had been a long running joke that they didn't really need to. Tornados weren't that long and often the cows wouldn't produce milk after them anyway. It had been a brilliantly prescient idea, but Alex wished his father had provided a bit more room in the underground tunnel. As a kid, he'd liked using the tunnel to get to the barn without going out in blizzards, but his shoulders were much wider and he was several inches taller now. He guessed he was just as glad to not have to expose himself to radiation for the cows' sake.

The storm barn stank after 30-odd hours, but the air handling system was still chugging along, so he wasn't gagging and his eyes weren't burning ... yet. The four barn cats had taken up residence just inside the fan shroud and their fear ruffled in the slight wind. If the wind died down, the windmill would stop providing power. He'd just have to hope that this would be over soon. He milked the goats first so they wouldn't pester him and then moved onto the cows. It bothered him to watch the white fluid drain away into the muck on the floor, but they couldn't drink more than the one pail and he had no way to refrigerate it. He was almost done with the last cow when he heard something outside. He left to join his family in the storm cellar. Mark had armed himself with a baseball bat while Alex took his shotgun down from the nails where he'd hung it out of the reach of Alice Ramirez, who was too young to understand the dangers of a gun. Whoever it was had walked up into the sunporch and they could hear him walking around.

"Maybe it's someone coming to tell us it's safe," Keri whispered.

"Or they've come to kill us," Mark muttered.

Poppy signed, "Radiation?" It was a new sign, made up since the bombs.

Alex spoke as he signed one-handed. "Quiet." Keri began explaining what they could hear.

The footsteps went into the kitchen.

"Did you not lock up?" Kerri asked.

"I did," Alex insisted. He gestured for Pete to give him a clear shot to the inside door. They could hear someone coming down the stairs, scuffing against the door.

"Alex?" Shane's deep voice called out.

Alex lowered his shotgun, thumbing the safety into position, before opening the door.

In the uncertain lantern light, Shane looked like he'd been in a fight and lost.

"You okay, man?"

"Yeah, I'm fine." Shane casually blocked Mocha's escape with his knee. "Rad level is dropping. It's in the safe zone now, but it might be safer to keep the baby down here until evening. Don't let any animals out until you've checked the water. I was coming from Jericho Springs and thought I'd let you know."

"How'd you get into the house?" Keri asked her brother.

"He hasn't changed the place where he hides the key and I don't have dementia. Do you have a Geiger counter?" he asked Alex.

"Cai gave me one as the only one out to this end of town who could hear the storm siren. What happened with that anyway?"

"I don't know. I have to get to town to find out."

Alex handed the shotgun to Keri and scrambled up the stairs after Shane.

"Could you stop moving long enough to talk to me, please?"

"No, not right now. Something's wrong at City Hall. They aren't answering and nobody has set off the storm sirens. I'll swing back by after I've taken care of that. We do need to talk. I'm not avoiding you. I'm just busy right now. Make sure you check everything for radiation before you let the animals out."

Shane drove off, leaving Alex to watch his trail of dust. A huge hollow formed in the pit of his stomach, absorbing the smaller one that had taken up residence there Wednesday night.

They'd been in City Council meeting when Bart Rawlston had strode into the room to whisper in Rob Delaney's ear. Alex knew the mayor pretty well, considering he was his father-in-law, and was surprised to see his face drain of color. Rob always seemed unshakable ... the sort of man who could witnesses a cataclysm and organize the cleanup committee without breaking a sweat. They'd continued the conversation in his absence, discussing the junk yard on Willow Creek Run, and then Rob had come back in to announce that he needed to end the meeting. There had been some sort of terrorism attack in Denver and possibly Kansas City and he needed people to go home and provide calm in their neighborhoods.

Alex knew there had been a whole life before that moment, but be perfectly honest, he couldn't yet remember it.

Quiet After the Storm

Emmaus, Delaney House

*T*he silence woke Rob first. The rain beat against the metal flashing for hours on end, so its absence was stark. He shifted to see his watch. Jill mumbled and tried to move into a more comfortable position. This shelter had been built for tornados, not double overnights. Thank God the kids and Jacob had stayed elsewhere. There was only one cot and it barely slept two average sized people if they were very friendly. When this was done, he would expand the storm shelter into the old coal bin next to it. This was ridiculous.

"What is it?" she asked.

"It's stopped raining. My arm is asleep."

"Sorry." She sat up, turned on the battery powered lantern. Her red hair was tousled and she was obviously not expecting company. He sat up, shaking pins and needles out of his arm. "That was actually a lot of fun last night," she remarked with a Mona Lisa smile. "It's the first time in 30 years that we've known for certain that nobody would walk in on us."

"It was fun." He twisted around to give her a kiss. Glister stood staring at the door, wagging his tail. "I know you want to go out, boy, but it's still the litter box for you."

Glister would figure it out eventually, as he had every time in the day and a half they'd been stuck in this storm shelter. Yesterday Rob had opened the wall vent between the storm cellar and the coal bin to show a bag of shredded newspapers out of their living area. The Geiger counter hadn't budged. Could be the whole basement was safe ... or not. He wasn't risking their lives to find out. Rob tossed Jill her bra and found his underwear. Three of his fingers were still tingling like he'd been bitten by fire ants.

"I'll see about some breakfast," she said while he powered up the walkie talkie.

"Bart, you got your ears on?" Static. "Hey there, City Hall, someone up yet?" Nothing. He switched channels. "Anyone got their ears on?"

A moment passed and then Jacob came on.

"We're still here," he announced. "Rain's stopped. Keep expecting to hear that storm siren any moment. Over."

"It might take a while for the radiation levels to drop. Have you heard anything from Bart? Over."

"No. The radios weren't working there for a while. Maybe radiation interferes with them. I gotta go. There's two women squabbling over something. Over"

The radio went dead. Rob tried unsuccessfully to raise anyone else. Finally, he decided to save the radio and eat some breakfast.

"The milk's starting to turn. Just starting to take on that ice cooler flavor."

"I brought some powdered. That's the last of what was in the fridge. I wonder where the kids are."

"I think Marnie and Cai are at the health center. Keri is presumably with Alex. Shane ... well, that's always a question." Jill nodded, then stared into space. "Worrying about him won't make him one bit safer."

"I know. That's not .... Remember those stupid drills when we were kids?"

"Hiding under our desks if the bomb went off. Yeah."

"Just wondering if it happened that way and when I wonder it, I see our kids not knowing to hide under their desks."

He put his arm around her. He didn't know what to say and sometimes it was better to say nothing at all.

We Interrupt This Disaster for Some Important Announcements

New York City, Casa Blanca Hotel

*T*he mercenaries still waited on the corners as Katherine Sullivan turned back onto 43rd Street. A well-dressed woman walking at a moderate rate with a designer bag over her shoulder drew only slightly less attention from them as a terrorist in full tactical gear might. She kept reminding herself to breathe. Stanley frowned at her when she reached the Casablanca's entrance.

"You were gone a long time," he said.

"All the ATMs were closed. I had to visit a bank."

Inside Mr. Gillam, the manager, smiled falsely at her, explaining that she hadn't needed to get a bank manager to call him ... her credit was good *forever* ... not to worry.

"Of course, Mr. Gillam," she replied. The wine service was already underway, so she slipped into the lounge.

She shouldn't be surprised that the Sullivan name proved to be as good as gold. Ren had more money than God.

For all I know, Ren knows the people who did this. Certainly many of the radicals he finances want to see the country destroyed ... sent back to the dark ages. Luddites, everyone.

Nuclear explosions in dozens of cities ... an unprecedented ecological disaster. Surely, Ren would not want to see something like that. He had always seemed to care about the environment ... on the North American continent anyway. He owned his own game reserve, for heaven sake, and sponsored a kids' wilderness camp there every summer.

You're just over-reacting. There's a lot of stress right now. Maybe take a sauna after dinner.

She sat down in the lounge, weak with relief. This evening's vintage was a Vieux Château Certan pomerol, quite a nice red. The television drew her, even though the news hadn't changed since Thursday. Multiple-city attack, estimates of 30 million dead, Washington DC was among those hit, shelter in place until directed otherwise.

Unless your credit card is suspect, then you are put out on the street with your baggage and a smile.

She looked up at a screen shot of the UN. One of the men held the remote and bumped the sound.

"Marshall Ellerby, the head of Homeland Security, is scheduled to speak at the United Nation shortly. Stay with us for the coverage."

"Is it possible to change the channel?" Katherine asked.

"It's not," Julian Raines replied. They'd met over wine last night. She was practically on first name basis with the entire hotel now. Julian was a software engineer from Seattle, stranded here because the planes were grounded. Katherine wondered how good his credit was. "CNN and MSN are both test patterns. The commercial stations are playing old movies. This is the only game in town."

"Fox slants the news so much," she grumbled.

"Yes, they are the worst at that ... except for all the rest," Lillian, a blond vintner from California's Central Valley, said. "It's starting."

News broadcast –

"On December 7, 1941, President Franklin D. Roosevelt addressed the United States to declare the Japanese attack on Pearl Harbor, Hawaii as a day that would live in infamy," Marshall Ellerby began. Katherine wasn't sure she would have recognized him without the caption at the bottom of the screen. "On September 11, 2001, President George W. Bush faced a terror threat on the mainland. This week, we have experienced multiple attacks with a death count higher than all US wars and terrorist attacks in history.

"It is estimated that 30 million people died in the initial blasts from small, high-yield nuclear weapons placed in 16 US cities – Houston, Dallas, Washington DC, Chicago, San Francisco, Portland, San Diego, Denver, Kansas City, St Louis, Cleveland, Atlanta, Miami, Detroit, Pittsburg. There were two bombs each placed in Los Angeles and New York. The ones in New York were discovered and disarmed before detonation. New Orleans levies were taken out with conventional bombs. Some cities near the target cities, like Baltimore, have been rendered uninhabitable.

"The bomb in DC killed the President, the Vice President, the majority of Congress, most of the cabinet, and all of the Joint Chiefs. The whereabouts of the Speaker of the House are unknown. As the selected Designated Survivor, I may be the only survivor in the line of succession. Much of the surviving countryside is dealing with fallout and radioactive rain. We do not yet have an accurate accounting of those who have died or been made ill by fallout. Please continue to seek shelter when the radiation levels rise and to be especially wary of rain in the coming weeks.

"In more than a dozen sites around the nation, military construction crews and construction contractors are working to seal in radioactive hotspots, to reduce the risk of future contamination. It is a heroic effort, assisted by the international community. It may take several weeks to fully contain these sites, but work is ongoing and it will be accomplished.

"Although the bombs here in New York were intercepted and disarmed before detonation, we still do not know who is responsible for this unprecedented act of terrorism. More than a half-dozen groups of various philosophical stripes have issued statements of responsibility. Federal investigators are pursuing several lines of inquiry to try to bring these criminals to justice. I apologize to the people of New York for the current curtailment of travel. As soon as we have located the bombers, things will be more normalized. I know it is difficult under current circumstances, but these curtailments are necessary to apprehend the suspects and I ask for your continued patience and cooperation.

"These are dark times for the US. Things could be worse. Whether by good luck or good planning, the majority of our crop lands have not been irradiated. Unfortunately, farmers face difficulties in getting harvests to market because major transportation hubs have been destroyed.

"I thank the international community for stepping forward to assist in these difficult times. In the coming days, we'll be discussing the forms of assistance we need most and setting up avenues for delivering it."

"Above all, I want the people of the United States to recognize that everything that needs to be done is being done. Please bear with us in the coming days and weeks."

The camera shot away to a Fox News pundit who began talking about Ellerby being the head of Homeland Security and who was his boss now that the President was dead.

"I'll bet it will be months before they get those hotspots capped," Julian said.

"It sounds like the Central Valley might not have been affected," Lillian observed. She hadn't said much about how worried she was, but the rush of relief Katharine had felt upon hearing that Kansas was probably fine had probably surged through her as well.

They sipped wine and discussed the news report. They now knew exactly how many cities had been hit. Katharine trusted that since it had come from Ellerby's own mouth. What the pundit was saying about the groups that had claimed responsibility for the attacks didn't impress her one bit. It was all media spin by the master of media spin.

The excellence of the wine had done nothing for the discomfort in her bra. Katherine decided the sauna was calling her. When she got to her room, she pulled the six $50 bills and five $20s out of her bra and snagged an envelope from the supply of hotel stationery. Where to hide it? The safe didn't seem safe. Changing the combination didn't overcome the manager's override. The Moroccan inspired shutters were just for show. It would be hard to retrieve an envelope from behind them and, besides, you could see the wall behind the decorative slats. The backside of the valance was an amateur's hiding place, as were the underside of a drawer or the toilet tank. The desk had an actual vanity panel. She slid her fingers under it and was relieved to find a slight ledge where the envelope could rest. She put the chair back in its place and breathed a sigh of relief. It had taken her only an hour to walk to each of the banks where Sullivan had money and get $100. It was unfortunate the banks would be closed tomorrow for Sunday, but at least she had some cash now and could get more on Monday. She pulled her lap top out of the safe to research what other banks were close to Times Square. Eliminating the ones she didn't have credit cards for, she planned Monday's outing.

How much money would it take to win free of the city and get to Kansas? Assuming her plan worked, she'd have $1000 by close of business on Monday. $600 a day .... Perhaps Joseph would get here before she had what she needed, but ....

"You can't cross the ocean by staring out to sea," she murmured. She glanced at the clock. She would go to dinner and play the role of the clueless socialite. Afterward, she would ask Lillian or one of the other women to go with her to the sports club. She would thoroughly enjoy the sauna and steam room and come back and sleep like she hadn't for the last two days. She'd take her time and then, when she was ready, she'd head home to her daughter.

Not Yours

Emmaus Kansas, Huffman's Market

*M*ae (Huffy) Osimowicz looked up from the book she was reading. Jos hummed as he made a meal on the camp stove. So long as they didn't run it too long, the boiler room had enough air capacity that it didn't make them sick. Jos was faster than she was. She shifted on the air mattress, and pushed herself up using the wall. Her legs ached. She stretched, her knees popping.

"Does it feel longer to you than it should be?" she asked.

Her grandson slid the food from the pan onto two paper plates. It was some mix of thinly sliced meat and eggs.

"I have no idea how long it takes for radiation to fall to a safe level, Granmae. I haven't heard the storm siren, so I think we should just stay patient."

He turned off the stove and set one of the paper plates on the crate they were using as a table, then sat down on one of the two camp chairs with his own plate before him. She sat across him. They said a prayer together and then started eating. He wasn't a bad cook.

"Hopefully, when we can go out again, the long distance lines will be up. We can call to talk to (his mother's name)."

"Granmae – stop," he said around a mouthful of eggs. "I know you don't want to deal with this, but Atlanta was one of the cities. We need to face the possibility ...."

Huffy wiped a tear from her cheek. My, she felt tired. You weren't supposed to outlive your children ....

CRASH!

They both turned toward the sound of shattering glass.

"That's the front door," Huffy identified. In a second, she had crossed the room and grabbed up the shotgun. "Stay here. They're not getting the store."

She opened the door and slammed it shut before Jos had gained his feet. She ran across the store room and into the main store. A man was squeezing through the shattered front door. She had a clear view down Aisle 4. There were two men behind him. Huffy ran to the end of the aisle and let go with a load of bird shot so as not to hit the cash register. The guy trying to climb through the door screamed. His friends grabbed him and dragged him back out of the store. Huffy put the shotgun up to her shoulder again to fire her second round, but they were running, hauling him away. She heard a vehicle start outside and as she got to the door, a white panel van roared away down the street. Then she felt hands on her shoulders and pulled away, yelling, trying to pull the shotgun around. Jos pulled the shotgun free of her grasp.

"Stop! They're gone."

"I hit one," she announced gleefully.

"With bird shot. It wasn't fatal. Granmae, you ran out into nuclear fallout. What the hell did you think you were doing?"

"Saving us. If they took it all, we'd starve. Don't you realize that?"

"Starving? You risked dying of radiation poisoning right now in order to avoid starvation later?" He shook his head. "You're a marvel, Granmae, but please, don't ever do that again."

"You shouldn't be out here," she told him. "You have a lot longer for the radiation to catch up to you."

"I'm fine. If you thought I would huddle in the boiler room while you took out the bad guys, you had another thing coming."

He set the shotgun on the counter next to the cash register. His steps crunched on the glass all over the floor. Beyond the broken door was a glorious September morning.

"We need to secure this," he announced. "I'll get some plywood from the back. You stay here with the shotgun. We can talk about what to do the next time while we work."

After he strode away toward the back, Huffy grabbed a broom to begin cleaning up the glass. Only then did she realize just how hard her hands were shaking. Was that nerves or was she already dying?

An Eerie Quiet &
A Deadly Scent

Emmaus, Main Street, City Hall

Shane couldn't remember ever seeing the town completely deserted during the day. He drove for blocks without seeing anyone. The people of Emmaus had been very efficient. He didn't see domestic animals either. Apparently, the whole town had gotten under cover in time. He could hope. The dead squirrels on the road reminded him of why he needed to qualify his observations.

He pulled over to the curb and stared at the front of City Hall with its 5-story clock tower, three stories of banded windows and dormers in the hipped roof. Built with Sullivan money, he remembered, back when Emmaus and Beulah had been in competition as site for the federal courthouse. It was way too grand just to be a city hall and had served as the federal courthouse for a couple of decades before some patronage had caused the court to move to Beulah.

Shane tried the front doors, but they were locked. He hadn't really expected them not to be. He knew another way in, up to the roof, but he preferred not to use it. He tried other doors along the way. These were locked with solid hardware that he doubted he could pick. Finally, he reached the back of the building where the 2-story maintenance wing joined the original building. A drain pipe ran up the brick façade to the roof overhang.

It wasn't like when he'd been 12 and Alex had bet him he couldn't do exactly what he was doing now. In his stupid small-town-bored fashion he'd proved Alex wrong. His legs were longer now and he weighed more, though it was offset by stronger muscles and actual skill. He had done a fair amount of rock climbing in college, but it had been three years since he'd last conquered a rock face. His arms were protesting long before he made it to the overhang. He flung an arm up over the parapet, swinging free of the wall. For a moment, seeing the town laying out before him and the long drop to the ground, he thought he'd done something really stupid, but then he got his heel hooked and the rest was easy. He slid over the parapet to the roof deck and knelt there panting for a bit.

He glanced at the weather vane on the top of the clock tower, pleased to see the wind was coming from the north. Then he became aware of the stench of rotting birds. Townhall's pigeons hadn't fared too well in the rain. Ignoring the odor, he examined the Geiger counter just under the overhang of the stairwell house. He could see the cable running under the door and down the stairs. It looked to be intact. He tested the Geiger counter. It showed the same numbers as his, reporting, that the rads were just within elevated, but safe levels. He headed into the stairwell, which wasn't locked because it never occurred to anyone in Emmaus that someone would climb a drain pipe to the roof and let themselves into the building this way.

The building echoed with silence, which caused him to pause to think for a moment. The generator was located at the very back of the maintenance wing. Had he heard it when he drove up? *First things first.*

A short corridor beside the stairs led to a room behind the stairs that housed the storm siren apparatus. By the light of his cell phone lantern, he located the power switch. The dials lit up. The batteries were fully charged. Shane pushed the pig-pink button and the siren on the roof wailed out in long mournful tones. He set the iteration for 1 minute bursts every 2 minutes for half an hour. Then he headed downstairs. In the mayor's office, he took a handheld radio from its charging cradle and tried to bring up anyone from the basement. Nobody answered.

At the top of the basement stairs, he froze. He hated going underground and somehow the wide open stairs to the basement sucked the air out of his lungs.

There will be other people here soon to do this. You don't have to.

"Hello, is anyone out there?" a ragged male voice cried out from deep within the halls. Shane forgot all about his claustrophobia and headed downstairs.

Emmaus's two cells were behind a locked metal door.

"Get me out of here," the kid yelled. Shane could see him through the reinforced glass window, but the door was not budging without a key. The kid's name was Danny. Considering he'd shot someone on Thursday morning, Bart had apparently felt it wasn't appropriate to take him into the fallout shelter. He didn't look any worse for wear. The basement was below ground, beneath a concrete building. Shane's Geiger counter said there was almost no uptick in radiation here.

"I haven't got a key," he told Danny. "Settle down. Someone will get you out soon enough."

He continued to the pressure doors. He banged and didn't get an immediate response. Anxiety began to play with his stomach. He cranked on the wheel latch. It groaned and the door opened. He tasted the bitter scent of carbon dioxide and suddenly felt like he'd been buried alive. He backed away until Jacob's heat registered on his back.

"Sorry, you need to handle this," he said to Jacob. "I need to go check on Cai."

He fled.

When the Air Runs Out

Emmaus City Hall

*L*ife ticked away one breath at a time as one by one they yawned and found a place to rest on the floor, backs to the walls, heads in each other's laps or upon each other's shoulders.

They thought they were just settling down to sleep, to wait out the toxic rain and then face what had become of their world fully rested. They didn't sense their ensuing doom. Occasionally someone protested that it was stuffy or hot, but few others were awake to hear them.

The hours ticked by and soon all were asleep. Nobody noticed the mouse curled in the corner, breathing its last. They didn't wake when the lights went out. The people died more slowly than the mouse, smothered by the lack of oxygen and the increasing carbon dioxide level. Bart Rawlston suffered convulsions causing his wife to open her eyes briefly, but when he stopped jerking, she soon closed her eyes and sank closer to death.

They'd worried about the radiation, not the ventilation. Had they been awake when the power went out, they would have been more worried about getting the lights back on than concerned that the ventilation belt had shredded. They didn't know. It was those little things that modern man had lost in his technological advance that would spell their deaths in this new world. They knew how to set up a remote sensor to monitor the radiation levels, but not how to check a belt to assure it was still processing air.

Jacob and Jazz went from person to person, checking pulses. They found some clinging to life -- several children, young women, teenage boys -- those with more efficient breathing, stronger hearts and smaller bodies. Once carried out into the fresh air, they began to revive. They were the lucky ones. Over 75 people had suffocated. They would not be the last to die, Jacob knew. They might not even be the first. How many people had been missed and died in the radiation storm? Not that trusting to concrete had been much better. Jacob watched as men from the school shelter, pressed into service, carried the bodies out. He watched dry-eyed and wished he had thought ahead and saved his friends, but wishing wouldn't make it so. It was like so many battles that had gone wrong in the past ... you had to analyze them, grieve for those who didn't make it, accept what could not be changed and move on. Like war, he doubted they'd have time for the grieving part. Dealing with the central situation of nuclear apocalypse would likely grab most of that attention.

Jazz didn't weep either at first, until they carried out Marv Groseclose and then she turned aside to puke in a garbage can. Jacob was holding her while she wept, fighting back his own tears for Bart, when Rob and Jill arrived. Jill went immediately to help care for those who could be saved.

"Where's Marnie and Cai?" Rob demanded with rigid control. "And has anyone seen Shane?"

The Shack

Emmaus Kansas, Sullivan Mansion

Warren "Ren" Sullivan poured coffee into a mug and sat back on the sofa, wondering where Joseph might be. It had really been a foolish decision for him to take the helicopter when the storm was predicted. Ren would have to do something about it when he caught up with his son. Men in their 40s really needed to stop being so impulsive.

Allison swung in through the door.

"Coffee," she drawled, holding out an eager hand. Ren grinned at her and poured her a mug as she swung to the table and eased herself up on the stool. Her first sip made her grimace. After adding milk, she sighed in contentment. Generally, Ren preferred coffee you could stand a spoon in.

"How is everything out there?"

The cellar of "The Shack" was high-end accommodations for the most part. Carpeted floors, a small kitchen and Ren had been fairly generous with his wine. The wood paneled walls and professional lighting design belied the subterranean as his hundred "guests" rested on comfortable couches in turns and watched videos on a television while others listened to the stereo.

"Most everybody is asleep," she reported. "What do you think is going on outside?"

"Not sure. Not even sure we can hear the siren from here. Rob Delaney promised me he'd send someone to us if he hadn't heard from me after a few hours. How are you doing?"

"Worried for Mom and Dad," Allison admitted. She'd been pretty good about not outwardly worrying since her father had taken the helicopter, but he knew her well enough to recognize that she was hiding her emotions.

"Your mother is fine. She was in New York. Joe will likely be fine too, until I get my hands on him."

"What's so wrong with wanting to make sure my mother is safe?"

"Nothing, except that in doing so, he put himself and Perry in danger. I still want to know why Perry complied. The man has no family. Why risk his life on Joe's whim?"

"You still can't raise them on the radio?"

"I haven't tried since yesterday. No reason to get lathered up until we can do something about it."

She tucked a strand of honey blonde hair behind one ear and sipped some more coffee.

"How's your leg?"

"The same as it has been for six weeks now. I was supposed to get the cast off day before yesterday, actually. Friday, the 28th."

"It's not going to hurt anything to go a few extra days."

She hid her blue eyes behind dark lashes. He wasn't going to argue with her about it. There was nothing he could do to make the time go faster.

She looked up and stared at the wall.

"Do you hear that?" she asked.

He listened. At first, he didn't hear anything, but then he teased out the rising and falling wail of the storm siren.

"I'll get on the horn to Rob Delaney, make sure we're hearing it correctly. Best not to wake the others until we know for sure."

Jazz Reprised

Medical Center

Shane got Cai on the radio before he reached the medical center, but Cai reported that they couldn't get the fallout shelter door open. Shane's hands shook as he picked the back door and let himself into the deserted building. The health center pressure door did not have a wheel latch and after several tries to get the lever latch to pull to the right, Shane admitted he couldn't budge it.

"I think this is going to need a cutting torch. Where's Ross Winther?"

"He'd be at City Hall."

Shane leaned his head against the door, wanting to curse, but he refrained since he'd only panic the people who could hear him on the other side of the door. Panic was not conducive to oxygen control.

"If I can't find him, who else has a welding rig and knowledge?"

"The salt miners have welders and – well, that artist woman who lives out at the ranch."

"Artist woman? No, never mind. I'll see what I can do about getting more air down to you and then getting a cutting rig in here. Just hang on."

Rob found him hammering the outside cover off what he was pretty sure was the air filtration system.

"What are you doing?"

"Trying to get air to the people here so they don't end up like the people at City Hall. The door is jammed and I am concentrating on priorities."

Between the two, they pried the cover free and Rob held his belt while Shane hung upside down to pull several layers of filtration material out of the duct

"We can hear you," Cai confirmed. "And there's air." Through the radio, Shane could hear the people behind Cai cheering.

"Good. We'll get you out as soon as we can," Rob assured while Shane sneezed from the decades of dust coming off the filters.

"What about the school shelter and mine?" Shane asked, slapping dust out of his hair and off his clothes, sneezing again.

"The school shelter folks are helping at City Hall. I talked to the mine on the radio. They're fine and coming out. Not everyone at City Hall is dead. You saved a few."

"If I'd not stopped at Alex's or if I'd gotten brave sooner ...."

"Stop! You are not responsible for the entire world. You had no way of knowing this would happen. If anyone is responsible for that, it's me. Nuclear attacks were history. It never occurred to me to have Maintenance make sure everything was working. It was just excess storage."

"Hence why doors close and refuse to open, I guess." Shane took a deep breath and blew out his cheeks. "The pump house is flooding. I tried to get in to stop it, but I can't pick an industrial lock."

Rob paused for a second and let the comment go. He pulled out his key ring.

"I think this master key will open it. Flooding?"

"The storage tank is overflowing. Jusilla's is an actual creek now."

"I'll try to find Jason Welton. He mentioned something about the pump house a while back. What can you do?"

"My mechanical mind hopefully will see what to do when I get inside. You got this?"

"Yes. You don't need to be on body detail. Go take care of the well."

Shane hooked the key onto his ring and turned toward City Hall and his Jeep. The front lawn was covered with people recuperating from their ordeal in the bomb shelter. The dead bodies were being kept inside. Jacob was leaning on Shane's Jeep with a young woman Shane had met. Odd name ... Jazz?

"You okay?" Jacob asked. Embarrassed, Shane scrubbed fingers through his short hair and tried to produce a believable grin.

"Yeah. Thanks for handling that. The smell got to me."

"It always will," Jacob assured softly. "For me it is the smell of blood. And you were panicked for Cai and Marnie. They okay?"

"They have air and Dad is getting someone to cut open the door."

"I'd be willing to bet I was the last mayor to order maintenance of those shelters. Not blaming Rob. He is just the most recent of folks who didn't think it was necessary."

"I wouldn't have wasted the money on it either," Shane admitted.

"I probably wouldn't have either, since the Soviet Union ended. It didn't look like there was a need. So what now?"

"I've got to go figure out how to shut down the town well before it washes out the hill and floods the hotel."

"The tank is overflowing?" Jazz asked. Shane nodded. "There's an electric solenoid that has probably been off long enough that it's no longer metering."

"Sounds like a young lady who needs something to do might have found a job," Jacob suggested.

What are you up to, old man? But, hey, you do have a point!

"Sounds like you know more than I do."

"I can try." She shot an odd glance at Jacob. *She's wondering too.*

Shane drove around the block and headed back toward Lufgren's Crossing.

"Jazz, right?"

"Shane."

"How did you spend the rain?" She laughed and he joined her. "This passes for a new weird form of small talk."

"I live in the apartments above the old factory, so I ended up with Jacob."

"Oh, how'd that go?"

"A bunch of strangers crammed together in an inadequate structure for two nights and a day? Challenging. I did thoroughly enjoy your grandfather."

"He's a cool old guy."

"So how did you spend the rain?"

"In a concrete bunker at the Jericho Springs Hotel." Her forehead creased in confusion. "I own it. The bunker is really the boiler room."

"I took a tour of Jericho Springs and the pump house with my students last spring. That's how I know about the solenoid. Ross Winther didn't know who owned the hotel, just that someone had remodeled it."

"That would be me."

"I probably look like the Nightmare on Elm Street." She flipped down the visor for the vanity mirror. Paperwork dumped into her lap. "Sorry," she said immediately and began gathering the pages up.

Don't freak out! Don't grab for them! Relax!

"Who is Joel Rhys? And why do you have his property deeds?"

"Those weren't for you to read." She blushed at his tart words, smiled apologetically, and put them back where she'd found them. "Sorry, it's just personal business" An awkward silence followed.

"So change of topic. Who hit you in the face?" It took him a second to follow her segue.

"I did ... technically. I was trying to shut down the well. The storm siren was screaming. I slipped and landed face-first in Jusilla's Creek." When he laughed, she laughed. *Maybe she won't be a problem.* "It was at that point that I decided to lock myself in the boiler room at the hotel."

People emerged from their homes, standing on their lawns, some standing in the streets. Shane slowed to go around one crowd, then stopped when Vin Barrett waved him down.

"Is the crisis past?"

"The most recent one is," Shane said. "Stay tuned for the next one. Where are Lila and the kids?"

"Lila is at the medical center and I told Melanie to keep the younger ones in the storm shelter."

"Lila's fine then," Shane assured him. He thought better of mentioning the situation at City Hall. *That's Dad's job.* "We're headed to fix the town well pump. My dad would say you shouldn't open the gas station until you've talked to him."

"I'm staying here with the kids then. Try to organize the neighbors so they don't go making a bad situation worse."

"You might want to get some folks together to clean up the streets. The local squirrel and bird populations didn't have concrete."

"Good I kept that stupid dog inside then. I'm guessing eating a radioactive squirrel isn't real good for schnauzers."

Shane grinned at him and headed back down the street.

"Jacob kept saying the hard work starts when the rain stops," Jazz said, gazing at the people standing on their lawns.

Shane just drove. What really was there to say? Jacob was right.

Sleeping with the Enemy

Wichita, Kansas
Eisenhower Airport

*T*he darkness pressed him on all sides, but the thirst was worse. He'd been two days without food or water and starting to feel it rather badly. Occasionally one of the Army non-coms would come in and ask him if he was ready to confess his crimes.

What crimes? I didn't do anything wrong.

He'd been amusing himself for the whole time dreaming of his girlfriend's raspberry scented hair and how his daughter's smile made her whole body convulse with glee. He'd wanted to get them a bigger apartment. That had been the whole reason for becoming a National Guardsman. He'd been saving for a house. And now ... and now .... Occasional gunfire suggested that he was never getting out of this alive.

When the key rattled in the lock, Kris Lawson opened his eyes. He refused to groan as he pulled himself up off the floor, though his ribs were still painful. He supposed he should be glad to be alive at all. Not all the National Guardsmen from the trailer that night or from the state line earlier in the evening were.

The E-6 who entered carried a police baton, but it was the canteen at his belt that got Kris' full attention. A long time ago, when Kris had been a kid, he'd felt the sting of one of those for mouthing off to a cop. He never wanted to feel it again, but his need for water was becoming paramount, making him bolder than the situation warranted.

"Can I please have some water?" he rasped.

"As soon as we get some business out of the way." The E-6's patch read COLVER. "Stand at attention."

Kris tried as best he could with cracked ribs. Colver observed him coolly.

"You can choose this day whether to live or to die. The National Guard of Kansas is being absorbed into the United States Army after several unfortunate incidents where Guardsmen have refused to follow critical orders. Are you willing to recognize the authority of the US Army?"

If the Army is offering water ....

"I am," Kris said.

"You understand that this might mean you will have to restrain or even kill some of your former colleagues?"

Kris swallowed. His daughter needed him to live.

"Yes."

"Repeat after me. I, Kristoffer Lawson, do solemnly affirm that I will support and defend the United States against all enemies, foreign and domestic; that I will bear true faith and allegiance to the same; and that I will obey the orders of the commander of the United States Army and the orders of the officers appointed over me, according to regulations and the Uniform Code of Military Justice. So help me God."

This is not the code. It's different.

"...so help me God."

The E-6 unhooked the canteen from his belt and handed it to Kris, who greedily sucked down half the water before wiping his mouth, feeling his empty stomach cramping.

"I could use some food," he told Colver.

"Come with me."

Kris followed Colver out into the airport's TSA hallway. As they walked down the hall, several National Guardsmen now wearing Army uniforms nodded to him. A couple tried to smile, but most didn't exactly meet his eyes. Colver led him into another office as another E-6 was asking another Guardsman if he would swear allegiance to the Army under this new oath.

"I won't," he said.

Colver pulled his service pistol and handed it grip first to Kris.

"This secures your oath," he explained.

"What?" *No, you don't mean ....*

"This man is guilty of treason. You must execute him. It is your duty as an Army enlisted."

Kris didn't know this guardsman who was now sweating, but still standing at attention.

"I'm not the one committing treason. You are," the guy said. Kris almost admired his courage, except that it was going to get him killed.

"If you meant that oath, this should be no problem for you."

"Has he had a trial?"

"We're under martial law, soldier. If you're not up to the task, you can stand next to him and we'll get it done more quickly."

My little girl needs me to live.

Kris brought up the pistol.

"I'm sorry," he told the guardsman.

"I'm not. You're going to burn in hell for this."

Kris sucked in a deep, deep breath and squeezed the trigger. It was really easier to kill someone than he had thought it would be.

"Come with me. There's food," Colver said.

Kris thought he wouldn't be able to eat, thinking about that guardsman, but the fact was, he'd been without food for two days and his little girl needed a father. He licked his plate clean.

Who Is Eric Faraday?

Emmaus Medical Center

*E*ven with fresh air, the bomb shelter smelled of too many people who had been without adequate ventilation for too many hours. The sharp tang of sweat bit at Cai's nose as he distributed water. Dell Conopher was on the other side of the door with a cutting torch and they would be free from this tomb soon enough. Cai wondered what had happened at City Hall. Something bad since nobody was talking about it. If anyone else had guessed, they were holding it close to their vest. Cai was more concerned about Shane.

He hadn't meant to be snooping. That was what he told himself anyway. Shane had been needed for direct blood transfusion of the pilot. He'd tossed Cai his keys and said to get the car back to town. Bart had met him and Jacob at City Hall to take the prisoner. Jacob had gone inside to give a statement and Cai had only meant to get into his own bag for toothpaste before going to see Marnie, but Shane's duffle bag had tempted. There was a scripture about that – it wasn't the temptation that got you into trouble. It was entertaining the temptation. Still, he could have turned away from it before he unzipped the bag.

Who the heck was Eric Faraday? Cai had stared at that badge with his brother's somber face staring out from it for a good long while before seeing the exact same badge with Shane Delaney's name on it. He'd been too busy to think much about it until now. Eric – their uncle's name. Faraday -- Jill's maiden name. It was the sort of thing an actor did when asked to come up with a stage name. Only Shane wasn't an actor … was he?

The smell of sweat now comingled with the acrid stench of burning metal. Marnie had been busy with their most critical patient, the pilot from the commuter jet. Cai saw her cover the man's face with a sheet and then sit down on the floor with her head between her knees. He rushed over to her.

"Are you all right?"

Lila Barrett kneeled beside her.

"She's just tired," she said. "It hurts to lose a patient."

"I couldn't control the infection, not under these circumstances," Marnie whispered.

"You did the best you could." Of course, he knew she wouldn't be comforted by that. Good doctors wouldn't be – not immediately.

A rush of cool, fresh air swirled through the shelter as light poured in from the door. A ragged cheer came up from those who had sheltered here, who immediately began to gather belongings and kids. Cai sat down next to Marnie.

"We can wait here for a moment," he suggested.

"I'll have Martin help me take the body upstairs," Lila offered. Marnie nodded, leaning her head back against the wall. Tears rolled down her cheeks.

"Is that your first?" Cai asked.

"No. There was one during my internship, but I wasn't the lead then. And, I know I did everything I could, but he lost too much blood and he had a reaction to the antibiotics. It still feels like I failed."

"You didn't fail. The kid who shot him failed. Come on. Let's go upstairs and breathe some fresh air."

Cai stood up and held his hand out to her. She caught it and rose up off the floor.

"Dr. Morton will want to do an autopsy. I could sure use a shower ... and a pizza. I'm starved."

Cai smiled like an idiot and let her ramble. He doubted they'd have access to a pizza today and who would want to eat one before, during or after participating in an autopsy?

Designated Survivor

New York City, Javitz Federal Building

*M*arisa Woodruff's heels clicked as she walked through the Javitz Building. The Americans were clearly unprepared for this. They were dashing about, trying to cover too many tasks. She supposed it was to be expected after such a crisis.

What would England be like if our major cities were bombed? Better than this, I believe. We've been through it before. The Americans are simply spoiled.

Rose Kriswell, Marshall Ellerby's new secretary, was coming out of the office as Marisa walked up, so she caught a glimpse of the Secretary of Homeland Security staring out the window at Broadway. Medium height, medium build, his hair starting to bald, he was not unattractive, but he missed the wow factor somehow.

The only way that man could be the President of the United States in this media era is for nuclear bombs to take out all other contenders, even though he might be the most competent of the slate.

Marisa had never met Rose before. She knew her only from the nameplate on her desk. After introducing herself and while waiting for Rose to alert Ellerby of her presence, Marisa amused herself by wondering who Rose had served before Ellerby. Some lower government official, no doubt – a mere director of something. She had a regal carriage. She deserved better than Ellerby, Marisa was certain.(*When he falls, I'll ask her to join me at the UN.*

Ellerby didn't bother to turn from the window as she came in. This hastily acquired office space had a thrown-together look. That desk had been around since the 1970s, she was sure, and the executive chair had clearly been cleaned of storage dust just minutes before Ellerby's arrival.

It must gall him incredibly.

She knew Ellerby well enough to know that he wouldn't complain ... not yet anyway. He had his eyes on a long view, seeking to be accepted as president. Americans liked to believe their leaders were their idea, so Ellerby would take his time. He couldn't seem to be rising above his station too quickly.

Unfortunately for him, her employers were unlikely to allow him the long game. He would have to act soon or risk their support. The United States was too large an asset to allow to languish now that its people were being awakened.

Ellerby looked up from the briefing documents in his hands and favored her with a serpent's smile.

"To what do I owe this visit?" he asked. They embraced.

"Nazem hoped I could get a straight story from you, darling. Surely you know more than you said this morning."

"Tell me truthfully. Is this office bugged?"

Marisa laughed. Ellerby was clever.

"I'm sure it is. By who is the question."

"Not your boss?"

"As if I am authorized to give you that knowledge. No, darling. You'll have to uncover that on your own. So don't waste my walk over here. Tell me something I can take back to Nazem."

"I'm still getting reports as more areas are able to report in now. The military has coordinated with contractors to enclose the hot spots. That's the major effort at this point in time. Cleveland is already 80% contained."

"What do you make of the groups taking credit for the attacks? A green organization executing a nuclear bombing seems counterproductive."

"When I was with the FBI, I investigated several eco-terrorism attacks. They are not above hurting people. They believe people are harming the earth. They're quite capable of violence. But you're right. It's hard to reconcile their love of the planet with nuclear bombs. And then there's the other groups. Militias plot, but almost never execute. They can get their hands on conventional explosives and certainly they've committed major acts of terrorism by conventional means, so why risk something that could spin out of control? The Islamists plot and carry out far more attacks and they care little for the harm they do to others. But what those three groups would have in common ... I don't know. Plus, the groups we're discussing appear to be taking credit for only single attacks, which doesn't account for the other 10 or 12 attacks. So, what do I make of them? I need more evidence before I make anything of them."

"We're hearing there may be problems further west."

"I've been told by some military commanders that as Secretary of Homeland Security, I do not have authority to direct their efforts. If the President and Secretary of Defense are dead, they prefer a military commander. We'll give them time to come to their senses. This is still America and there is an established chain of command. It appears they are working in Denver and Portland to cap the hotspots. I can afford to give them time."

"Actually ...." This was the whole reason she had walked from the UN Building, to give her time to formulate how to say this to him. "Your request for UNDAC teams is suspended until you get the chain of command under control." His eyes widened. "When we put teams into war zones there needs to be some assurance of stability and at this time, you cannot promise that."

"This is not a war zone."

"Of course it is, darling. You just don't know who your enemy is yet." She looked at her watch. "I really must be off. I'll drop by on Monday to see if you know more. I wouldn't expect any aid until after the first of year in any case."

She said this as she was opening the door, so she was through the reception area and striding down the hall before Ellerby could react to that revelation.

She almost felt sorry for him. He didn't realize the currents swirling around him.

Frightfully Civilized

Emmaus, Delaney Ranch

Kim smiled and set aside her brush. Nevada looked up from staring at the wall.

"Are you finished?"

"I am." Kim turned the canvas so Nevada could see what she'd done. The painting was of a humming bird with its proboscis in a sunflower.

"The colors are fantastic," Nevada told her. "You could work on the shadows a little. It's hard to fix the sun direction in your mind when you're indoors. But you did a much better painting in details than I can do."

Kim smiled, but her happiness faded. No matter what they tried, the reality continued to assert itself. This was nuclear Armageddon. Life as they knew it would never be the same. Nevada turned on her cell phone to see what time it was. Midmorning on Saturday. When would they hear the storm sirens?

She had enjoyed the time together in the storm cellar. Kim had arranged it without guidance and so it had a sleepover quality to it – a futon mattress on the floor, supplies lined up under the single cot, a hand-cranked radio that so far hadn't picked up any signals and a gravity light that cast a surreal light over everything. They could go another three days on the food they had. Hopefully this would be over by then.

The banging came as a profound shock to the system. They both stared at the door to the stairs as someone hammered on the bulkhead doors. Nevada grabbed a flashlight, told (Daughter) to lock the door behind her and ventured up the narrow stairs.

"Who is it?"

"Max Albright. It's okay. The rain has stopped and the siren sounded. Come on out."

Max Albright? The last thing she had expected was for him to show up at her door. She unlatched the bulkhead and pushed it upward. Max added his strength to the effort. Fresh air rolled down over her, renewing her like water.

Max nodded, grey eyes somber.

"He's not with you then?" Nevada stared at him. Of course, that explained why he was here. "I know you two were together and I know why. I'm not going to go diva on you. I just ... he didn't come home."

Nevada breathed deeply, suddenly worried about Drew. She hadn't really thought about it before, assuming he'd been with Max.

"We left Chicago at the same time, but we took different routes back. I guess we didn't need to do that."

"All men cheat," Max informed her. "He may not know that I have, but ...." He had the grace to blush slightly. "He thought he was hiding the credit card statements. So, just so you know ... when he comes home, you two don't have to sneak around."

"Good to know, I guess. Do you know what's going on?"

"No. I came right here after I heard the siren. When he wasn't the first one to the door, I knew he wasn't with you."

"He's probably holed up somewhere on the way. I got caught in Phillipsburg overnight. He probably got stopped along the way and he'll be here as soon as he can."

"Yeah, probably." Neither of them was certain they weren't lying, but it would suffice for now. "Well, I'm going to City Hall to report him missing."

"If he contacts me, I'll tell him you're worried." That felt so odd to say. Max was spouse to her lover and they were being so frightfully civilized to one another. Max turned toward his BMW. He paused before climbing in.

"If you need something, while he's away ...."

She nodded and he got in his car and drove away.

That was freaking weird! No weirder though than a gay lover or nuclear Armageddon. All things are relative now. Everything changed on Wednesday.

She turned back to the shelter to let Kim know she could come out now.

A Well in Emmaus

Jericho Ghost Town

Jusilla's Stream ran full and now water poured from under the well house door and from the storage tank on the roof. Although a mess of flowing mud, the hill still hadn't washed out, probably owing to the scrub brush that had grown up its flanks. Jusilla's Stream was a one-foot-deep torrent of mud, grass and leaves. They paused on the bridge to watch it for a moment.

"Where does the stream go after it flows through the gold town?" Jazz asked.

"It's never flowed. Not since they capped the spring. But you have a point. If it had been filled in farther downstream, it would be backing up by now. Let's take care of this here first and then decide if we need to be concerned about it."

The normal approach to the well house was a slippery torrent of mud. When Shane went to put the key in the door, Jazz stopped him.

"That door opens outward and you have no idea how much water is behind it."

She felt the metal door. Shane put his hand at the bottom and worked his way up.

"About there." That was about 18 inches up the door. "Back up. This is going to be tricky."

He stood to the side, turned the key and let the door fling open. He jumped sideways, barely avoiding the water as it rushed out. The door slammed wide open against the concrete wall as the water boiled downhill. Jazz found a large rock to block the door open. Water flowed over their shoes as they entered. Inside a large pipe came out of the back wall. A mechanical valve controlled the flow, but just after that a black box straddled the pipe. Aluminum flex conduit ran from that to a box on the wall. Water poured through a vent in the roof. Jazz pointed to the black box.

"That's the solenoid. It's supposed to close when that storage tank gets too full and there are no fire hydrants calling for water. Its default must be open, because when the electricity was off for long enough, it stopped metering the water. If it continues at this rate, it's going to blow out the hydrants."

"Not to mention collapsing the well house. What about people in town? Does this provide water to their taps?"

"Yes, but there's a backup well under Beulah Park and most residential areas have individual wells that are still functional."

"And you know this because …?"

"In addition to the tour, one of my students wrote a paper on it – quoted your dad and everything."

"My dad – you mean the guy who didn't maintain the fallout shelters?"

"I thought you said …."

"My dad and I have a complicated relationship." He pointed to a wheel valve on a stand pipe that ran up to the roof and then to the larger wheel valve on the main pipe which dove back into the ground before leaving the building. "So we need to stop the diversion to that tank and we need to close the well head."

As he spoke, he grabbed the turn valve to the diversion. With a groan he slowly turned it to the closed position. The flow outside did not stop yet, but it would. Jazz had already grabbed the big valve to close the well head, but it hadn't moved. Shane now added his strength to the effort. It didn't budge. While he struggled to get any movement, Jazz went to the cabinet against the back wall. She returned with a crowbar and a long piece of pipe. He wedged the crowbar under one of the cross braces and tugged. The wheel moved a quarter inch and stuck. Further effort just caused him to slip on the wet floor.

"Damn it!" he hissed. "Fiscal conservatives suck!" He fitted the pipe over the end of the crowbar and threw his entire weight backward against it. It moved an eighth of an inch and stopped. Jazz tried to add her strength to the task, but her shoes just slid on the wet floor. Then she put her back to the lever and braced her feet against the pipe before it plunged into the concrete. Slowly, painfully, the valve wheel began to move. It slowed and then stopped as Jazz lost power as she stretched out.

"Switch places," Shane suggested.

The muscles in his back and legs screamed as slowly and painfully, the valve wheel finally moved to the closed position. He heard the water stop flowing.

"Wow!" they said in unison.

Water no longer poured from the roof hatch. Shane climbed the ladder, but the hatch refused to open and he took a shower for his trouble.

"The roof is probably an inch deep in water," Jazz suggested. She picked up a push broom. "Should we clean up?"

"We should go inspect the damage to report it to Ross."

"Ross died at City Hall," Jazz reported. *Who didn't die at City Hall?*

"Then we have plenty of more important things to do than sweep up mud. You don't have to come with me."

"I'm not afraid of heights," she assured him. She followed him up the outside ladder. Behind the low parapet, water stood an inch deep, slowly flowing out the scuppers. The tank seemed to be intact. Water was still coming out of a relief port, but it was slowing. Shane fished the diversion hose out of the roof lake and climbed up to reattach it. Jazz went back inside to find a spanner wrench to make it easier.

"Was this what you were doing when you tripped?"

"Yeah, more or less. This was obviously a two-person job. I couldn't have closed that valve without your help. We'd better head back."

"You're soaked."

"I'm fine. I've got clothes in the Jeep, but it's not really that important right now and it feels kind of good to rinse away days' worth of sweat."

They walked toward the Jeep. She caught up the Geiger counter and told him to hold still while she scanned him.

"You're fine."

"It's a closed tank and there was plenty of underground water washing that roof." She frowned at him. "You didn't think I didn't realize all open water sources are suspect right now?"

"You didn't act like it worried you. So, what about the stream?"

"It should dry up now that the water is shut off. We don't really have time to mess with it."

"So, do you really think this is your Dad's fault?"

"No, not completely. Like Jacob said, nobody thought the shelters were needed after the Soviet Union fell. There are engineers responsible for this well house. Dad should kick someone's butt for not thinking of a days' long power outage."

"And it's all the fault of fiscal conservatives?"

"No, that was me venting. I pay plenty of income tax and when I got my first property tax assessment, I became a fiscal conservative. I usually count to 10 before I erupt these days, but most people in town will tell you I'm a hot-head. Hence, getting pissed off about the paperwork. I can't really explain who Joel Rhys is, but I shouldn't have left private paperwork in the visor."

She gawked up at the sky behind him. He turned to see smoke billowing up beyond Jusilla's Ridge.

"What do you suppose that is?"

"We should go find out. I'm starting to see why we needed a four-person police force."

Seeking a Soul

Hardwick, New Jersey

Javier stared at his face in the mirror, memorizing the lines and contours that had been hidden under his beard for two years. Had his lips always been slightly crooked and his forehead so high? It didn't look like he was losing any hair, but that was a 5-head if ever he'd seen one. Shaving his beard had been a deliberate choice. Buzzing his hair had been an impulse. Shedding the identity of an Islamist terrorist should have felt good, but he just felt less hairy.

I had a soul once, didn't I?

Maybe your soul ceased to exist when you helped to kill 30 million people.

Rigby was supposed to stop it. How? There was no way for us to stop it. It went too deep. If Rigby got the message, he's analyzing the information. We'll bring people to justice ... if San Diego is still there.

Javi sighed and turned from the mirror. Anything he did now would never make up for all the death. Beyond this motel room was a new life and a new identity. He'd done this before and he might do it again, but the guilt would always be with him.

Hardwick, New Jersey seemed like a nice town, a good place to change his identity. Javi was pretty sure he'd like it if circumstances were different. It reminded him a little bit of his hometown, just normal Americana post-apocalypse. He was Martin Pulgarin, a Columbian-American from White Plains, divorced with two kids, worked as a maintenance man. His ex-wife lived in Colorado Springs. He was headed there to see his kids when this all happened. He was desperate to go see his kids.

The best cover stories were the simplest. He didn't need more than that. Too many lies were too hard to remember and he'd built those kids up in his mind so that he could cry on cue about his worry for their safety.

Checkout time was noon. He picked up a map from the bed and spread it out to look at it. Sure, his laptop could access websites that nobody else had access to right now, but he didn't want to risk it until he was further away from New York. The authorities were looking for a bearded Hispanic man who fit his vague description. He didn't need to wave any red flags by showing up in the middle of someone's wireless network seeking information other people couldn't access. Besides, Javi liked paper maps, liked how you could open them up and see a whole area rather than resizing. It reminded him of something from when he was a kid ... riding in the middle seat of a car while a woman told the driver how to get somewhere. He thought that might be his only memory of his parents.

Today, he would cross the Delaware into Pennsylvania and some of the danger of being caught would ease ... maybe. Months ago, Javi had bought a car and stashed it under his chosen identity. It was too old for GPS and had a clean registration. He thought he'd be all right, for a while ... maybe.

Every state-line crossing meant showing his ID to whichever authority was guarding the checkpoint. Traffic was always backed up for blocks as soldiers checked identification. It was a very dangerous situation for anyone with something to hide.

He held absolute confidence in his paperwork that included a carefully crafted clean identity engineered over the last several months and activated it just after he hit New Jersey on Wednesday night. He'd stayed the night at a motel, claiming to be on a trip to see his kids. The credit card had worked; nobody was looking for Martin Pulgarin, but if they had checked, Martin rented an apartment and paid utilities in White Plains. A college student who vaguely looked like him was getting a sweet house-setting deal until a week ago. Like everyone else, Martin had complied with the shelter-in-place order ... making appropriate concerned comments about his kids in case anyone was wondering. With the order lifted this morning, he felt certain he'd get across the bridge – in two days. By the time he'd heard the order had been lifted, the queue was already two miles long. He wanted to be west of the Delaware River two days ago, not stuck in traffic today. He hadn't fully anticipated the blowback from the New York attack. He'd figured they'd concentrate on the city and the routes in and out, not throw a net hundreds of miles inland. Sure, he sort of matched the description of one of the men who had delivered the bomb to Central Park, but his ID was solid. It was. If only he trusted his own work and – well, frankly, it would take two days to clear that bridge at the rate they were processing vehicles. From what he'd overheard on the scanner, it was better to find another way across.

Javier stared at his map, calculating. I-80 looked like a nice safe route, not near anything that had blown up. Once across the bridge, he could easily get there and head west. Except ….

The black-suited mercenaries worried him. He knew Knight Industries, of course. They did much of the fighting in the Middle East these days and were the defacto security force stateside. The typical crony capitalist entanglement on steroids, it made so much sense that they were mixing with the Army personnel. They had different sources of information than the military, which made Javi's identification less secure. It might be safer to swim the river and regroup on the other side.

Risking the bridge held advantages. He wouldn't have to secure a new set of wheels or locate food. Hardwick had a perfectly nice grocery store and he'd already bought the supplies he needed. Assuming he could get across the bridge, he needed to decide on a destination. Rethinking his paranoia about the internet, he used his notebook to pull up various safe houses. That hollow feeling in his chest meant he grieved for the folks lost in the conflagrations. Raised in foster care, he didn't have folks to mourn, but he'd had friends ... once.

Concentrate! Where wouldn't they be looking? His entire career had been spent in South America and urban zones. He needed somewhere rural. Two sites in Nebraska. No, they were activated. He couldn't trust the people there were on his side.

Whoa! The Emmaus house has gone active? I thought the firm sold it after they disbanded the McAuliff militia. Who would be assigned there and why? Rigby was in charge of that op. Could it be?

He opened one of his many email accounts and sent a message to one of Rigby's secure emails.

Are you at the well? J

Of course, there wouldn't be an answer immediately. He'd have to wait until he was across the Delaware before he risked checking. If Rigby was indeed in Emmaus, he might have hope of redemption.

Confusion on a Platter

Emmaus, Lufgren Farm

Keri Lufgren filled her car with gasoline from their private pump, staring as Shane pulled into the driveway, wondering why in the world Jazz Tully was exiting the passenger seat.

"How do you two know each other?"

"Nice to see you too, sis. Jazz and I met the other day," Shane said, like it was the most normal thing in the world. When she frowned at him, he explained. "Dad's sending us to Mara Wells and to make a wide sweep around town to check things out. Can I borrow some fuel?"

"Sure. Alex asked me to do those things, but he could use my help here, so go for it. Just remember to stop at Lufgren farms, because they can't hear the storm siren."

He rolled his eyes at her and signed "Know that." Alex came over wearing rubber boots and carrying a shovel, smelling strongly of cow manure.

While Shane explained the new plan to him, Keri drew Jazz away.

"Why are you two together?"

"Shane needed someone who knew something about the well house and I needed something to do to distract me."

"The apocalypse isn't distracting enough?"

"You don't know?"

"Know what?"

"Close to a hundred people died in the City Hall shelter when the air handling system failed."

The world turned on its side, the sun went behind a cloud, all the air was sucked out into space and Mocha licked her fingers while Jazz helped her sit down on the porch stairs.

"You're sure?"

"I helped find the few survivors. Shane found them. I think we both needed ...."

"Cai and Marnie? Mom and Dad?" Jazz flinched as if rebuked for attending to her own trauma.

"They were in other shelters. I haven't seen Cai or Marnie, but Shane talked to them."

Keri swallowed nausea.

"I knew people would die in the aftermath of this, but ...."

"Yeah. Marvin Groseclose was there."

"Oh, God. "Keri's throat felt choked as she blinked back sudden tears. "Marv was such a nice guy!" Tears spilled down her cheeks. Although Keri was an elementary school teacher and Jazz and Marvin were high school teachers, they all worked on the same campus and attended the same Christmas parties. Jazz sat beside her, waiting for the storm to subside.

"Whoever did this deserves a special place in hell," Keri muttered, wiping away tears to put her grief aside. "I have work to do and you and Shane should get those others out of those shelters before there's more tragedy."

"We will."

"Also ... be careful with my brother. Shane is not Cai. He never gives any thought to the danger he's putting himself and others in."

"We're all in danger right now, Keri. Which doesn't mean I am not hearing you, but that I think you forget that we're both adults. Trust me. I dated Paul Osimowicz. I can handle myself."

Shane had finished filling the Jeep. What had he and Alex been discussing because Shane looked irritated and Alex looked uncomfortable.

"Hey, sometime soon, you need to actually come talk with us," Keri told her brother.

"I had planned it," Shane assured her. "The end of the world got in the way." Poppy came out of the house with Keri's shoulder holster and 9 mm. She handed it to Shane, who held it out to Jazz, who donned the holster and checked the gun's status. "We'll get this back to you, Ker. I just think, given the circumstances, it's best if she's armed and we didn't plan on that."

"Of course. Jazz, you be careful out there." Jazz nodded as she cocked and locked the gun before sliding it back into the holster.

"You look really familiar with that," Shane complimented.

"That would be true," she agreed. "I'm ready. We probably should get going."

"Sounds good. Out of curiosity ... who are they?" Shane asked, nodding toward their new family members.

"Mark and Alice Ramirez and their two kids," Alex reported. "They were working here when the bombs hit. I couldn't leave them in a camper during the rain."

"They look like hard workers. We're going to need people like that." Then to Jazz. "Let's go."

"Spread the word about the meeting tonight," Alex told him. Shane nodded and he and Jazz headed to the car.

Watching Shane drive down the driveway, Keri noticed the documents in Alex' hand.

"What are those?"

"Confusion on a platter. Your brother has this whole secret identity that includes owning two corn fields that means he must have a net worth in the millions. I mean, I could buy that he's rich enough to buy the old Jericho Springs hotel and remodel it, but this .... He wants me to harvest the corn. And he's right that the town may need the food, but ...." He handed her the documents to read.

They were land deeds for Joel Rhys. The fields were just to the west of the ridge.

"You think he's lying to you, convincing you to steal corn?"

"No. I think he's telling the truth. That's what freaks me out. Who the hell is Shane Delaney? I do not recognize this man as my best friend since kindergarten."

"Yeah. I know what you mean and I have no idea what to tell you. Whoever he is, he's uniquely suited to this disaster, so we should probably be grateful he's here."

Alex heaved a sigh.

"Can you run these into the desk? I have to get back to work. I think best when I'm working and I need to prepare for the cooperative meeting tonight. Shane says we have to get rid of any open water sources because the rain would have contaminated it. Can you take the Geiger counter and go check all the stock troughs?"

She did what he asked. On this gorgeous September morning, it was almost impossible to believe that bad things were still working to kill them, but they had to keep that in mind now. The world as they had known it had ended and a new more dangerous one was dawning.

World Gone Mad

Seattle Washington

*T*he parking lot of Quality Food was packed with a winding line of desperate people who just wanted food. Geo wished he could just throw open the doors and let people get what they needed, but there were procedures that must be followed.

Geo Tully read the woman's address and keyed it into his laptop. Nothing. She looked tired and stressed, holding a toddler by one hand and an infant on her hip.

"Charlie, can you check this address?" he asked his partner. Charlie smiled at the man he'd just cleared and did as requested.

"Nope," he said.

"I'm sorry, ma'am, but you are not assigned to this grocery store," Geo explained.

"This is the closest grocery store to my home and I've already been to Safeway and Markettime. Where am I supposed to get food?"

"I don't have that information, ma'am. I have to ask that you step out of line."

"My children are hungry. We're out of milk." Her volume increased as her voice became shriller. She was about to cry. The baby whined. "I'm almost out of gasoline to drive to another store. Can't you tell me which store to go to?"

"I would have said Markettime, but I don't have where you go in my database."

Charlie spoke in his radio.

"Ma'am, our commander is going to come out and speak with you," he said. "Please step out of line and we'll try to help you."

Maybe I'm not the right person for this. Calling the commander didn't occur to me.

Geo was clearing someone else when a sergeant came out to speak to the woman. He gently guided her toward a trailer off to the side of the screening area. As she entered, two MPs followed. Geo shivered in the sun. He'd seen a few people go in there, but nobody ever came out smiling. They didn't come out at all. There was a back door, but somehow he didn't think it was the exit to paradise.

His family flickered through his mind's eye. He'd tried to reach them on the telephone, but the lines were down. He was fairly certain Jazz and Michael were fine. Mara Wells was far enough from Denver and Kansas City that they should be fine in the basement. The folks concerned him. They'd been headed to Florida. Had they been there when the nukes detonated? Were they still alive? Stuck on a road somewhere?

What was going on across the street? He looked sideways at Charlie when the guy in the front of the line asked him "What's wrong?"

Charlie's freckles stood out starkly against his white skin and ginger hair. He fumbled with his earpiece, mouth drawn back in an expression of shock.

"What's wrong?" Geo asked, but then he heard gunfire from the trailer. He sprang to his feet, drawing his service weapon. "Get out of here," he yelled to the crowd that had started to mill lazily. Charlie was on his feet now too, drawing his own weapon, but before he even had it clear of his holster, he was thrown back against the wall of the store by two slugs to the chest while Geo flipped the table and dropped to his knees.

Chaos reigned beyond his temporary shelter. A man dragged his middle-grader behind it with him, covering the kid with his own body. Geo saw a wave of black suited men headed their way, sheathed in Kevlar and carrying deadly firepower. Some of them were targeting US military personnel while others were targeting the fleeing civilians. Bullets dented the table top. A gun materialized from the father's jacket. Geo combat crawled over to Charlie. The E3 was past saving, but Geo grabbed his gun and checked for additional mags before crawling back to the table.

"I'll draw them off. You and the kid go the other direction," Geo told the father.

"God bless you, sir," the man said. He whispered to the boy, who shook with terror, but nodded. The father looked at Geo.

"We'll break right. Think it's worth it to go for my car?"

Geo fished in his breast pocket.

"See that APC over there?" The father nodded. Geo handed him the keys. "You'd be better off with that. The doors are unlocked. Don't stop. Roll over whatever gets in your way. Go on three."

"Wait. Son, I know you're scared, but I need you to have your wits about you. We're going to that truck. I'm killing anyone who gets in our way. Stay behind me on the left and don't let go of my belt. We're not stopping for anyone. Got it?"

The kid's frightened blue eyes widened with new knowledge of his father. He sobbed once and then nodded, his soft boy's mouth stiffening.

"One, two, three. Go."

Geo stood and sprinted for the far end of the store. Bullets began whizzing by his head, ricocheting off the concrete. He cut in behind a car and fired at the nearest black suit. The APC roared to life and lurched forward. The mercenary fell. Another turned toward the truck. Geo drew down on his neck and his head exploded. The APC picked up speed, headed toward the exit. Geo headed for the next car, where another soldier lay unmoving. He collected the dead guy's 9 and mags, knocked a mercenary down with two bullets to the chest and moved on. A mercenary stepped into his path. Geo fired into his face mask. The guy rolled on the ground until Geo plunged his knife deeply into his throat. Now he had a Mac 10 and a half dozen mags. Geo was on the move, clearing his path with the Mac. He was vaguely aware that an MP had joined him, armed similarly by scavenging. They ran around the edge of the shopping center.

"Where to?" the MP asked. *Okay, if you think I should be in charge ...*

"See that old truck over there? I can probably hotwire the thing. We have got to get out of here."

"Go. I've got your back."

The MP shot a mercenary as they were moving, but they covered the rest of the distance to the truck unmolested. It obviously belonged to a landscaper. An elbow to the wing window got the door open and hotwiring it was a matter of seconds. It was old enough not to have a steering lock. They drove out of the back of the parking lot and roared away from the bedlam.

"What the hell was that?" Geo demanded, power-sliding around a corner. Civilians were fleeing in all directions. He braked for a gaggle of children led by an older child with a blood-splattered dress. As soon as they crossed, he powered forward.

"I have no idea. They just suddenly came out of nowhere. I was monitoring radio transmissions and

I picked up chatter just about the time they hit the parking lot."

"We need to get off the road. These uniforms identify us as their prey."

"There's a sporting goods store two blocks up and a few to the right. We can get clothes and more ammo. I'm Marcus, by the way. Wes Marcus."

"George Tully. Geo."

"It's not nice to meet you, but I'm glad you've got my back. You're clearly not a standard clerk."

"I'm actually a Navy SEAL. They asked me to fill in for the day here and suggested I wear the uniform just so I wouldn't confuse people."

"Turn left here."

A couple more blocks and Marcus told him to turn right and stop in front of a strip mall. The sporting goods store was about halfway down. The front window had been smashed and two men emerged with bulging duffle bags. Marcus caught Geo's arm as he moved to get out and confront them, so they waited for them to drive away before entering the store. They were trying on jeans and shirts when they heard the loud speaker informing people of martial law by order of the mayor and ordering people to shelter in place. Geo pulled his feet up into the changing booth and held his breath. There were voices noting that the place had been cleaned out and then they faded. After what seemed like forever, he heard Marcus creep across the store and then come back.

"I guess they have bigger issues than looting that's already occurred.

"What do we do?" Geo asked.

"We get the hell out of here. I'm not staying some place where they're killing soldiers."

"I'm pretty sure those were Knight Industry mercs. They don't do anything without someone crossing their palms with silver."

"But why?"

"I don't know. That outside said it was by order of Mayor Sollis. He never seemed like an insurrectionist."

"Nobody ever nuked most of the cities south of his before," Marcus said, but he was distracted by his ear piece. "Okay, I think they're blocking most of the bridges and I5. We can't stay here and we can't run, but I know a place where we can hole up for a few days, figure out how to get away from the city. What are you doing?"

"Stowing my gear." Geo shoved his Kevlar and weapons into a duffle bag. "It's a liability right now, but it might not be later."

Marcus stared at him a moment and then grabbed another duffle bag.

"Why were you wearing it?" he asked. "I mean … my job … you do, but a clerk …?"

"SEAL paranoia maybe. I don't know. Never thought I'd be in a war in my own country. Let's go."

They looked cautiously up and down the deserted street before crossing to the truck.

What to Do with a Murderer

City Hall

Behind City Hall, pairs of men loaded bodies into the back of the Big I, the large truck normally used by Jacob and Rob to haul feed supplies. The back door was still locked, but Cai had a key, so he let himself in to join his father on the third floor. Rob and Jacob were trying to get anything on the old Emergency radio, but they weren't having a lot of luck.

"Dad, I need to talk with you ... and Granddad too, I think."

"Marnie tell you what's going on here?" Rob asked.

"Yeah. Shane has nerves of steel, that's all I can say. I'd have been in a panic."

"That crystal clarity passes for panic for some people," Jacob remarked.

"What's up?" Rob asked.

"The pilot died."

151

"What pilot?"

"Commuter aircraft landed on the field, the kid shot him ...." Jacob prompted.

"Oh, right, Pa, sorry. So much has been going on! Kid's still in the holding cells. Bart was in the shelter. Normally I'd ask him what I should do with him, but ...." His voice grew hoarse with grief.

"He'd usually go to county for the real jail," Cai said, clearing his throat.

Jacob shifted, blinking tears out of his eyes.

"Pa?" After all, the man had been a three-term mayor himself.

"I think this is martial law, Rob, which means the military ought to be rolling up soon with some directives."

"They aren't here yet and we've got an evolving situation. We should go check the Homeland Security manual. I think we report to Fort Riley under martial law."

"What are we doing about ... about the dead?" Cai asked.

"I asked Vern Carlson to open a section of Beulah with a backhoe," Jacob reported. Rob blinked at him. "We gotta be realistic. We don't have refrigeration for that many bodies and we can't bury eighty people in the traditional way."

Rob nodded, swallowing his distaste.

In his office he set the DHS manual on his desk, then used the indexed tabs to find the section he needed.

"Looks like Ft. Riley. That takes someone out for the rest of the day."

"Do we have to take him today?" Jacob asked.

"We don't need responsibility for him."

"If this isn't martial law, we'd usually take him to the Beulah County Jail pending State charges," Cai said.

"You're thinking like a civilian, son. Of course, martial law is coming."

"Is it?" Jacob asked. "There's no president to declare it nationally and we haven't heard anything from the Governor's office, so logic dictates that we follow the usual procedure."

Rob stared at them both, not sure what to say. Sometimes it was best just to walk through things.

"We have a shelter-in-place order from Homeland. That's the last thing we heard, so ... that lets out Ft. Riley and Topeka, for now. Cai, radio your brother and ask him to swing over to Beulah on his sweep. It's just plain weird that they're not answering."

Cai went out to the lobby to get Shane on the base station since the hand-helds didn't reach all the way to Lufgren's Crossing. Jacob lowered his rump onto the edge of Rob's desk.

"You need to consider that we're on our own," he said softly. "The structures we were used to are gone. We may have to deal with our young murderer on our own, as well as a whole lot of issues we never thought we would face before."

"You think this is anarchy?"

"I think we need to be prepared for that, yeah."

Rob stared at the wall, overwhelmed by the thought. After a moment, he summed up his feelings on the subject.

"Damn," he said calmly.

"Yup, what you said."

Knowing Your Neighbors

Delaney Ranch

*T*he horses kicked up their heels as Jill let them out into the paddock. Nevada and Kim had already removed the straw bales from the stable's front door before Jill got there. They worked together to open the back door so the horses could be let out to run. The troughs here were under wide eaves, so the Geiger counter didn't show any increase of radiation above the background level which was not that much higher than ordinary.

Kim set about feeding the horses while Nevada worked with Jill to mix the feed for the coming week.

"How did it go in the shelter here?" Jill asked.

"It was fine. Kim is really pretty easy to spend time with. What about you?"

"Rob and I enjoyed a couple of days just the two of us. I suppose it was a nice break before we had to deal with this mess."

"It's awful," Nevada agreed. "What is wrong with people?"

"I don't know. It's hard to fathom any of it. I never felt it was my place to ask. Do you have family out there somewhere?"

"Not really. Kim's father has been out of our lives for a long time and my parents are both dead. It's just the two of us. I have a brother at Ft. Lewis, but we don't talk much. There's a lot of years between us."

"I grew up in Seattle. Met Rob when he was stationed at Ft. Lewis."

"Really? Small world. Is Seattle still there?"

"Not sure. I saw a list on Thursday that didn't have Seattle on it. I think that might be a good sign." They nodded and smiled. Jill usually did this by herself, but found this was pleasant. It reminded her of coming to visit Vi when they'd lived in the apartment above the stables. "What brought you to Kansas?" she asked.

"When my dad died, I got his life insurance and retirement, which he hadn't touched yet. So we had money and I wanted to try to make a living with my art. I'd met Mrs. Sims' daughter on the Internet and she kept talking about what a lovely town this was and then how her mother was retiring from the dance studio. I thought I'd come and operate the school and do art and raise Kim."

"You thought of it as an adventure?"

"Yes. I've never lived in the country before."

"Do you like it?"

"I do. When I got here the other day … I was away when the bombs hit, so I got here just as the rain was coming. Your son Cai was here making sure Kim was okay. That never would have happened in the city. I was absolutely amazed. And that's what I love about living here."

"We are a neighborly bunch."

"We are. After two years, I almost feel okay to say 'we'."

"That's about right. It took me about that long too. So, you're really here all on your own."

"Mostly. I – well, there's a man I was, uh, sleeping with."

Jill thought it was cute that Nevada seemed embarrassed to say that.

"A local man? Don't worry. I don't want to know who."

"Yes, he's local. I found out today that his spouse knows about us."

"Oh, my! Sounds awkward."

Why do you young women get yourselves into these messes?

"It was. Um, his, uh, spouse said something curious. 'All men cheat.' My ex did. And my lover is. Do you think that's true?"

"Statistically speaking, a lot of men cheat. To my knowledge, Rob never has on me. I don't think Jacob ever cheated on Vi. So, ALL men … I don't think that's true."

"What would you do if you found out he had?"

"I'd be angry and he'd sleep somewhere I wasn't for a while."

"You wouldn't divorce him?"

"We've been married nearly 40 years, so no, probably not, but we nearly divorced in the early days."

"Why? Or, er, that's probably none of my business."

"No, it's fine. Rob had a tough time after Vietnam and that was hard on our marriage. We lost a baby and we were fighting all the time and for a while there he was dangerous. We separated until he got his head screwed on straighter and then we came back together."

"How'd he convince you to trust him again?"

"He serenaded me night after night for weeks until I agreed to go on a date with him and then things just gradually resumed."

"Wow. I never wanted to see him again."

"Yes, but Rob didn't cheat on me. Cheating is different. Adultery really changes the dynamic. If that had been the problem 30+ years ago, we might not have been able to repair it."

"So you just forgave him and that saved your marriage?"

"No. Rob accepted God's forgiveness which made him willing to make amends. For us, the relationship is definitely bound by our faith."

"You believe in God?"

"Yes."

"Even after all this?"

"Oh, yes. More so. God told us millennia ago that we would do horrible things to one another. This isn't a surprise."

"I thought God was about making people better."

"He is, but mankind is not warm and fuzzy. We invite destruction. We conjure it up. God could lead us not to do these things to ourselves, but we refuse His guidance and it leads to this."

"Or the Crusades."

Why do they always try to change the subject?

"You have a point," Jill said, while washing her hands at the sink. "The Catholic Church, which did not represent all of Christianity even at that time, turned a defensive action into a holy war and that was wrong. But don't mistake the work of an ecclesiastic body with that of God Himself. The two are not one in the same."

"Doesn't the Pope speak for God?"

"No. The Bible speaks for God. Popes are just men who have been given power and wrapped in ceremony and myth. Some of them have been godly men and some of them have been anything but."

Nevada frowned and Jill couldn't think of anything more to say.

Take the Holy Spirit's hint, Jill. Don't push.

"If you ever want to sit down and discuss what I believe, let me know. For now, I need to get back to the house." Kim was standing at the fence watching the horses cavort. Rocket was still bucking like a foal.

"I really need to be headed back. Can you put them away this evening?"

"Yes, ma'am," Kim assured. She and Jacob had worked out some sort of monetary arrangement that included being allowed to ride and she'd done a good job feeding and water and shoveling manure. Jacob enjoyed mentoring young people.

"Thank you." Jill waved at Nevada and headed back to the house, taking the old farm road through the cottonwood grove rather than the roundabout paved roads.

Mara Wells

Old 24 West of Lufgren Crossing

Jazz stared out the side window as they drove Old 24 toward Mara Wells. Shane wished he could enjoy the bright blue sky and rain-washed air, but he had to keep dismissing the feeling of his cells breaking down. He didn't want to interrupt her deep thoughts, so he caught up the Geiger counter to operate it himself. She stirred.

"I think that may constitute distracted driving. Give it over."

He obeyed, though the road was completely deserted and mostly straight and he saw no signs of IEDs.

"It's a little higher here than in Emmaus, Townhall was just under 300 there and we're now at 300 here."

"What did you know about radiation exposure a week ago?"

"I didn't. I would have been freaking out at this number a week ago. Now I know we can get cancer twenty years from now if we're exposed to this level for 90 days."

He slowed at the town sign.

"Check the radio. They're supposed to be on Channel 7."

They weren't. Jazz felt panicked by the time she got someone on the radio, on Channel 5.

"Glad to hear your voice, Emmaus," Stan Osimowicz, Mara Wells' mayor, said. "Are we back to normal radiation levels? Over"

"No, but we're at survivable levels," Jazz explained. "And the levels should continue to drop. Keep young children in the shelters until levels drop to 100. Uh, over."

"Roger that. Who is this? Over"

"Jazz Tully. You should check on your people. Emmaus had one shelter fail. Over."

"Are you okay, Jazz?" another voice said, squelching badly.

"I'm good, Paul. Thanks for asking. Where's Michael? Over."

"Not sure. He's not here with me. Over."

"Emmaus out." When Paul started speaking, she turned the radio down to a murmur before she set it on the consol. "Can we go to my house?"

"Sure." Then he asked a question he didn't think he'd ever asked anyone in Emmaus before. "Where is that?"

The streets were eerily empty. They drove to a farmhouse Victorian on the northwest edge of town. As they got out, they heard a weak meow. A pitiful ball of fur lay on the lawn.

"Oh my! That's the neighbor's cat."

It had obviously been exposed to a lethal dose of radiation. Fur was shedding. It was bleeding from the nose.

"I'll meet you at the front door," Shane said. "You don't need to see this."

She didn't ask what he was going to do and Shane tried to be quick about it. After the big rock came down on the cat's head, he saw a shovel leaning against the wall of Jazz's house. He was just tapping down the dirt when Jazz came out of the house with a gangling young man who was clearly related to her. He had the same dark hair tinged red, though his eyes were more gray than green. They shared a similar mouth. *I thought she rinsed her hair to get that reddish tone. So much for my observation skills.*

"My brother, Michael," Jazz introduced. "It was Tinkerbell," she explained.

"I'll let them know. They tried to find her before they went to the shelter and I promised I'd catch her if I saw her, but I didn't see her before the storm sirens sounded."

"It's not your fault.

"I know, but it still feels ... sad."

"I'm Shane Delaney, by the way. I assume you had a basement to stay in."

"I did. Dad would be proud of me, Jazz. I spent the time reloading bullets."

"Cool. I'm just going to get my guns and be right back, Shane."

"So you're not staying?" Michael asked.

"No. I have a job at the moment."

Jazz headed back to the house, leaving two strangers standing together over a cat's grave.

"Delaney. You're related to the mayor?"

"His son."

"What is Jazz doing? This job? You guys aren't trying to have school in this mess."

"She volunteered to sweep up to Donovan's Elevators and across to Brady's Tanks than back down 83 to check out Beulah with me."

"Sweep?"

"Just making sure people heard the siren and start to harvest their fields. We need to assume the government is not showing up to guide us through the process."

"Yeah, that's why I was reloading bullets. If things are going to hell in a handbasket, my dad would say you can trade ammo for food and fuel."

"You're not wrong there. I'll suggest to folks they start collecting their brass."

Michael nodded. Shane guessed he was about 20 – the kid left at home to watch the place while the parents took a retirement trip. His parents had left him with Keri one summer when he'd been back from college. He'd been an okay home caretaker, but Keri had spent more nights alone than not. He'd had to cover up one party that could have gotten her into a lot of trouble.

Jazz came from the house carrying a duffle bag filled with, he assumed, guns, with a rifle over her shoulder. She'd found a large plaid shirt to pull over her tank top. It partially concealed the 9 mm. And she had donned a gimme-cap to cover her unwashed hair. Or maybe it was to shade her eyes. It was a bright and sunny day the other side of Shane's sunglasses.

"Michael, could you go get the box of ammo from the entryway?"

"Sure. You know we're only 15 miles apart, right?"

"Your arsenal is always 20 minutes away when danger is right there in front of you," she quipped. He laughed at her reinterpretation of a gun culture meme and headed for the house. Shane opened the trunk to the Jeep so she could stow the duffle bag. She set the rifle on top.

"That's an old World War 2 issue," Shane remarked of the 30-06.

"My great-grandfather served. He and Jacob actually knew one another."

"Yeah, it's rural Kansas," Shane scoffed.

"No, over there. Jacob told me stories about him. They knew each other here too, but Jacob told me stories I'd never heard before. GPa gave my dad the gun and Dad passed it to me a couple years ago because the boys thought it was old-fashioned. I knew he'd carried it in the war, but I didn't know he actually saw combat. He was part of your grandfather's unit."

Shane could see the pride in her green eyes.

They lived through hell and the ghosts of the fallen follow them through a lifetime. Why don't they ever tell those stories?

She stepped from around the Tully house garage. He needed to change the subject before he started obsessing.

"You weren't joking about being a gun culture girl."

"No. Those NRA training courses were how I paid for college. What about you?"

"Student loans, which was stupid, and driving truck for Breen." She shot him a sidelong look. "I know his reputation, but it's largely undeserved. He hauls liquor to some of the dry communities, but that's about the only illegal activity I ever saw."

"Wasn't he involved with a militia?"

"No, some of his guys were involved with the militia – including his son Josh. Jason is actually an anarchist like my grandfather."

"But he's a felon!"

"Nope! He was accused and arrested for a crime way back when Marnie was little, but two juries hung and he was released. He hires felons, but he himself is not a felon."

Michael came out of the house lugging a backpack bulging with boxes.

"It's a good thing I reloaded. You're not going to be able to turn around in your apartment."

"Says the man with enough weapons to arm a small nation."

"They don't all belong to me. Of course, this shotgun and AR don't belong to you either."

"Dad won't mind and you know it. Have you heard from Geo or Jim?" Michael shook his head. "Mom and Dad?" Again the answer was negative.

"They're probably fine." Jazz sounded more certain that Shane suspected she was. "How are you fixed for food?"

"The folks laid in a lot of food before they left, thinking they'd not have to worry too much about it in their first year of retirement. I probably have enough to get through the winter. You?"

"I might be back to dip into the family stores. You take care."

They hugged. A car slowed and turned into the driveway next door.

"I guess I'd better ...."

Shane and Jazz nodded. While he got into the car, Jazz paused a moment to scan the front of the house. Then she got into the car.

"Let's go."

"I probably know this because of what's in the cargo area, but if you want to stay ...."

"No. I moved to Emmaus for a reason and I have a reason for staying there."

Well, that's obscure, but I'm not one to judge …
being the master of obscurity.

"Just thought I'd give you a choice."

He slid the shifter into 1st gear and headed out of town.

Moving in the Right Direction

East of the Delaware River

*J*avi's every instinct screamed of the stupidity of this idea. *Don't get stuck in traffic!* But there was really no other way forward. He left enough of a gap between his Isuzu Trooper and the car in front of him so that he could take to the ditch if he absolutely had to. The line might see him over the bridge by sundown. That was bad, but at least it gave him time to listen to the radio. The mayor of New York gave a speech before the UN. Javi wondered who was pulling his strings. That he was alive was proof enough that he was a puppet.

Is it Rigby in Emmaus? And if it is, can I trust him? You've trusted him for years. And look what's happened? You don't have a choice. Why would he choose Emmaus? The water. Remember that? Of all the safe houses, it is the one with the most secure water source. Water is life. The house is too close to a community.

Javi watched as a Knight walked up to his window. All he could hope was that this was just a standard check because killing a Knight right now would be his death sentence.

The Knight asked for his identification and registration. Javi cooperated. He knew how Martin Pulgarin would act.

"Where you headed?" the Knight asked. He was watching his tablet while he was engaging Javi in conversation.

"Colorado Springs."

"Why? This says White Plains."

"My kids are there."

"They with your ex?"

"Yeah. I was headed there when this happened."

"Gotta make sure they're safe." Something came up on his tablet. He handed Javi back his identification. "You can move into the left lane to go forward. Just so you are aware, Pittsburg and Cleveland are both irradiated. You want to stick to I-80 through Youngstown. Going west St. Louis, Kansas City, Chicago and Denver are all hot zones. You have iodine tablets?"

"I do."

"Good. There are posts along the way that will suggest routes around the danger zones. It's not as easy as it was, but you can still get there." The Knight cleared his throat as his voice suddenly grew choked. "When you see your kids hug them tight. Mine were in Detroit." He took a deep breath and let it out slowly.

"I'm sorry, man. I hope it turns out they went on a trip or something."

"Thank you." The Knight clearly knew that wasn't the case, but Javi knew Martin would hope for the best. "The left lane is clearing pretty fast. Ought to have you across the river by sundown at current rate."

"Thank you."

Javi steered into the open left lane. Soon enough he was behind another car, but that was fine because the car was moving and that meant things were going in the right direction. He wanted to be across that river by night and headed toward Emmaus within the next 24 hours.

An Unusual Request

Emmaus City Hall

A crowd gathered on the front lawn of City Hall. Jacob watched, wondering what Rob expected to do about it. Joe offered coffee, which he was making in a French press to save electricity. Jason Welton had come to check out the system and reported that the overheated air handler in the shelter had caused the generator to "self-protect" and shut down. The time it had been down had partially drained the battery backup, so Jason had recommended they not use electricity for much.

"One's my limit, thanks. How's your head?"

Joe had been clubbed in the head during a small gasoline riot day before last. He touched the bandage on his forehead.

"Been too busy to even think about it," he admitted. "The school shelter was pretty well maintained, but that many people together in a tight space for 30 hours .... How were things where you were?"

"About the same. We were above ground, but the old factory kept us safe. Still, people forced to spend that much time together in a confined space get bored and irritable. You doing okay?"

Joe sighed deeply and his eyes grew shiny for a moment.

"I am the entire Emmaus police department at the moment. Bart died. And umm, well, Shell Davis is still alive." He barked an ironic laugh.

"Where was he during the rain?"

"In the shelter, but he's just one of the ones who survived. And, the kid who killed the pilot ... he sat the rain out in the cells and he seems fine too. Doesn't really seem fair."

"No, it doesn't, but life is not often fair, much as we would like it to be."

Rob came out of the office.

"I'm going go down and talk to the crowd, see if I can get them to go home."

"Most of them aren't townsfolks. They sheltered here after they came off the interstate," Jacob explained.

"Then we should ask Donna to open the motel again."

"She was one of the people who died in the shelter," Joe announced.

Rob closed his eyes for a moment and just breathed. *You look like a man who could use a drink.*

"Are we collecting personal effects from the dead?"

"We are. I asked the volunteers to tag them."

"See if we can find Donna's keys and then … Pa, can you go open the motel?"

"Of course. I'll get on that right now and let those folks on the lawn know what I'm doing." He leaned in for a little privacy, though Joe was known to assuage gossip of any sort. "Son, take a minute, count to 12. If I see Lemuel, I'll send him your way."

Rob shot him a surprised look, then nodded. In the 30 years he'd been sober had he ever been under so much stress before?

"Thank you, Pa. Speaking of that … you'll be headed in that direction. If you see Maggie, ask her to keep the bar closed, please. I know the others have the sense not to open, but she's the one I worry about."

"I'll make the request, but you should probably remember that you have no real control over private businesses."

"It's a request. We just don't need drunks right now."

"You're right there."

Jacob headed down the stairs. At the back door, he saw Ren Sullivan crawling up the loading dock.

"This does not look good." The billionaire watched as a pair of volunteers carried a body to the waiting truck. "What happened?"

"Air handling system failure. What brings you here?"

"You remember how I let you qualify on the EA-500?"

"I'm old, not senile."

"Would you fly me to Wichita?"

"I only fly solo these days."

"I know that, but this is special circumstances and if you were to die in flight, I could still land it. It's just that I haven't got a license and I don't need the hassle of explaining myself to the FAA."

"Why can't your own guy fly you?"

"Joseph absconded with him right before the rain. I think he was worried about Katherine, who is perfectly safe in New York. I can't get my office on the horn and I really don't like being out of touch."

Control freak!

"I got a few things to do before I can say 'yes' and then I should probably let the mayor make the call since right now, I'm serving at his pleasure."

"Since when do you serve at anyone's pleasure?"

"What was the last year I was mayor? I took an oath and I'm not sure I can rescind that now. I'm on a mission. Go tell Rob what you're asking and we'll see what he says."

Donna's keys had already been tagged. Jacob took them and let himself out the front door of City Hall. The crowd almost immediately began to coalesce around him. They knew him from the factory shelter and trusted him.

"We don't know what the larger situation is, but for those who want to stay here, the mayor has authorized me to open the Ranch Motel. I'll need a volunteer to run the registration until I can find someone from the town to take over the job. You're welcome to stay, but you'll have to clean up after yourselves and figure out the food situation. We are a small town. We don't have resources to operate a shelter."

"I'll volunteer," said a pretty dark haired woman with a riot of curls. Jacob knew her as Kristine. She was originally from Egypt, but had been an American citizen since she was 12. "I stayed there my first night."

"Thank you. I'll be at the motel in half an hour."

His 64 Dodge truck waited in the parking lot. He drove to Callahan's Bar and Grille, where Maggie was smoking a cigarette and trying to start the generator.

"Are you trying to blow yourself up, woman?" he demanded.

"You don't need to go lecturing me about smoking," she complained.

"No, I'm lecturing you about trying to start a generator with an open flame in hand. Go stand over there." He cleared the choke and pulled the starter. It cranked, sputtered and caught. "Rob's asking that you don't open, or that you at least don't sell booze."

"That sounds like your son. Folks are going to want something to drink after all that time underground. You want a beer? They aren't cold yet, but ...."

"I have never bought drink by the glass and I never will."

She laughed.

"I was offering a bottle. Your grandson will take one."

"Maybe I'll stop back by for a cold one if you're acting like a package store. Gotta go. I'll let Shane know you're serving."

"Where's my daughter?"

"At the med center. I think she may be the head doctor at the moment."

First Things First

Emmaus Medical Center

Cai handed Marnie a glass of water. She pulled the rag off her forehead to drink it.

"Maybe Dr. Vashon will come back from Wichita," Lila suggested hopefully.

"And maybe unicorns will sprinkle rainbows over KC," Marnie countered. "And, I'm sure that will help with the nuclear radiation." She drank the last class. "Dr. Morton being dead makes me the lead here for the time being. I'm a second year resident. The ink is still wet on my license to practice. I haven't taken my boards yet." She covered her eyes with the heels of her hands. "This cannot be happening."

Cai and Lila didn't know what to say, so they held silence. Marnie wiped tears from her cheeks and swung her legs off the couch.

"Okay, first things first. We need to secure the medical supplies. Cai, can you go to Mac's and have

Genine help you bring everything here? Make an inventory. We'll reimburse Mac when we can ... if he's still alive somewhere." She covered her mouth with her hand, swallowed and let her breath out slowly. "Lila, find Martin and ask him to run a thorough check on the facility. Everything needs to be in good working order. Ask Vin if there's any way to access the diesel at the station because we need to fill the tank for the generator. Cai, can you also break the news to the copilot about his friend. I don't know how to handle that."

"I've got it. You're sure you're okay? I've never seen you faint before."

"It's just overwhelming." Marnie averted her eyes while she and Lila exchanged significant glances that Cai couldn't interpret. "Please don't worry about me. Go take care of things. If you see your mom, ask her to come talk to us. I'm going to need as many medical personnel as I can scrape together."

"I'll spread the word."

"And, could you also ask Anders for their supply of iodine. We need to be protecting thyroids here."

"Sure. The commuters went to the mine to shelter, so I have to go there anyway."

The medical center was quiet now that everyone had left for home or to help with the cleanup at City Hall or the burial at Beulah Cemetery. Cai paused in the deserted lobby for a moment and just took a deep breath.

God, just help us get through today. I don't think I want to look any further ahead until tomorrow.

And then he headed out to face the world. Ten minutes later, he was standing on broken glass at Mac's pharmacy. Genine, the clerk who had been left in charge when Mac had gone to fill their weekly order on Wednesday, wept, staring down the empty shelves. Acting automatically, Cai bent to put a smashed bag of diapers on the counter next to the open and empty cash register.

"It never occurred to me that anyone would do this during the rain," Genine admitted. "I went home to hide in the storm cellar. I locked up. I swear I did."

"I believe you. You had keys. Why smash the door? According to the readings at City Hall, the rad level got pretty high, but after it stopped raining, there were several hours where folks in chem suits or even someone not really afraid of cancer could have traveled about. I should go see if there are signs of any other looting. Could you go report this to Marnie? She's at the medical center."

"Yeah. People! They are so fucking stupid!"

Cai nodded in agreement, but what more could he say. He had looting to document. He'd barely gone a block when he found Jos and Huffy Osimowicz screwing plywood up over their smashed front door.

"Oh, no! How much did they get?"

"Nothing." Huffy handed screws to her grandson with one hand while bracing the plywood with the other. "There's someone trailing blood, though. I'm pretty sure I clipped him with the load of buckshot I blasted."

"We were in the boiler room," Jos explained. "The rain had stopped, but we were waiting for the storm siren when we heard the window breaking. Granmae risked herself to step out there and shoot at the robbers. They drove off, but that sure looks like blood there in the gutter."

Cai moved to where he directed. Sure enough, there were a couple of spots of drying blood on the asphalt.

"Either of you see the vehicle?"

"White panel van with a truck front," Huffy said. "Beulah county license plate."

"You should go to the medical center, have Marnie check you out."

"After we get things secure here."

Okay, so she might get cancer, but her heart is as strong as ever.

Cai did a quick surveillance of the downtown area. He was considering how far afield he should go when the radio crackled. Rob was just checking in, but none too pleased when Cai told him about the looting.

"You need to stay in touch with me when you get news," Rob chided. "Over."

"It's an evolving situation out here. I suspect my father-in-law might have something to do with this. Over."

"Let's not jump to conclusions. Jason's been accused many times and then he turns out to have been somewhere else with a dozen unimpeachable witnesses. Over."

"I'm headed to the mine, then. I haven't seen any other looting. The pharmacy and the grocery store make sense, which is why I expect professionals in this. They didn't go after anything you couldn't eat or sell for a lot of money. Over."

"I'll have your brother check the Box Belt on his sweep. Keep an eye out for utility folks. Shane reported that the lights might be on sometime today. Over."

"Roger that. Out."

Dying

Highway 2 North-bound

*H*ighway 2 stretched north, a ribbon of asphalt. Even on an ordinary day, it wasn't a heavily trafficked road, but the lack of traffic today just drove home the reality of their situation. Here the corn fields were interspersed with soybean and hay fields and stock lots. Jazz's stomach growled and Shane stopped the car to introduce her to Meals-Ready-to-Eat, Chicken Pesto.

"These are pretty good, but way too much for me to eat it all. You want some?"

He took the oatmeal cookie and wheat snack bread.

"I already ate one this morning ... or, er, last night. You should know they have ... mmm, side effects."

"I can imagine with this low fiber content, but it surely beats canned soup and tuna fish on pilot bread. I can eat while you drive."

"Just drink lots of water. It helps."

They stopped at two farms to make sure people knew they could come out of their shelters. They found one family grateful for the respite and the second farm empty.

Shane pulled up before the house, but nobody answered their banging on the bulkhead doors and shouting. They walked around to the front porch. Jazz pointed to a name sign by the front door.

"I think the Gimbles were in City Hall," she croaked. She took off her hat to run her fingers through her sweaty hair. "Their son Jeff was in my …."

Shane grabbed her arm and forcibly pulled her into the center of the driveway.

"Ow! What are you …?"

Something large and powerful struck the fence to her right, bellowing. She instinctively put the Jeep between her and the Angus bull, who snorted, wild-eyed, and circled back into the pasture before running at the steel rail fence again. Bloody sores dripped gore from its back while it glared at them with whitening eyes.

"My god!' she gasped while Shane reached into the car. "What's wrong with it?"

Shane didn't say anything at first, just scanned the pasture with the Geiger Counter.

"He's hot," he reported. She couldn't tell what he was looking at because of the sunglasses, but then he pointed to a shed across the pasture. "I'd bet he escaped from there, maybe during the storm, maybe drank from that stock trough which is also peaking. Listen. You hear the cows?"

The bull slammed his chest into the rail fence again. If there were cows, Jazz couldn't hear them.

"You got ammunition for the 30-06?" Shane asked, putting the Geiger counter down on the hood.

"Yeah. You want to shoot it?"

"He's an enraged bull defending his harem in pain and therefore dangerous. I'd like to also bury him so we're not poisoning what birds survived the rain. Can you shoot him while I get the tractor or do I have to do it?"

"I can do it," she assured him. What was it with guys and small women? They always seemed to think she was delicate.

While she loaded the 30-06, she considered the best way to handle this. She pointed out a swale in the ground at one corner of the pasture lot. Shane agreed and headed over to the tractor while Jazz skirted the fence.

The bull made several runs at the rails, bellowing, foaming at the mouth. Jazz stayed well back, heart hammering in her ribs. This wasn't going to be like taking a deer. This would be more like shooting fish in a barrel. Despite the overwhelming feeling of violating hunting ethics, Shane was right. The bull was in pain, dangerous and not salvageable. Blood issued from its nose and it had trouble seeing. She finally got into position, rapping the metal railing with a rock to gain the bull's attention. It lowered its head and snorted blood, then stormed toward her position. Just shy of the swale, Jazz shot it between the eyes and it tumbled into a pile of dead flesh five feet from the fence and right in the swale.

Shane drove the tractor over to the resting place of the bull and began scratching out a basic grave. Jazz went back to the Jeep and drank some water. While Shane used the bucket attachment to roll the bull into the grave he'd dug, she took the Geiger counter to the stock tank. Sure enough, Shane was right about it having captured a radioactivity level somewhat higher than was healthy. She was actually kind of surprised that none of the bodies of water they'd encountered weren't higher than this. They seemed to be higher north of Mission Ridge, but still not as high as the book she'd read in captivity had suggested. She could see how to release the water on the tank, but hesitated, not sure if that was the right thing to do. She was eating a portion of the MRE at the Jeep when Shane joined her.

With the tractor silent, now she could hear cows. Shane pointed to the barn which had been heaped up with dirt.

"We need to drain that cattle trough and see if one of the nearby farmers can come take care of those cows. They probably need milking."

"We shouldn't let them out?"

"Not until the trough is empty and probably somebody besides a teacher and a pilot ought to do it. How much do you know about cows?"

"Alex let me milk one once. She stepped on my foot and kept swatting me with her tail."

"Like I said." They both laughed.

She showed him the lever for releasing the trough and they watched the water drain off into the grass. The radiation levels immediately dropped, though they were still above normal background.

"We can probably find someone at the Elevators to take care of this for us. Let's get going."

The next farm had people at it and Hiram Shore was glad to take care of the beeves at the Gimble place. He seemed to know about them and to know the bull as "a great loss for herd diversity."

"He was a tricky one, Hercules. He busted out more than most. Too bad for that."

"Just know that if any Gimbles show up, the beeves don't belong to you."

"Ah, yeah. I know that. I'm going to feel guilty folding them into my herd, so it's no problem. Thanks for letting me know. We can't be wasting anything that might be food after all of this."

"We need to get the crops in too. Winter's coming," Mrs. Shore said. "What did we do to deserve this?"

Jazz watched Shane tilt his head as if she were a curious bug he'd never seen before.

"I don't think it works like that," Jazz offered. "God doesn't punish people in that way."

"No, I mean what did the State do to some other country that they decided we deserved this for not stopping our government?"

Shane chortled.

"Yeah, you got the right idea." Mrs. Shore's eyes widened.

"I didn't – of course, you're in the Army. Are you AWOL?"

"No, but I was a military contractor and I can tell you ... if we didn't do this to ourselves, we've done enough overseas that some groups might have done this. Jazz, we should get going. If we stop to talk at every farm, this is going to be a really long day. Remember the meeting tonight."

Hiram agreed that he would and they continued driving through sere corn fields.

How to Run a State of Emergency

Anders McAuliff had to admit that Rob Delaney knew how to run a state of emergency. Sending Cai was so much less authoritarian than sending a deputy. The request sounded like it came from the medical center rather than the mayor. Of course, he'd share the iodine supply. It was a state of emergency and he was a good citizen.

Fortunately, for Cai, the copilot had not gone to seek lodging at one of the local motels, so Cai was able to break the news of his friend's death to him. By this time, Anders knew to call him Dennis. He seemed sad to hear of his coworker's demise, but admitted that they didn't really know each other well. He wondered how he was supposed to let the bosses know so that they could let his family know.

"Have they heard anything about elsewhere?" asked Click Michaels, the *Chicago Tribune* reporter who'd been on the commuter airline.

"Not much, yet," Cai admitted. Something flickered behind Click's eyes. *Of course, he has family, people he's worried about.*

"Can I tag along with you? You folks have media, right?"

"KERB, sure. It's not on right now."

"Maybe I can help with that. I need to be doing something. How about you drop me there?"

"I'll deliver that iodine to the medical center along with a handful of my guys to help distribute it," Anders told Cai. "Let me know if there's anything else we can do to help."

"Actually, I think there is. Bart and two deputies died in City Hall when the air handling system failed."

"Shit!" Anders hissed, Dennis and Rick echoing him.

"Yeah, about 100 people. So, there's no police force right now. Just Joe. Maybe you could assign some of your guards to watch the barricades at the ramps and see if Joe and Dad need other help from them."

"Of course. I'll send them to the barricades for now and talk with the mayor about other duties. My god, this is a nightmare."

"My wife would definitely agree with you. She went from being a 2nd year resident to being the lead doctor in the space of two hours."

Cai turned to head for the Subaru, then paused, staring at the building on the other side of the parking lot.

"You missing any of those?" He indicated the neat line of delivery trucks.

"Um, one didn't come back on Wednesday. I figured the driver got caught up in the disaster, was maybe sheltering in place somewhere else. Why?"

"We had some looting during the rain. A white panel truck with Beulah license plates was spotted. Someone winged one of the crew with some buckshot."

"Well, except for that driver and that truck, all my crew and trucks are accounted for. You can check my records."

"No, it's fine. Just keep your ears open, okay?"

"Of course. People in crisis do some shitty things."

"They do at that." Cai looked at Click. "You ready to go?"

"I am."

Ander waited while they drove out of sight and then turned to his fleet of trucks to count them and assure he had not just lied to the mayor's office.

End of Life as We Knew It

Highway 2 North-bound

As they continued driving north, Jazz ran her fingers through her dripping hair before settling the cap again.

"Does that air conditioning work?"

Shane kept his eyes on the corn fields.

"It does, but it also reduced gas mileage and we need to be thinking about that. When the tanks at the station are empty, we're all walking."

"You don't think help is coming, do you?"

"Something that looks like help at the front end might come, but what comes out its ass may look a lot like slavery."

Jazz stared out at the passing pastures. *There ought to be beeves out there now, getting fat for slaughter.*

"You were in the military, right?"

"I was a military-affiliated contractor. Why?"

"I'm just wondering what we actually do overseas."

"You just spent two days with Jacob. You know what he'd say to that?"

"I'm not sure."

"it's not 'we' who are doing it. It's the government, which ceased to be under your control a long time ago."

"So, we don't have to feel guilty for what our leaders do?"

"You don't have to. I was complicit. And when the nation building abuse comes home to roast ... well, I think it probably looks a lot like this."

Far to the north, they could see a squadron of jets scooting westward.

"What do you think that's about?"

"Looks like F-16 Falcons," Shane reported.

"You can see that?"

"Yeah. Can't you?"

"I see fighter jets, but no, I don't know one from another."

"I don't know what they're after though," Shane murmured, looking off to the northwest now. A lot went unsaid with him. He was very different from Cai in that regard. *Is this what realism in the apocalypse looks like?*

On the horizon, she could see the top of tallest elevator. Shane turned into another driveway. This family had already come out of their storm shelter and were draining their water troughs, so they spoke briefly with the farmer's wife before heading north again.

"God, it's hot," Jazz complained. "Aren't you hot?"

"At 10 am – no. In Miristan, it's often 120 degrees by noon. It's only about 80 right now."

He wasn't dripping with sweat like she was. He smelled like he'd had access to adequate water and soap over the last few days. He'd shaved. *Who shaves for Armageddon?* Shane paused at the railroad tracks. Jazz heard a shot and flinched. Shane pressed on the gas. The Jeep leapt forward, flailing rocks into the undercarriage. A denim-clad man pointed a revolver at a kneeling woman's head and cocked the hammer. Shane leaned on the horn as they roared up to where they were gathered beside a hole he'd obviously dug with a nearby backhoe. The man looked toward them as Shane stopped the Jeep and both he and Jazz popped out with guns drawn, running up to him.

"What the hell are you doing?" Shane yelled. He was definitely not keeping his gun pointed in a safe direction. The way he handled it spoke of a lot of experience at pointing it at living people.

Clem Burroughs stared at them like they were space aliens. Sweat stood out on his forehead beneath his strawberry blond hair. The veterinary opened his mouth to explain when the man kneeling next to the woman croaked.

"Don't stop. Give us mercy. Release us."

Jazz looked from the woman to the man to the dead baby the woman held in her lap. She'd seen this before. Bleeding from the nose, hair falling out, skin peeling. She'd seen it in photos and recognized it in Snowball and Hercules. Her breath stopped as she imagined her own cells breaking down.

"They came from Denver and then tried to shelter in a metal shed." Tears ran down Clem's cheeks. "I can't help them. Nobody can help them. It's too late. Don't you see?"

Shane lowered his gun. A moment later, Jazz followed his lead, her hand numb. *That poor woman. Her baby.*

"Marnie must have treatments." Even to herself, her voice sounded very small and weak.

Shane stood stock-still, staring at the family. There were already two bodies in the makeshift grave, an another man and woman. Surely this wasn't the first death Shane had seen. He'd taken the whole scene in a matter of moments. She saw his Adam's apple bob up and down, but he didn't seem shocked.

"Please kill us. It's so painful," the woman whispered.

Shane holstered his 9mm.

"Jazz, there's a first aid kit in the back of the Jeep. We'll try to give them some relief while we take them to Marnie. Could you go get it, please?"

Jazz turned gratefully toward the vehicle. They were going to help these people. *Clem didn't know what to do. Shane's experienced in matters of war.*

More practical. She found the plastic tool box labeled "First Aid" behind Shane's duffle bag. Just as she wrenched it free, she heard two shots ring out. Smoke rose from Shane's gun as first one body and then the other fell into the ditch. The world seemed to lurch precipitously off-kilter as air sucked away into a giant vacuum and a mighty roaring filled her ears. *No, this can't be happening. Oh, my God! This is not happening!*

Shane holstered his weapon and put a hand on Clem's shoulder as if congratulating him on a job well done. The world had ended and no one was normal any longer.

Jazz let go of the first aid kit and sat down on the ground behind the Jeep, weeping. Through her sobs, she heard the backhoe and Shane and Clem talking.

What am I supposed to do? He killed two innocent people. Shouldn't I call the cops, or ....? They were too far gone. You read the brochure. They wouldn't have lived. It doesn't matter. It is wrong to kill people who aren't trying to kill you. They were in pain, suffering and there was notihng you could have done. God, what am I supposed to do about what Shane just did?

"Maverick, this is Malacai. You got your ears on? What's your 20? Over." Jazz wiped tears from her cheeks and crawled to the passenger door to get the radio sitting on the seat.

"Shane, where are you? Over."

"This is Jazz Tully. This Cai?"

"Yeah. Jazz ... where's Shane? Over."

"Um, Shane ... I ... he ... oh, God. Cai, he killed two people just now."

"What?"

A shadow fell across her arm and she looked up in horror as Shane reached across the car to wrest the radio from her hand, his face contorted in rage. She flinched back to protect her fact with one hand while reaching for her gun with the other.

Crime Doesn't Pay ... Usually

Mara Wells, Old Osimowicz House

Paul Osimowicz plunged the knife tip into Trey Conopher's shredded skin. Chuck held him down as he screamed. Another ball of lead shot tumbled into the bowl.

"Shut up!" Paul snapped. "I told you two to stay away from Huffman's. It serves you right."

"You didn't tell us that old bitch had a shotgun," Trey retorted.

"This is rural Kansas. Everybody is armed."

"You also didn't tell us that they had an onsite shelter," Chuck said.

"Why would I need to tell you that if you weren't going anywhere near there? Sit on him. We got one last one."

Trey bellowed and swore. This pellet was deep and blood welled up, but eventually Paul dropped it into the bowl.

"Quit your whining." He poured rubbing alcohol over the wounds. Trey screamed expletives while Chuck continued to sit on him. Paul ruthlessly began to bandage each of the wounds. It really wasn't that bad. Just the right upper quadrant of his back had been peppered, and only the one wound looked like it could use stitches. Paul pulled it together with steri-strips and called it good.

"You might want to take some aspirin," Chuck told him.

Trey growled and poured himself a shot of tequila. Paul and Chuck headed into the garage.

"So let's take a look at the haul." Paul stepped up into the van and pulled the tarp off what was there. The tote sacks were filled with bottles and boxes. He upended one for a better look at the contents.

"You ripped off a pharmacy?" Paul shuffled through the bottles. "We got some good stuff here. Not sure what some of it is, but things like anti-biotics will be worth a bit in these circumstances. Of course, if Huffy got a look at you, you won't be able to enjoy the haul."

"She didn't see us. We still had the chem suits on, including the face masks. Besides, she doesn't know us."

"You'd be surprised what that old broad knows. You do not want to ...."

A banging came on the front door. Paul dropped to the garage floor.

"Stay here. Don't make any noise."

His grandfather's house was more garage than house. Paul always wondered how his father, brother and three sisters had grown up in a two-bedroom house. Randi Osimowicz stood on Paul's doorstep.

"What's up, big sis?" he asked, opening the door just wide enough to talk to her.

"Dad wanted me to come check on you. Everything okay?" Randi was a tall brunette, a mixture of their father and mother, with amber eyes and a haughty attitude.

"It's fine. Jazz still at the shelter."

"You need to leave Jazz alone or someday when you annoy her, she's going to shoot you in the face."

"Now why would she do that?"

"Because you're a creep and she doesn't want to be on the third chorus of 'Every Breath You Take.' So, everything's good. I'm gone then."

As Randi strode away toward her car, Paul turned back to Chuck.

"It's fine. Bossy bitch doesn't suspect anything. Before the cops over in Emmaus get organized, we need to hit the Walmart. Think of all the food there that's just going to go to waste."

A Single Pulse

Bluffdale, Utah Mission Data Repository, Camp Williams

From Jerome Mellor, Data Analyst

To Hal Holbinger, Group Chief, MDR

RE Operation Sunset

Sir, my analysis of the terrorist attack(s) suggests that none of the groups taking credit for the bombings were in communication with one another prior to the events. It might be they were using confidential software, but at this time, I cannot say they are related to one another in any way, but one ....

Exactly one second before the bombs went off, a single command was sent from 16 different IPs through Telegraph Messaging. Two of them did not trigger because the bombs had been disabled, so the messages remained open longer than normal and allowed me to trace the others. It's very much like a Thunderclap campaign. Brilliant in its simplicity, really. To set something like this up would take a high degree of coordination, which suggests someone was talking to someone.

Aunt Joyce's House

Ballard, Seattle Washington

*T*he small tract house had been adorned with some Craftsman details to give it pizzazz. Geo didn't much care except that you always paid attention to your surroundings. He filed the image away in his memory, then focused on the moment as they pulled into the alley garage and sat there in the echoing dark for several moments. Marcus stirred first, reaching for the door handle.

"What is this place?" Geo asked.

"My aunt's. She was on a business trip to Portland, so I don't think anyone will disturb us."

"I'm sorry for your loss."

Marcus nodded and got out of the truck. Geo followed because it seemed like the only course of action. An enclosed breezeway connected the detached garage from the house. It contained a washer and dryer and shelves for items you might not want in the house. Geo flinched as a black

Labrador pushed its way through the doggie door, growling low until Marcus said his name, dropping to his knees to ruffle "Duke's" ears. While the two got reacquainted, Geo noticed the dog's water bowl was empty. He filled it at the sink and the dog forgot all about Marcus. The backdoor was locked, but Marcus knew where the key was. The small bright kitchen shined with colorful tiles. Marcus closed the lace curtains.

"I don't think anybody will question us being here, but it's better if they don't see us. Let them think it's Joyce."

Geo nodded. He looked in the fridge. The power was on, so even the milk was still fresh.

"There's two bedrooms. I'd rather not sleep in my aunt's bed, so you get the front room." He opened the basement door.

"Where you going?"

"My uncle died maybe five years ago and I don't know if she kept any of his stuff, but it might be useful if she did."

"Can I come?"

"Sure."

Narrow stairs under another stair accessed the unfinished basement. High windows opening into wells provided uncertain light. With some fumbling, Marcus found the pull chain, then smiled when he saw the shelves lining one wall.

"Fred was a bit of a survivalist," he explained as he pulled out a citizen's band radio base. "The antenna is still up, so we ought to be able to monitor frequencies."

"They got any weapons?"

"Probably not. Joyce was nervous of guns. I wouldn't it put it past Fred to have hidden one or two, but where ... I don't know."

"I'm going to go check our security, make sure nobody can sneak up on us."

Duke met him at the top of the stairs, but apparently, providing him water was the key to friendship, because he let Geo pet him. Out of curiosity, Geo checked the telephone. The dial tone still hummed. The largest room in the house, the living room fronted a convivial covered porch, visible through the sidelight. The oak front door secured with a double-key deadbolt and chain. The double-hung windows locked. Geo closed all the curtains as he went to keep prying eyes out. The front bedroom had sheets and blankets and a door to the bathroom as well as a patio door to the side yard. The bathroom connected to the guest bedroom, which had also been made up. An exercise bicycle sat in one corner of the small room. That brought him back to the kitchen.

He considered going back to the living room to take the stairs to the attic, but Duke nuzzled Geo's hand and encouraged him to follow him back to the breezeway where he made it clear food ought to be in his bowl. Geo found cans of dog food on the shelves beside the door and a can opener. Duke licked his hands as he spooned the food into his bowl.

An odd vibration got Geo's attention. He went back to the living room to peak out the curtains. An MRAP rumbled by, black uniformed mercenaries standing up in the back, rifles at the ready. Geo hadn't set down his Mac 10, so he stood there wishing it were a M-16 or at least an AR-15. He stopped breathing momentarily upon feeling warmth at his back, but it was only Marcus. The MRAP was passing out of sight now.

"I never thought I'd be hiding in my own country," Marcus whispered as if the mercs could hear them.

Geo shuddered.

"I used to laugh that the folks who said 'It can happen here. 'Of course, it couldn't,' I'd say. The military would stop them."

"We don't know the situation. There might be more of us. Unfortunately, we have short-range radios. We can't reach any of the military bases here."

"Your aunt have a radio ... you know, standard FM-AM?" Marcus opened the television armoire and turned on the Bose system. "Try AM 570 or 770. If anyone's talking, it's them."

There was only so much they could do from a bungalow in Ballard, but for now, they had a base of operations and a few tools at their disposal. First order of business was to find out what was happening. Second was to turn it to their advantage.

Duke walked up and licked Geo's hand. It was easy to rub the dog's head and appreciate the calm assurance. Marcus' aunt had died and he'd be sleeping in her bed tonight. Geo felt a big hole in his chest when he considered his own folks and thought a faltering prayer for them as he turned to get to work.

In the Wind

New York City
Javitz Building

Ned Merriman pushed down the corridor, aiming for Ellerby's office, the dispatch clutched in his hand. Wisdom said he should have emailed it, but he'd been so excited by the contents that he'd printed it out and ran.

Ellerby's secretary, Rose, gave him a sharp look as he approached.

"I've got urgent information for Secretary Ellerby."

"Just hold a moment," she said, ringing into Ellerby. Ned moved toward the door. "Sir, please wait a moment."

Ellerby opened the door.

"What is it, Merriman?"

Ned directed him backward, closing the door crisply.

"Wednesday night, while we were all distracted by the nuclear bombs, there was an incursion at Lakeland CDC facility in update New York."

"What do you mean, incursion?"

"A well timed attack with multiple players. Their identification seemed authentic. They made it into medium security before a low-level security officer asked for verification. They got the rest of the way in with brute force."

Ellerby gazed at him, searching.

"The lab ordinarily would have told them to hold for verification, but in crisis, the protocol failed. This crew was well credentialed. They had CDC ID and some of them had Homeland Security badges. They would have been allowed all the way into the most sensitive areas if not for the young officer who died for his curiosity. That alerted the others, who managed to keep them out of the deepest security levels. What they got away with was bad enough?"

"What did they get hold of?"

"A variety of viruses, a couple of them weaponized."

Ellerby nodded, sitting down in his chair.

"Do we know where they went from there?"

"No. Traffic cams were down. We're seeking satellite telemetry in hopes of tracking them, but we've only known about it for a few hours."

"How did we lose sight of this? If it happened Wednesday, why am I hearing about it on Saturday?"

Ellerby's self-control was admirable. Ned had soaked his shirt with sweat in his haste to get the news to him, but Ellerby dealt with the news dispassionately.

"Normal channels of communication had been severed. Rain from Pittsburg swept the area on Thursday morning, forcing a lock down. They've just been able to communicate with the outside world since last night."

"We need to get ahead of this. What do we know about these viruses?"

"That information should be coming shortly."

"We need an inventory of all remaining CDC facilities to assure that there are no other nasty bugs in the wind."

"Yes, sir."

"I need to speak with the administrator from Lakeland."

"As soon as possible, sir."

"We should plan a ceremony, honoring those who prevented the full incursion."

"Of course, sir."

Ned's phone dinged and he looked at the screen.

"I have the administrator for the lab on the line, sir."

Ned handed his phone to Ellerby and stepped back.

"I'm sorry we're meeting under such difficult circumstances," he said to the lab administrator. "What can you tell me .... Yes, I understand about the rain. Now, what can you tell me about these viruses?"

He listened for a bit. Then he nodded.

"My Latin's a bit rusty, but it seems like you're describing flu viruses." Ellerby listened for a painfully long time. "I see. Weaponized. What? A second-wave attack? Are there any treatments? I see. I will have someone call you from the Institutes of Health. We must develop treatments as quickly as possible. Yes. All resources will be made available to you? Thank you for your sense of urgency in this matter."

Ellerby hung up and returned the phone to Ned.

"Three of the viruses are a concern. One is a variant of the Spanish flu that wiped out millions in the early 20th century. Another is a variety of swine flu. Neither has been weaponized and both are treatable with anti-virals. The third one is a variant of the standard flu virus, but it has been weaponized to make it more virulent. The initial infection is normally not life threatening, but it is designed as a second wave attack. He's getting me the details, but it could incapacitate about 25% of the population if it gets out."

Ned stared at Ellerby, wondering how he could be so calm. He personally felt like he needed to sit down and put his head between his legs. Weren't they dealing with enough without adding weaponized viruses to the mix?

My lord, what is happening to us? Why are we under such unrelenting attack?

Remade by War

Emmaus City Hall

When the power came back on, the telex spat out a statement that, among other things, directed them to a certain frequency on the Emergency Broadcast radio. Rob and Ren began fiddling with the old machine. So far they could hear some stations, but were not able to broadcast and ask questions.

"Pa's real good at this sort of thing," Rob noted. "He should be back here in a few minutes."

"I think it's really interesting that they have relocated the governor to Wichita. He was supposed to be at a fund-raiser in Kansas City on Wednesday night."

"You seem certain of that."

"I was invited to speak, but Joseph and I were trying to correct a situation with the natural gas plant in India and so I canceled last minute."

Rob turned to see Marnie and Joe embracing in the lobby. They'd grown up together in the same class as Shane and Alex. Joe had hung out with them until Junior High when Marnie and Shane had gone dark. Alex had been up to healthier hijinks, but Joe had been too good a kid for that sort of nonsense. Still, Joe and Marnie had to know how each other felt right now being the apprentice suddenly promoted to journeyman by tragedy.

A beautiful woman – tall, athletic, with lustrous chestnut hair and striking blue eyes with unusually prominent irises, Marnie somehow managed to make scrubs look sexy. Separating from Joe, she followed Rob into his office.

"How bad is it?" he asked.

"It's not good. We have very limited supplies of antibiotics and I have two patients on insulin and a handful on heart medications and I have maybe a week's supply for them. I have three patients on various chemo regimes. The hospitals they were using in Denver are now gone. Someone has got to go refill that pharmacy order, though I don't know how that helps those three. I'm not qualified to treat them."

"Yeah," Rob agreed. *I probably should have thought of that before I let Shane go north. On the other hand, that boy doesn't need more stress in his life.* "Ren's headed to Wichita if Pa will agree to fly him. They could fill the pharmacy order."

"I made a list of what we need urgently. The problem is that there are a lot rules for filling pharmacy orders. I've included the right numbers, but if they can't be verified and -- What's he doing here?"

Rob followed her gaze to where Carl Sullivan had come into the lobby.

"Member of the public wants to talk to his mayor," Rob said, and left her to greet Carl. The man smelled like an ashtray and he needed a shave, but that was Carl. "Hey, Carl. What's up?

Despite his disheveled appearance, Carl's eyes were clear. He might be a schizophrenic, but he was also Ren Sullivan's brother and Rob's childhood friend. Looking back, there'd been clues to his illness in high school, but even now it was hard not to flinch at what he'd become ... and give him a little dignity by listening to see if he had something important to say. You might have to wade through the delusion to get to the brilliance, but sometimes it was worth it.

"Jacob asked me to monitor the radios."

"With your shortwave? Pa told me about that. What did you get?"

"That guy Rutherford is back. He's calling shots for the Army. First night, he ordered the liquidation of people in cars near the cities."

"Shane got Cai out of the Denver Containment Zone."

"I heard. But lots of others died. They napalmed them." For a moment, he seemed to see the scene. Rob knew it was probably the same scene he saw when he entertained it. You could come back from the Nam, but you always carried a part of it with you. Carl shook himself. "So, then during the rain, I wasn't hearing any chatter, but this morning, it started up again. Rutherford has ordered confiscation of food stores and securement of water resources."

"Hang on a minute, Carl." Rob went back to his office for the telex. "Is this what was said?"

"Kind of." Carl rubbed his jaw. "What I heard was more orders – Rutherford talking to colonels about the units. Thought you might want to know what he said."

"I do. This is a big help, Carl. Thank you."

"I'm not done yet."

Rob waited patiently while Carl referred to his notes.

"The colonel – Hutchison – he said people would resist since there was no formal martial law. Rutherford said quote You may have to kill a few, then word will get around and folks will be more compliant. Unquote. Hutchison replied quote we can't treat Americans like Iraqis. Unquote. Rutherford We can't trust the American people with these decisions. They'll make stupid mistakes every time. Make it look like it's a cooperative effort. Talk to the governors and use the National Guard so that they're under the command structure, but move on those supplies. If people resist, be decisive. Unquote"

Rob's stomach turned over like a lead weight rolling down a muddy hill.

"Until we hear from someone directly, we don't have this information," he told Carl after a moment's contemplation. "You understand?" Carl grinned, nodding. On his meds, the man was good at keeping secrets. "Go back to monitoring the radios. I'll deal with this."

"Sure thing. There's one more thing."

"Yeah."

Carl took a deep slow breath and let it out as slow.

"I got a couple of months' worth of meds, so I'm pretty sane right now, but when it runs out ... I'll tell you a few days ahead – because I'm going to want you to shoot me in the head."

Rob stared at him, hoping he was joking. Carl stared back with an expression that wasn't.

"I mean, you could be gentle, if you can OD me on tranqs or something, but you don't want me alive in a crisis situation if I'm not on my meds. I just thought someone should know that and that brother of mine ain't going to want to hear it. You have a couple of months to wrap your mind around it."

Rob nodded because he didn't know what else to do. Carl sighed.

"Look, I know it's unfair of me to ask, but these aren't normal times and I don't want to be a burden on the town, not when it needs people who have their wits about them." Carl turned and strolled out the way he'd arrived. After a moment, Joe came to Rob's elbow.

"Crazy ole coot." Rob startled. "Back when I first got back from the Police Academy, he told me that suicide-by-cop seemed like an interesting way to die."

"So you think he's just saying stuff?"

"I hope so. Because honestly, who here is really going to shoot him in the head?"

As if to answer that question Rob's radio crackled at his belt.

"You know you got a crowd gathering on your lawn?" Stan Osimowicz observed.

"You're here?"

"Yeah, freshly broke loose of the living grave. Can I come up?"

Joe had already headed down the stairs.

"Meet the deputy at the back door."

Marnie glided up to Rob's elbow.

"I'm going home to take a shower and sleep for a week ... or until someone calls to say they need a doctor, whichever comes first. Just my opinion, but Cai would be the best person to send to Wichita. He's the City attorney and he helped me with my pharma exams so the list will seem familiar to him."

"That's a good suggestion that I wouldn't have come up with on my own."

She shifted from one foot to the other.

"Um, you know Shane and I talked the other day, right?"

"He mentioned it. He seemed not to be too upset about the news."

"After he calmed down, maybe. I just want you and Jill to know that I'm going to do my best not to make him uncomfortable. Cai and I talked about maybe going to stay at the ranch for a while."

What the hell are you talking about? Why are you at all concerned about Shane? You're married to Cai!

"We don't have time to discuss this right now, Marnie. On the scale of urgency ...."

"Of course." She had the grace to blush. Even red face looked good on her. No wonder men fell in love with her.

Cai was naïve to think her heart could be tamed. Shane came closest, but he seems over it now. Did Cai wait for Vi to pass just to avoid her assessment of their union? The rest of us just politely accepted it. She wouldn't. She'd have said you were a wool-headed idiot. Careful, man, she's a family member. Your daughter now too.

Marnie passed Stan as he came through the door. Rob watched his gaze and gave him a pointed look, which Stan greeted with a laugh.

"She's got way too nice an ass to be a doctor." Now it was Joe's turn to blush. Rob tried not to snort. *It's true.* Stan poured himself some coffee, putting Joe at ease by remarking that he loved hazelnut vanilla, then followed Rob into his office. A tall, lanky man, he wore his age well. He hadn't grown a beard like Rob, but he had sported the same biker mustache since 1976.

"Does he realize that to old Nam vets like us, this tastes like candy?" Rob shrugged, shaking his head. "Thought we should talk about coordination."

"Yeah, we did say we would do that. We had a hundred people die of asphyxiation in the shelter here."

"Well, shit, son, that's just the first and you know it. When the Costco shipment is done, everyone but the farmers will be licking postage stamps for the calories."

"I'm sending a crew to replenish the pharmacy stock. We got robbed while we were hiding from the rain."

Stan's sharp blue eyes narrowed. The sun coming in the windows briefly made his eyes glitter silver.

"The med center?" he asked.

"Mac's pharmacy. They hit you?"

"No, but the Costco is a pretty secure building. Mac's ... big windows. How's the Walmart?"

"Don't know yet. Joe is the entire police department. I've got Shane sweeping the outlying areas and Cai checking the town."

"Do you need guards on the highway ramps?"

"I think the mine's going to loan us some."

"I can cover the ramps west of you for now, so the mine can cover the eastern approaches. Where are you replenishing the pharmacy from?"

"Wichita."

"Good. They relocated the governor there from Topeka. Your boy ... he's a do-what-it-takes sort of soldier."

"Shane's not going to Wichita. I sent him to sweep the outlying areas to make sure everyone heard the sirens and to let the farmers know that Alex is calling a cooperative meeting for tonight."

"Well, at least you're not wasting his skills."

"I thought you might not like Shane."

"No. That deal with Paul – it was wrong what my kid did. He's lucky yours didn't shoot him. So, I've been talking to my people – what else you going to do in a bomb shelter for 30 hours when nobody brought a Risk board? I thought we'd be organizing to secure our communities, but you have bodies to bury. I'm guessing that's why your doors are locked. Are they still here?"

"We've moved about half out to Beulah Cemetery. The volunteers are eating before they continue. I've got folks making temporary markers so we can reinter the bodies later."

"Have you talked to the folks on your lawn?"

"Yeah, Pa did. Most of them are travelers, stuck here during the rain, who want to know what they're supposed to do now. I don't have an answer for them. The interstate is still closed. As far as I can tell, we're still under the shelter-in-place order. You get the telex?"

Stan nodded.

"It's bull. We're not giving up our food stores to the National Guard or Win Dixie. You?"

"Nobody is offering me any food stores. Huffy paid good money for most of what she has and she's not sharing unless people want to pay her good money in return."

"That's my sister-in-law. Gotta love her. Your farmers?"

"I asked Alex Lufgren to work through the Cooperative, but my guess is they aren't going to share for free either. Why should they?"

"Right. I got folks working on getting the sorghum and dry beans in. We are lucky in a way that we had the cold spring because everything is harvesting late. Most years, the fields would be cleared and the grain gone to the elevators."

God looking out for us?

"Makes you wonder if the attacks were timed with the idea that crops would already be harvested."

Stan raised an eyebrow, then shrugged.

"Could be. Never really thought the ragheads would consider all that."

"Who says it was Middle Easterners? Last I looked, Iraq gave up its nuclear ambitions."

"We think." Stan set his mug aside and unrolled the map he'd brought with him. "So, I spent 30 hours chewing this over. We blocked these ramps, but what happens when people come at us from this way, or this?" He indicated the west and north of Mara Wells. "You folks are somewhat protected by Mission Ridge, but not to the east." He showed that on the map too. "There's no fences. It's just wide open range."

"You have a plan?"

"People will stick to the roads. Americans are not the Viet Cong. They aren't comfortable going off road. We need to block the roads in these places, directing them around us, along 36 and down 83."

"That's the entire township, an ambitious area to try and control."

"Not control. Protect. These are mostly small farmers who attend our churches and shop at Huffman's and the Costco, buy feed from you."

"There's Lufgrens here and here and Dell Conopher's place is here and there's 3 or 4 Bennett farms here. True. What about Donovan and Brady?"

"I just sent my daughter to ask Donovan. She's also going to warn Luther about what's coming their way and invite them to join us if they want. They're outside the township, but they're going to take the brunt of our redirection, so we should warn them. After we're done here, I'm headed to Beulah to find out what's going on there. It's downright weird that nobody is answering."

As the mayor of a central and larger town, it made sense that he stayed put. Besides, they had bodies to bury.

"I was going to have Shane do it once he gets back into radio range, but it's probably better if you do it. He's not really what you would call a diplomat."

Stan smiled into his coffee.

"Do you think your group will get anywhere talking to the Governor's Office?"

"I think Ren is a billionaire who probably gave to the man's campaign, so – yeah. Is there anything I can do for you?"

"Talk to the utility company about turning on our power too."

"It just came on. I had nothing to do with it."

"Well, good then. We're off like a galloping herd of cantaloupe. It may not be going in the right direction, but it's moving and that's not probably a bad thing."

Cai came into the lobby. One look at his face and Rob was on his feet to meet him at the office door.

"I need to talk to you, Dad, alone!" His pupils were enormous. Stan stood, weighing the situation.

"I got places to be," he announced. Rob swept the door closed right behind him.

"Shane just killed two people up at the Elevators," Cai announced.

Rob blinked at him. The words made no sense. Cai wiped away tears.

"How ... how do you ... how do you know this?" Rob managed.

Cai explained what Jazz had told him when he'd called from the radio station since it sat on a high point of land. Rob reminded himself to breathe even as the stench of napalm poured from the past.

You could come back from the Nam, but there was no grave deep enough to bury it completely. Similar circumstances always resurrected the corpse.

"Did you talk to him?" Rob wiped sweat from his forehead.

"He took the radio from her and said (quote) I did what needed to be done. Judge me if you like, but best hope you never have to take the same responsibility. He must have turned off the radio because it went dead then."

"How did he sound?"

"Like he was discussing taking out the garbage. Dad, who the hell is this guy? He's not my brother."

"That is your brother remade by war, Cai."

"You and Grandpa went to war. You wouldn't … you wouldn't."

"Yes, I would. Probably Pa would too. You see things differently when you've been in truly life-threating situations. You may hate what you had to do, but you do it because it's what needs to be done."

Cai scrubbed tears off his cheeks, staring at Rob like he'd never seen him before. Perhaps he hadn't. It was a side of Rob that had been laid to rest years before Cai was born. *Is it about to be resurrected?*

"Are you going to try to call him? You might be able to get him from the base."

Good question. What would be the purpose of that call?

"No. He doesn't need to feel like anyone is second-guessing his decisions and, truthfully, he doesn't need you judging him by talking behind his back." Cai's mouth dropped open. "I know, son, that you don't mean it that way. Your tears are for Shane and what you see as the loss of his soul, but Shane won't see it like that. He'll see the judgment part of it and he isn't wrong, because that is part of it too."

"So you just let him do it and do nothing?"

"It wasn't murder, Cai. Jazz described a mercy killing. Clem wouldn't have done that unless it needed to be done and honestly, I don't think Shane would either. I will talk to him, but not over the radio, not to question what he did, but to sympathize that he had to do it."

Cai sat down with his head in his hands. Rob waited. When he sat up with a resigned sigh, Rob sat down.

"You want to pray?" he asked.

Cai's eyes widened, his lips moving as if seeking words.

"I have no idea what to pray," he admitted.

"Your spirit does," Rob assured him.

They bowed their heads. Silence descended on the office. Rob waited, biding his time, praying silently. It took an hour for the clock to tick a minute and then Cai croaked out his soul's cry.

"God, my brother needs You and I don't know how to make him see that."

That was all. Cai fell silent and then Rob finished the prayer.

"Jesus, Lord, Savior, seek Shane where he is and bring light into his life in whatever way necessary."

Together, they whispered "In Jesus's name we pray, amen."

Rob sat up, feeling peace settle over him for the first time since Jacob's call on the radio that he was needed at City Hall immediately. Had that only been three hours ago?

Cai's eyes were dry now.

"Why do I feel like I shouldn't tell Marnie or Mom about this?"

"Because you shouldn't. If Shane wants to share that pain with them, that's his business ... but he probably never will. If you feel like you need to talk with someone about it, I'm always here, but it shouldn't go any further than the two of us."

Cai nodded. He licked dry lips.

"We really don't have time for this right now anyway," Rob explained. "I need you to go with Ren and Pa to Wichita to fill a pharmacy order for the medical center."

"Marnie suggest that?"

"Yes, she did," Rob said, surprised.

"I helped her with her pharmacy exams. Practically memorized the PDR. It makes sense. Power's on, so let me use your computer so I can write a letter of delegation for you to me. Looks like Ren and Grandpa want something."

Rob joined them in the lobby while Cai moved to boot up the computer.

"What have you decided, boss?" Jacob asked. *At least you still have a sense of humor. I need to remember that.*

"You're flying to Wichita. Cai's going to fill the pharmacy order and talk to someone about what to do with our young murderer. The governor's there. Anything from that radio, Ren?"

"I think it's broken. It won't broadcast."

"Pa, Cai, I'm going to deputize both of you and Shane when he gets back to act on the town's behalf." Rob picked up one of the shields from his desk, retrieved from the shelter. "Pa, I'm going to ask you to bend your principles for a short-term mission."

"I'd rather we had a town meeting and confirmed everybody was happy with that, but I'll do it this one time." Jacob looked at the shield. "Not that one. Cai's the statist here. Give him the honcho shield."

Ouch, Pa. You have a point, but ouch!

Cai took Bart's shield, trying not to mist up as he did so.

"This should probably go to Joe," he remarked after clearing his throat.

"We'll discuss that when you get back. He needs some time to grieve."

"When do we leave?" Cai asked Ren.

"As soon as we can be fueled." Ren looked at Jacob.

"An hour." Jacob turned toward the door. "I gotta go talk to Jason about opening his part of the field so I've got enough runway. Fueling and pre-check will take an hour. When we get a minute, we need to get that commuter jet off my field. And, speaking of Shane, do we know where he is?"

Jacob looked from Rob to Cai, gaze dwelling overlong on Cai.

"Should I ...?" Ren said.

"Nope. We're good. Whatever you boys have between you ... I suggest you get it settled because we don't have time for juvenile games. You got it?" Jacob said to Cai. After heaving a sigh, Cai nodded. Jacob turned to Rob. "And you don't need to be indulging them." Then the old man took a deep breath and actually smiled at Rob. "I am all for keeping Shane hereabouts and not making him play the hero, by the way." Rob tried to keep his face stone, but Jacob could read him like no one could, except maybe Jill. "It's like that, is it? That boy can find trouble in a monastery," he muttered. "Well, least I know what I'll be doing while I'm fueling the jet." He turned then and headed for the stairs.

Ren watched him go, then shrugged and turned to Rob.

"What does the town want me to say to the governor?"

"We need to know what's going on. I think between us and Mara Wells, we don't probably need a lot of immediate help, but we're groping in the dark."

"Sounds good. We'll get that pharmacy order filled too. I'm headed back to my place to make sure everything is squared away there and then I'm headed to the airfield. Cai?"

"Same thing. Marnie should know for sure that I'm going and I want to catch a shower and a shave."

Ren headed toward the stairs. Cai paused.

"Dad ... thank you."

"Everybody needs to be talked off the ledge from time to time, son. And, trust me. I'm not taking this lightly. My experience is just different from yours"

Cai nodded to himself and left Rob standing alone in the lobby. Joe came over with coffee in Rob's favorite mug.

"I don't know what's going on, but if you need someone to talk to ...."

"Thank you." Rob sipped the coffee. It was good, better than one could expect in a world where his son had just had to kill non-combatants. He looked up and saw Lemuel McAddams coming through the door.

"I hear you may need to talk to me," the gruff bear said. Lem and Rob had been each other's accountability partners for more than 25 years. One or the other was the sponsor depending on the situation. Most often, they just went fly fishing together.

"I do. Grab a cup of coffee while I close the blinds."

Snakes in the Grass

New York City, Javitz Building

The sun hung in the southwest by the time Rose announced that she had Cranston Rutherford's assistant on the phone. Marshall paused to consider his best course of action before sitting down at his desk and picking up the phone.

"Colonel Rutherford," he began, trying to strike a balance between used car salesman and politician. "Thank you for speaking with me. This is Marshall Ellerby."

"My aide told me who was calling. Get to the point, Ellerby. I don't have time to play politics."

Marshall had never liked Rutherford when they'd served in President Dotson's cabinet. He was a hammer of a man and everything looked like a nail to him.

Rutherford is the reason Americans separate their leadership and make the military answer to the civilian.

"I expected to hear from you earlier ... as soon as communications was restored."

"Why? I don't report to you."

"Of course you do. With the death of President Dotson, there is a line of succession."

"And the Secretary of Education, Anna Byers, is still alive and well, meaning you are at best the Vice President."

"You know that Anna is not qualified to be president."

"She's an American born citizen of the required age."

"Are you telling me that she's calling your shots?

"I'm calling my own shots with her guidance, at least until someone locates the Speaker of the House – Francene Maracle."

"You cannot be serious! Franc was an eye doctor in Alaska before she ran for office. She is no more qualified than Anna to protect our interests."

"Either of them is more qualified than Dotson was."

"it's not up to you to make a determination like that. There is a line of succession."

"And you're at the bottom of it."

I should appeal to a higher pay grade and not argue with this goat-roper.

"Perhaps I need to speak to Anna instead."

There was a brief pause and then a pleasant feminine voice came on the line.

"Hello, Marshall."

They're together? How did that happen?

"Madam Secretary, I am so glad you are safe and healthy. When I was selected as the designated survivor, I assumed everyone else had perished. How is it that you missed the speech?"

"My mother called me to her side hours before the speech. I was here with her when the bombs went off."

"Oh, is your mother ill?"

"No, but my uncle is prescient."

"Your uncle."

"Yes. Didn't you know that Cranston is my uncle? It's all very convoluted. My mother and Cranston were actually step siblings until their parents divorced. It's a sordid tale really, but Cran and Mom stayed friends and he's always been around in my life. Of course, being a Dotson appointee, you might not have known that. It didn't get a lot of press when we were appointed by President Meyer and Dotson seemed unaware of it. The man was really not well prepared for his job."

Marshall envisioned the delicate bone structure and blond hair of the Secretary of Education.

Speaking of people who are unqualified ....

"We need to coordinate," Marshall said. "I've been gathering my resources, locating people, getting reports on our situation. Of course, you're senior, but I believe my aid will be very valuable to your administration ... at least until the Speaker of the House can be located. How is it that Francene missed the speech, anyway?"

"Franc's husband was injured that morning and she flew home to Fairbanks to be with him while he underwent surgery."

"So, we do know where she is?"

"I don't know that anyone has actually spoken with her and she would have been in the air at the time of the attacks."

"We should make every effort to find her, don't you agree?"

"I do. Perhaps when she's been located we can all sit down and discuss how best to move forward. In the meantime, I believe we need to move our military forces back to domestic soil. We are vulnerable and there is no telling what might be in the works."

"We can begin a draw-down, but we cannot remove ourselves precipitously from some areas as it will destabilize other regions."

"I don't really care about other regions, Marshall. My sole concern is the people of the United States during this time of crisis. USNorthCom takes precedence at this time. The rest of the world will have to take care of itself. There are places we can withdraw from safely. Let's start with a 10% draw-down of our forces in EUCom. I want 6500 boots on the ground here in the US within the week."

"That's not possible, Anna."

"Cran says it is. I'll have him issue the order. As of this minute, he is acting Secretary of Defense."

This woman will risk chaos overseas.

"Where are they to be deployed?"

"I've already spoken to the Canadians who have promised their full support on the northern border. The Mexicans want to play 'Let's Make a Deal', but I don't think they really want to invade us right now. Somehow, nuked cities are not as attractive as the largest economy in the world was. Seattle-Tacoma is the only remaining West Coast port and the command there is under attack by some force they haven't identified yet."

What? Why am I just hearing about this now?

"What's the matter, Ellerby?" Rutherford asked. "Didn't you realize that the military is answering to me?"

Never let them see you sweat?

"I had heard there was civil unrest there, no more."

"It's not what we're hearing," Anna said. "It sounds like a highly coordinated non-state-actor, possibly mercenary force. We're repositioning satellites to get a better view. While they're fighting in Seattle, it appears other cities also have troubling mercenary forces ... including New York."

"We could not reach required staff levels with New York Police Department staff and calls for military aid were not answered."

"This is still the United States of America, Marshall. New York appears to be in a state of siege. Surely you don't need that many boots on the ground."

"Yes, actually we do. There has been sporadic violence in the city since the bombs were defused. We still haven't located the terrorists. While the police and military are seeking the terrorists, the security forces are necessary to secure the city. We need to discuss distribution. FEMA has food enough to feed 300 million people for two weeks, but the New York warehouse will be empty by Tuesday."

"What should I do about that?" Anna asked.

"Well, first, you should be speaking to the UN to release some of its stockpiles and second, the military can help distribute the remaining food, staring with getting a shipment into New York before supplies become critical."

"I've already spoken to the UN, Marshall. They feel that the US has enormous resources at its disposal, so we don't need food assistance until we've properly secured our food stores and begun redistribution."

"That's FEMA's job."

"Is it? I thought I heard you asking for my help. We prefer to keep the command structure tight and the military provides us with that control."

"What exactly are you saying?"

"You're welcome to stay on as UN ambassador and continue the search for the terrorists, but for the time being, there is no Homeland Security department. We really can't afford to complicate matters."

"You're not the president to make those sorts of decisions."

"According to the line of succession, until such time as Franc can be found, I am indeed the President. You can either get on board with my administration or find a friendly country to host your retirement."

Marshall felt a chill up his back. Those were the exact words Dotson had used right before he fired Rutherford.

My god, this is falling apart right before my eyes.

He knew how to manipulate events behind the scenes to get things to where he was in charge. The goal was still in sight. It just might take a bit longer than anticipated.

Questioning Alliance

Emmaus Airfield

*L*iberty Trucking's yard buzzed with activity as Jason Breen's drivers and mechanics cleaned up from the storm and found housing for the new people who had joined them. A few of the guys had wives and ole ladies and a few kids they'd brought to sit out the rain and were now thinking home was not really that safe a location.

Jason had always liked Jacob Delaney. When he'd been a wild teenager, Jacob had seemed like the only sensible adult. And when he'd been accused of murder, Jacob had paid for his lawyer. When he'd learned that going through something like that meant you were never trusted again and would have difficulty finding jobs, it had been Jacob who had suggested he open a trucking company, leasing part of the Delaney Airfield and starting with an old truck Jacob owned. Jason couldn't think of anyone who had ever been a better friend to him than Jacob Delaney. Still, the end of the world could make a man suspicious. He watched as Jacob's green truck pulled into the compound.

"Jason, hey, I've been hired by Ren Sullivan to fly his turbo prop to Wichita. That commuter is screwing up my runway. Can I get you to open the gates and move some trucks at this end so I can take off this way?"

"Sure. That was the deal when you leased this area to me. I'll get some of my guys working on it right away. While you're gone, we'll drag that plane into the old terminal parking lot. Looks like it'll fit. How are things in town?"

"I saw Maggie. She looked fine. So's Marnie."

"Good. They like their independence, but I still worry about them."

"Of course. You hear anything about a burglary in town?"

"Burglary? No, why?" *Old man, why do you suppose I know anything about that?*

"You sure? Someone smashed the window at Mac's pharmacy and cleaned the place out. They tried the same thing at Huffman's, but Huffy unloaded some buckshot into one of them and they ran. You got any guys trailing blood."

Jason stared at Jacob. The bigoted views of the town didn't surprise him anymore, but he had thought Jacob wasn't like that. On the other hand, maybe you should cut people some slack during the apocalypse.

"I'll vouch for my guys. We spent the rain right there." He pointed to the old fuel storage building with its concrete roof and boarded up windows. "And with all due respect, we wouldn't crap in our own nest. We're smarter than that. If we were going to take to looting – and some of my guys would be down with that if I let them – we'd be gathering resources for the town and selling them to the town at a reasonable rate. Okay?"

Jacob opened his mouth as if to say something, paused, looked up at the sky and then he nodded.

"I'm sorry. You're right. I just showed my knickers. The town may well need your skills. I don't want to alienate you."

"You haven't, but you'd best remember that in the 25 years since that incident, I've been accused a dozen times of crap and I've never been tried. Yes, I work in the grey economy, but I'm not a criminal."

Jacob nodded.

"Your guys are more likely to hear something than I am, plus I'm going to Wichita. If you hear anything would you let Rob know?"

"Probably not. I'll contact Marnie or Shane, maybe that idiot son-in-law of mine."

"Cai's going with me. Rob deputized us to act on the town's behalf. Shane's sweeping the outlying areas, making sure people heard the storm siren, carrying messages."

"If we hear anything, we'll take care of it then. I don't consider Rob to be my ruler and I'm not submitting to his authority. Why isn't Bart Rawlston investigating this?"

Jacob heaved a deep breath before speaking.

"Bart died when the City Hall shelter's air handling system failed. There were almost 100 fatalities."

The sounds of the compound faded as Jason felt sweat spring up cold and clammy on his forehead. He felt his pulse in his ears.

"Oh, my god!" As much as he disliked cops in general, he had respected Bart for being a peace officer rather than a dictator.

"Yeah. We might have lost the medical center shelter too except Shane decided to risk the elements without relying on the storm siren."

"He's the one who set it off?"

"Yeah."

"How'd he know the rads were down?"

"I don't know. We've all been too busy for a sit down over coffee to discuss it. Anyway, I gotta get to work fueling up Ren's plane. I know you won't submit to authority, but I hope you'll voluntarily cooperate with those of us who are trying to hold things together."

"I'll take it under advisement, " Jason said. Jacob had adjusted his attitude pretty quickly. So .... "I know it's not personal. Folks don't trust people who don't conform to society's rules. On the other hand, given that the apocalypse just began, my skills might be in higher demand than they were last week."

"Could be," Jacob agreed. "We'll know more when we get back from Wichita."

Jason watched the old man drive away. He was 99% positive that none of his guys had anything to do with ripping off the pharmacy because they'd all been in the same building for the entire rain, but he considered it wisdom to have a talk with them to assure none were considering something similar now that they were able to get around. *At least not in the township. The towns will be our best customers if we play it right, but not if we alienate them now.*

Rogue Unit

Beulah, Kansas - County Courthouse

A Kansas National Guard unit guarded the off-ramp into Beulah. They asked Stan a lot of questions before allowing him to drive to the county courthouse. During the short drive to the five-story Art Deco court house, he felt like he was back in Nam, driving into a forward base. There were snipers on rooves and the entrance to the lot was semi-blocked by an MRAP with a 50-cal mounted on the roof.

A E4 searched Stan when he got out of the car, instructing him to leave his gun in the truck. He was escorted into the building by two armed soldiers. The sergeant major turned out to be an old friend. They'd served together in the Reserves several years ago.

"Gus, you old coot! What are you doing here?"

"They called me up the first night."

"Not at the state line?"

"Yep. We were sent after a shooter – some rogue agent who busted out another agent from the containment zone. You know about that?"

"I've heard rumors from the ham radio operators." That was technically true if not the whole truth.

"Well, they're true. The Army liquidated the containment zone." Gus sighed, flinty eyes softening for a moment. "We were headed back when we heard the other NG units being wiped out for resisting the order."

"We heard about that too. So you survived and now you're here. What's up with the high security?"

"We're not here with Army sanction. From the radio chatter, I don't consider it in our best interest to turn ourselves in. So we're hunkering down."

"What about the county government? I've been trying to get them on the phone and there's no answer."

"Yeah. I asked them to go home for now. We don't want civvies in the crossfire if it comes to it."

"Right. We're trying to figure out what we're supposed to do with a kid who murdered someone in Emmaus."

"Yeah, well, we're under functional martial law, so the Emmaus mayor can make that decision. You know what I would suggest, right?"

Stan felt a cold fist form in his gut.

"Yeah." Stan nodded to the radiomen working in a glass-walled office. "What do we know about the world out from here?"

"It's going about how you would expect nuclear apocalypse to go. It's rough out there. Total chaos. Nobody is in charge and the people who think they're in charge ...." He shook his head. "The closest thing to a civilian leader is the Homeland Security Secretary, but there's a guy named Rutherford out of Cheyenne Mountain who seems to be calling the shots for this area. If he's who I think he is ... that's bad."

"How so?"

"I knew a Rutherford in Cambodia. He was a creepy guy. The point of the spear, if you know what I mean."

"I've met guys like him." *I was a guy like that.* "What's coming our way?"

"Real martial law. Gun to your head kind. Rutherford will see your food confiscated and your streets patrolled. It is a warzone from which there is no escape. Emmaus, that's where Sullivan lives, right?"

Stan nodded, remembering the smell of burning huts and the sing-song jabber of Vietnamese women begging for the lives of their husbands and sons.

"Bolster your borders. Harvest your crops. Ask Sullivan to help you get what you don't have and need. Don't accept Rutherford's offer of help when it comes. It'll be tempting, but if you do it, he'll stomp all over the Constitution. I've lived my whole life in the military, but I would not want me guarding your community with him giving me orders. I think if you're honest, you don't want to bring Vietnam to the streets of Mara Wells."

"My experience ... you can't turn down martial law."

"Do what you choose, but I'm telling you – don't let Rutherford in. He'll offer you food, fuel, protection. You got Sullivan to help you. Don't be fooled by Rutherford. His help comes with a price and you have a choice not to pay it. Better to go down in a hail of bullets than to submit to that devil."

Stan stared at his friend. *Such vehemence! What do you know that you're not saying?*

"I'll talk to Rob Delaney. We're coordinating with surrounding communities, so I think we're already thinking along those lines. Will you be all right with us using you as a listening post?"

"For as long as we're still here. If the Army shows up, we'll be gone one way or the other."

"I understand."

When he got to his truck, Stan stared out across the parking lot, feeling the world closing in like a dense fog. These men here were expecting death at any moment. He had emerged from the bomb shelter to see a world that had not really changed. It was the same buildings, same people. Nobody had died in Mara and the dead squirrels and birds could be cleaned up. The rain had been boring. As dangerous as it had been, it was over. Life would go on … except … when the Costco shipment ran out, everybody but the farmers would go hungry and life would never be the same again.

I need to talk to Ren Sullivan. If Gus is right about Rutherford, we need a plan before he gets here.

He started the truck and turned west, back toward Emmaus. As he passed the houses of Beulah, he realized he hadn't seen any civilians. That icy fist began squeezing his gut again. He trusted Gus to act honorably, but the memory of burning villages in a land faraway reminded him that honor sometimes was a relative concept.

I don't want to know. I can't do anything about it. I can only control what Rob and I are able to influence. Gus wouldn't do that. Just keep that in mind and don't dig any deeper.

He glanced to the left and saw a young girl standing by a house with a dog on a leash. The fist of ice dissolved. In a desperate situation, people were still basically the same. He hoped.

Water Under the Bridge

County Road N

Shane left Jazz in the car without saying a word to go bang on a storm cellar door. Jeremiah Lufgren finally emerged, asking questions about the radiation levels and whether it was okay to let the cows out. Shane's sign was rough, unpracticed, but Jeremiah provided the vocabulary when Shane resorted to spelling and Shane quickly began to renew his second language. He explained about refilling the water troughs and planning the harvest. While he used the Geiger Counter to assure that the radiations levels were down, he was aware of Jazz staring out at the gently rolling prairie.

I don't care what she thinks. I had to do what was necessary. Who is she to judge me?

"Something wrong?" Jeremiah asked.

There were probably signs for nuclear Armageddon, but Shane didn't know them. He was reduced to pantomime. Jeremiah shook his head.

"No, something else. You hold close to your chest. Your choice. But I see."

"World – it stinks. Some people think we still same. We're not. They argue about what needs doing."

Jeremiah took in what he said and then signed solemnly.

"You need do, not judge."

"Not me judging."

Jeremiah glanced toward the Jeep. He assumed he could read Shane's mind. It was easier than explaining reality.

"We should go. Oh, cooperative meeting 5 pm City Hall. Alex call it."

Jeremiah nodded. He signed to one of his older boys to take the truck and go let the other Lufgrens know they could come out now. Seeing that he seemed to know the details without asking Shane allowed Shane to remove Lufgren farms from the circuit.

Jazz didn't say anything until he turned down the road into the old missile silo.

"Why are we going this way?" she asked.

"Maybe I'm going to drop your body down the missile shaft."

She stared ahead, a stifled expression on her face.

"I was just under the impression this place had been abandoned."

"Which makes it the perfect place for drifters to stop and camp," Shane explained. "I want to shoot a couple more people today." He pulled up to the old gate house. The windows had been boarded up. The gate was securely closed with a sign directing inquiries to Anders McAuliff. Shane tested the gate, but it wasn't budging. The fence looked to be in good shape with gleaming concertina wire around the top. He stared down the fence line, contemplating the heat of the day. He could walk around the perimeter and assure everything was locked up.

You're just trying to avoid dealing with her.

That recognized, he decided the security of the missile silo wasn't worth hiking for a mile. Tossing his overshirt into the back seat, he sat down in the car.

"Stay put for a second," Jazz told him. Shane froze with his hand on the key.

"Rationally, I knew that anyone who had served in the military had killed people. Rationally, I know that there was nothing we could do for those people, that even they knew that. But, emotionally ... it shocked me and ... when I heard Cai's voice on the radio ... it felt like a life raft. It wasn't my place, but I needed ... I felt like I needed help. I wasn't really afraid of you. I was ... was ...."

"It's okay to be afraid of me, Jazz," Shane assured, staring out across the dashboard at the giant geodesic dome that capped the missile silo. "I'm a dangerous guy. I can kill people and not feel guilty about it. Despite how roughly I removed that gun from your hands, I have no plans to kill you, but you're right to be afraid of me. If you'd hit the safety, you might have died at the Elevators."

"I was reacting to something other than you. I'm not really afraid of you. You were angry about the radio. You weren't planning to hit me. I'm sorry I made you feel that I felt threatened by you."

Denial is not just a river in Egypt.

Shane sighed and turned the Jeep around to head back to the rural highway.

At the Bennett farm, doors were open and people milled about. Andrew straightened upon their approach, said a few words to the two young men he was working with and left the stock trough to meet Shane. That both were armed made complete sense now, though it occurred to Shane that Andrew had every reason to want to shoot him.

"Shane Delaney. I had heard you were back in town."

"Hi, Andrew. We were just checking to make sure people heard the siren."

"We did. It would be good for us out here if they'd get KERB up and running."

Shane nodded, then shrugged. That wasn't part of his assignment.

"No need to be awkward, Shane. What happened before you left last time ... water under the bridge."

"Seriously?"

"Yeah. Caleb had gone to the dark side, talking insurrection and pushing people around. McAuliff should have reined him in or sent him away. I'm not saying McAuliff deserves to be in jail, but Caleb broke the law, whether I agree with that law or not. And you were just a pawn in it all, caught up in the statist system."

Shane laughed. Jazz got out now and walked around to their side of the car.

"I hadn't heard it stated that way before, but yeah – that's about what happened. Thanks for understanding."

"So, your dad deputize you?" Andrew asked, favoring Jazz with a friendly smile.

"I volunteered. You two know each other?"

"No ... I don't think so."

"His kids homeschool," Jazz told Shane. She and Andrew introduced themselves. "I'm a fan of your Saturday show, though."

"Yeah? So you're one of our four listeners. I wonder ... if I showed up this morning, would they let me do the show? I'm feeling like a prophet right now. I've been talking about this for four years and never really thought it would happen." Shane looked blank and Andrew laughed. "You have no idea what we're talking about, do you?"

"No, but it doesn't matter. Look, I don't think my dad's here yet, but the town is going to need to band together and look to our own security. I know you don't like government, but the simple truth of the matter is that we need to plan for what's coming our way. So far we haven't done a very good job of that."

"What do you mean?"

Shane explained about City Hall.

"Jazz and I had to put down someone's bull that got left out in the rain and Clem had to give mercy to a family that sheltered in a storage shed."

Andrew rolled his eyes toward heaven. Like Jacob, he was a spiritually-minded anarchist.

"We have food and that's going to make us targets. I'm surprised we aren't already seeing bands of scavengers."

"The big cities are gone, so there's less need for resources," Andrew explained. "The survivors in the medium sized communities will use up their resources there before they head our way. We have a few weeks before it dawns on them that their resources come from the countryside. We don't object to communities organizing in a voluntary fashion, so we'll hear you out when the time comes."

"First things first. Alex called a cooperative meeting at 5 pm at City Hall. We need to get the corn and other crops in. Somebody needs to talk to the Elevators, see if they can store it for us. We didn't see anyone there and I don't know the community well enough to go banging on doors."

"I do. I'll head over there. Not sure what this whole storing the corn thing is for. We need food and most of my corn is dent. It ain't good eating corn. Corn in general is not going to keep us alive, not without some heavy alteration."

Jazz nodded.

"We'll need lye or wood ash to nixilate it."

Shane stared at them. They laughed.

"He has no idea what we're talking about," Andrew remarked. "Don't worry about it. There'll be OJT later."

It's just corn, how complicated could it be? Of course, I don't know what "nixilate" means and I haven't got Google to inform me.

"Jazz, you ready to go or do you want to see if someone here can run you back to town?"

"No, I'm good," she assured him. They got back into the car. "Are you sure you don't feel anything about what you did?" she asked as he turned the car around. He shot her an odd look. "Controlling your reactions is not the same thing as not feeling."

He could feel his cheeks getting warm and just hoped his tan covered the blush. He stared out over the hood for a moment.

"I can't afford to feel right now. We don't know that at the next farm, I might not have to do it again."

"So you just feel nothing?"

"I wouldn't say that." He started the car and backed around to head back out to the road. "I'm not a sociopath ... I've just learned how not to let feelings get in the way of what needs to be done."

"That's sounds painful, actually. So change the subject. Who is Caleb?"

"Caleb Jacoby, He was part of McAuliffe's militia. A good speaker. He jacked his jaw at some gathering in Montana and got the FBI looking at McAuliff. Dan didn't do enough to shut him up."

"How were you involved?"

Shane sighed.

"I was an informant. The FBI knew I had worked for Jason Breen, so they recruited me."

"So did Dan McAuliff really threaten national security?"

"Not in my presence. Caleb was saying some dangerous things. A couple of Jason Breen's guys agreed with him, but most of McAuliffe's militia were committed anarchists who favored philosophical revolution, not violent government overthrow. Unfortunately, McAuliff got caught up in Caleb's mess."

Shane slowed and stopped by the water tanks in Brady Tanks, a collection of buildings marking a town that had once been the first water stop as the rail line moved north from Emmaus. Nothing moved. Jazz joined Shane to walk door to door. Brady Tanks had been larger once, but people had fled decades ago, moved to Emmaus or one of the larger towns, or the big city. Shane didn't want to think about those who had left the old town visible in the abandoned storefronts to move to Kansas City or Denver. Better to be bored and poor than dead.

I never thought I'd say that.

The town had never been huge. There was no city hall. The wood-frame school now housed a diner. Somewhere out there in the corn fields were likely houses, but Shane had hoped to find someone here who could go wake the neighbors. If anyone was here, they were hiding under one of the buildings with a concrete foundation.

The wind sighed through the surrounding corn fields, rustling drying leaves and sending swirls of dust along the single street. Shane began to wish he'd worn a hat. He'd forgotten how intense the Kansas sun could be. Jazz's silence wore on him.

"Want to tell me what you're thinking?"

"I'm having a Children-of-the-Corn moment," Jazz responded with a smirk.

"That's why I keep expecting to see a bunch creepy kids in Amish clothing?"

"Let's hope they locked up the scythes."

He had to admit her sense of humor showed resilience. She could by lying. She probably was.

"'Outlander!' Shane mocked. She laughed. Maybe she wasn't lying ... much. "This is the last building." He mounted the steps to the diner's door. He looked through the front window and froze, pushing her back with an outstretched arm, staring down the barrel of a shotgun.

Conspiratorial Complications

Emmaus Listening Station

*T*he listening post had hidden in plain sight as a bed and breakfast with seven generous bedrooms, several baths, and some nice luxuries. Emily and Madelaine had made the beds upstairs and were finally unpacking the kitchen. Grant had assisted as much as he could, shifting boxes on the granite countertops and stocking pantry shelves. They seemed to have forgiven his father-in-law Jim and he hoped his generally supportive presence would cause them to thaw toward him, but they finally shooed him out of the kitchen, so he went downstairs to check on Dylan.

"What's up here?" Dylan asked, indicating a map on the screen.

"Tracking Shane's phone. I think it's a small crossroads town – a bar and a diner, lots of corn. Why?"

"He's stopped a few places along this route, but he's settled in here."

"Could be a simple reason. His behavior would suggest he's sweeping the area, maybe for the town. I texted him a while ago, but he's not picked up yet." Grant was not inclined to worry about Shane in rural Kansas ... at least not yet. He tapped the notepad beside Dylan's elbow. "What can you tell me about Rutherford?"

"Nothing that makes sense. He retired. He made some politically divisive statements against President Dotson and got fired. He showed up Wednesday afternoon at Cheyenne Mountain and he was suddenly in charge."

"On whose orders."

"That's the weird part." Dylan scratched his upper lip where he hadn't shaved yet. "The Department of Defense cleared his being there at 1:30 pm Wednesday. At 4:30, Ellerby sent a message that Rutherford was to be considered in charge, but ... it didn't come from a DHS server."

"Where then?"

"It came from an CSA server in Atlanta. I can't obviously hack a terminal that's been destroyed, so I don't know who sent it. I'm running a search now, seeing if I can back-track close enough to make an educated guess or run across some identifying fingerprints of the user. Also, the UDC is reporting that the bombs were set off by a single pulse over the Internet, emanating from several different locations. Someone worked really hard to make this seem like they were unrelated attacks that just happened to occur at the same time. Why?"

"Speculating? They were covering their own tracks, maybe so they could be placed in a power position in the future. There is no way these were all random. The people involved may have thought they were acting separately, but someone had to be in charge. The pulse gives us the first clue that there was a mind behind all this."

Grant looked at his computer screen.

"What's going on in Denver and Kansas City?"

"Military is attempting to cover the hot spots with concrete."

"So they're utilizing what was learned from Chernobyl. Good for them. What about the governors of nearby states?"

"The Governor of Nebraska did a radio broadcast an hour ago, directing farmers to start harvesting their crops. He's guarded by the Nebraska National Guard. The Governor of Kansas is guarded by Knight Industries, but the curious thing ... the traffic says nobody has seen him."

"There's traffic?"

"Yeah. The contractor's interweb is up and the Knights are talking to one another. Electricity and cell phones in this local area are also up. They can't call beyond the two or three towers working, but folks here can talk to one another."

"Oh, good. I won't need to redirect a satellite to talk to Shane. What's the video?"

"I've been working my way through Alan's data. I really wish I knew where it had come from because it is powerful. If I'd only been able to process this before the attacks ...."

"You'd be dead, son. So show me."

"It's part manifesto for the downfall of the United States and part hit piece on DHS, DOD and State. We're talking thousands of pages of documents. There were plans for civil unrest. I researched. The planned events ... some of them had already occurred -- violent clashes with police over – get this, planned officer-involved shootings, protests over gasoline prices, food shortages that created riots. There were apparently terrorist attacks planned as black flag events, but they weren't expected until later in the year. I guess they'll be canceled now."

"The purpose?"

"To allow the president to declare martial law and suspend the elections."

"Have you found out who was directing it?

"No. This almost comes off as a conspiracy theory except every document I've researched comes up as legitimate. I can see when the information was saved and it is before several of the events took place."

"Does it mention the bombings at all?"

"No. It's like there were two separate plots operating in isolation from one another. Alan's information feels like a black flag operation. What

Chavez sent you appears to be more like a terrorist plot the government had knowledge of."

Grant sat down abruptly. He had thought he had a singular goal – figure out who had done this to his country. Two plots complicated that task, but it also begged the question – what if there was more that they didn't know about?

Embrace of Big Government

Wichita

Jacob successfully took off, announcing that Wichita was about 250 miles away, so they would be there in about 45 minutes. The flight gave Cai a chance to mull over what he had learned of his brother that morning. He supposed, if he was honest, he knew that Shane was capable of it. He'd been a soldier of sorts and the memory of what he'd done to the soldiers at the Kanorado state line sure fit with what he'd done at the Elevators. Still, he hadn't killed the soldiers. As he'd said at the time, he dented their Kevlar. Assuming that was true – and Cai thought that might be served with a large slice of denial -- why would Shane kill innocents? Shane had always walked up to a line that Cai didn't believe should be crossed, but this stepped way over it.

Jacob had been talking on the radio off and on while they were flying and now he was actually talking to someone in pilots' code. Cai had never paid much attention to it, so he didn't know what they were saying. Ren was sitting right seat and he occasionally provided information into the headset too. He'd been a military pilot, so probably was privy to the code.

Off to the east, Cai saw a first-class electrical storm near where Kansas City might once have been. He shivered and checked his seatbelt. He'd seen lots of storms over the prairie, but he'd never seen anything as big as that. Ren turned in his seat.

"They say that's the ionized environment over Kansas City. Rads are a little elevated here." He showed the Geiger counter they'd brought with them. "But within acceptable limits. The whole world has gone mad overnight."

He turned back around and Cai returned to staring at the storm. Eventually it dropped away as they neared Wichita. He was always nervous on landing in any plane, but Jacob set it on the ground so skillfully that Cai didn't know they were on the ground until he saw buildings outside the window.

The terminal looked more like an office park with some hangers than an airport in a good sized city. A truck drove up to the plane and a man got out. He was very tall and fit, dressed in a sport coat and jeans.

"Thanks for being on time, Phil. This is Jacob and Cai Delaney."

"If you'll come this way, gentlemen."

"I'm going to stay with the aircraft," Jacob explained. "I'll have it filled up and ready to go when you get here. How long do you think it'll take?"

"We should be back by 2 pm," Ren said. "I've already called ahead to the Governor's office, so they're expecting me."

"I took care of that request, sir," Phil said. "Durant Drugs will fill that order for you. If you give me the list, I'll fax it to them right now and they will deliver it here."

"Looks like I didn't need to come," Cai quipped, handing over the list.

"You should come with me to the Governor's Office to represent the town," Ren said. "Lancaster is a friend, but I don't think it's a good idea that I be perceived as throwing my weight around. The requests should come from the town."

Cai tied his tie on the drive to Garvey Center, taking his cue from Ren, who certainly could show up however he wanted, but had spiffed for the occasion. Blocks before they reached the provisional state capitol, they began to notice security.

"The Army took the National Guard right out from under the Governor, so there was no choice but to call in these private security people," Phil explained.

"There's got to be hundreds of them," Cai whispered. *Is this what Shane was doing?* The black garbed figures with their Kevlar, black helmets and guns at the ready caused a cold fist to form in his gut. *No wonder he's so cold!*

"They're not just here guarding the governor. They're all over the city."

"How many?" Ren asked.

"Thousands, I think. There's also Army. I keep waiting for them to come to blows."

"Who would win?" Cai asked.

"That's of lesser importance than who would we want to win. If you can answer that question, let me know."

A block from the high-rise, they were stopped by a security checkpoint. When Ren stated their business, they were directed into a parking garage where mercenaries paid very close attention to Ren's credentials and far more attention to Cai's driver's license than he was comfortable with. *Were we somehow flagged by that dustup at Kanorado?*

After about 10 minutes, they were asked to step out of the car and submit to a pat-down search. The guy doing Cai's pat-down asked him his name, home address and Social Security number.

"Where's Emmaus?" he asked while he groped between Cai's legs.

"Out I-70, about two hours from Denver … what used to be Denver."

The mercenary stared at Cai long enough to make him nervous before calling to his commander that Cai was "clear".

"Sanchez, you're with us, then. Let's go."

They left the parking structure, passed through a sculpture garden with brass children playing crochet and entered the tallest of the several buildings in the complex. They discharged on the 9th Floor to enter a luxurious apartment. The unit commander went deeper into the apartment while they remained in the entryway. Cai had never seen so much travertine in his life and the wallpaper appeared to be actual fabric.

Sanchez kept shooting odd looks Cai's way. They seemed odd. Maybe the whole situation was making him paranoid? The unit commander Crispin came back.

"The Governor is willing to speak with you, Mr. Sullivan. Mr. Delaney, you may have a seat. Sanchez, make sure he's comfortable."

Ren and Cai exchanged glances and then Ren walked away with Crispin.

"Do you want a soda ... or something stronger? There's a bar over there."

"No, I'm fine." Cai sat down on the sofa. He almost felt guilty sitting on a sofa stuffed with down and covered with damask.

Sanchez sat down an arms-length away on the sofa and handed Cai his phone that showed a screen shot of Shane back-dropped by a long line of cars.

"Do you know that guy?" he asked.

Bigger Troubles Looming

Brady Tanks

Shane had just finished his hand-pressed burger and fries at the Whistlestop Diner when Dick Vance entered. Taking off the battered drover hat he always wore in his workaday world, he started to say something to Les Tanner, the owner and cook, but Shane's presence distracted him.

"Shane Delaney," he remarked.

"Probably won't do me any good to deny it then," Shane retorted. "How you been, Dick?" He turned around on the stool to shake Dick's hand. Dick was a little older than Rob, his hair still a deep black indicative of a lot of Indian blood and his beard a wonderful riot of chest-length grey locks. His had been the beard Shane had aspired to when he first started shaving, before he'd realized that he hated the feeling of face fur.

"Personally, I'm doing fine, though I think the country may need a handbasket."

"No argument there. I take it you heard the storm siren."

"I did. Mission Ridge doesn't come over far enough to block the sound. Your dad send you here?"

"Jazz and I are sweeping the township to make sure people know."

Dick nodded to Jazz. He loved to harmlessly flirt with young ladies, so Shane wasn't surprised they knew each other.

"How are we doing?"

"Mixed bag. We lost 75 people when the City Hall shelter lost its air-handling system." Dick's brown eyes took on a sad cast. "Had to shoot a bull that got out at the Gimble place."

Shane suddenly couldn't meet Dick's gaze and found his own drifting up toward the ceiling. There was no way he could finish the next part of the report.

You did what you had to do.

"These times are going to be hard. Some of us are going to be called on to do things the rest of us don't want to do. If you got your heart right with God, you'll know better where the lines are."

Somehow, of all the people in the world that Shane could have lecture him on faith, Dick was the one who didn't immediately make him prickly.

"So, your dad may want to know what's going on over the northeast." Dick's gaze included Les and Jazz in his report. "You can see it from the water tower."

Jazz gave Shane a questioning look.

"You can stay here. It's hotter than blazes out there."

"I'll make some lemonade," Millie Tanner, Les' wife, offered. They were trying to use up things that might melt when their generator ran out of fuel.

Heat shimmered off the drying corn fields and made Shane's head ache while he and Les followed Dick toward the water tower. He could feel his tan getting deeper just walking 100 yards. To make matters worse, Dick knew it. When they reached the stairs for the water tank, he grinned at him from under the brim of his drover's hat.

There's no way I'm wearing that, but a hat would have been a good idea. I wonder if Emmaus was ready for a do-rag made from a t-shirt or a keffiyah?

The water tower set off some bad thoughts about Marnie's sister's suicide jump from another water tower in Emmaus, but provided a great view of the prairie to the north and east. Standing on that side of the tank meant the sun no longer baked Shane's uncovered head. Beyond the polarized lenses of his sunglasses, the sea of corn nodded sere and still, golden ripe for harvesting. He needed Dick's field glasses to see the APC waiting at a crossroads.

"There were a bunch of them earlier, pulled up there at the crossroads and then they dispersed east and north." Les pointed to the crossroads that had brought Shane from the west. The cook had served in the 1st Gulf War and thought he knew a thing or two about the military. Shane wondered if he'd recognized that the men with the truck were not wearing Army issue.

"I drove over to Massey to check on our daughter," Dick explained. "On the way back, I saw that truck. When I stopped to ask what they were doing, they told me some bogus story about being an advanced team from the government, checking for looting."

"I'll let my father know, but that is very much out of Emmaus's jurisdiction. That's gotta be Bethlehem Township. He only authorized me to sweep Jericho Township and I doubt we have the resources to even protect that much. If we can all cooperate, we might be able to do something. Of course, we have no power over you folks out here, but it makes sense that we all work together for our own protection."

"So they scare you too?"

Les was a short fellow with a round belly and a bald head, but he'd made up for pointing a shotgun at Shane's head with some of the best hamburger and fries Shane had ever eaten. Shane felt he was owed a little respect for that pleasant lunch. Of course, after three days of eating MRE gourmet, he'd have taken a tough steak with lima beans just for the variety.

"Yeah. That isn't military. The truck is. The men aren't. So, like I said, the corn needs to be harvested. We can't wait. Another rain could drive us underground again and we will have missed our window or come out to find it's been taken by someone else. Maybe those guys."

"You're sounding a lot like your grandfather," Dick said. "Figured your father would be a bit more dictatorial."

"So did I, but that's not what he told me to tell people."

Les pursed chubby lips.

"I'll let everybody know around these parts. Dick and I will. What should we do if they get closer?"

Shane thought about that a moment and then shrugged.

"The corn isn't worth your life, right? I gotta get going."

Jazz was waiting in the diner when they got there. While they'd been outside, the power had come back on and the air-conditioning had kicked in. For a moment, the coolness made Shane dizzy.

"Ready to go?" she asked as his phone buzzed. He pulled it out of his pocket.

"Looks like we have some cell service again." He scanned the messages to see what he should deal with now and what could wait for later. "I need to check a few of these."

"Why don't I pour you a lemonade?" Millie asked Jazz, who had pulled out her own phone. She agreed, but turned aside to a booth to deal with her messages.

Shane went into the bathroom to get rid of some MRE. Apparently Grant had a tracker on him. He explained what he was about. He hesitated over even opening Mike's message. In the end, he decided that Mike was probably loyal and Joel Rhys's email was hidden behind a lot of encryption.

He figured it out? Naw, Alicia told him. But what's he talking about 'whack-a-mole'?

Mike had included two GPS coordinates that turned out to be Kanorado and Wichita.

It was evolving, making shit up as I go along. Is A safe at mom's?
And, how'd you find out?

BW had stopped harassing him, so they must think he was trapped overseas. CSA wasn't under that impression. There was reports of Rigby's death in San Diego and demands for him to report to the nearest duty office, but they didn't say which one, which suggested they didn't know where he was.

Rigby does a great job.

He drank the lemonade, thanked Les and he and Jazz headed for the Jeep.

"My folks sent me a text Wednesday night saying they were okay and waiting at a rest stop in Tennessee," Jazz told him.

"That's good, I guess. At least you know they survived the initial attack. I heard from my friends.

They had left San Diego, so they're good too. Well, let's get headed to the Box Belt."

"It feels good to be getting back to normal."

Shane paused, adjusting his sunglasses.

"Yeah, I don't think normal is where we're headed, but it's good to know people we care about are still out there."

He hit the starter, slid the Jeep into first gear and headed south.

Don't Break Curfew

New York City

*T*he receptionist at the gym's front desk stopped them as they approached the door.

"The police just announced a curfew," she explained. "We tried to get all the members."

A sign announced a 7:00 pm curfew. Katherine glanced at her cell phone. They had five minutes. Lillian looked at her curiously.

"We can make it if we walk fast."

Outside the sun had set and the canyons of New York City were deepening into purple. It took her a moment to recognize the eerie background noise as a lack of street traffic. She couldn't hear cars or feel subways far beneath her feet.

"Where are the street lights?" Lillian asked.

"I don't know," Katherine admitted as the hair on the back of her neck tingled. "Hotel is that way. Let's not waste time."

She stepped out toward the curb to avoid looming alleyways. Lillian fumbled with her cell and then the lantern came on.

"Best not to do that," Katherine insisted. "It's a beacon for anyone looking for us."

"Why would they be looking for us?"

"Not us specifically. Anyone who is still out and about. Stay behind me. Walk fast and if someone gets in our way, be prepared to kick ankles and knee groins."

"You're kidding?"

Katherine shook her head and started walking, glad that she had decided to wear her tennis shoes instead of her pumps. She could hear Lillian tapping behind her as they rounded the corner. *We need to move faster, but I can't leave her behind.* They were a block and a half from the hotel. What could possibly go wrong?

A truck came around a corner two blocks up, the headlights bright in her eyes. She heard the engine rev and dropped to a crouch behind a postal box. Lillian didn't follow suit. In moments the truck was upon them. Loud speakers ordered "Do not move!" Katherine chose to disobey. Staying low, she sprinted toward the hotel as the soldiers focused on Lillian, who screamed and began protesting.

"Stop. You are under arrest. We will fire," the loudspeaker ordered. Back home in Emmaus, she had run five miles every day, some of it flat out in an effort to keep her figure. Now she ran harder than she had run since a high school track scholarship had been her way out of the slum she'd been born in. She shot across the intersection as bullets ricocheted off the building beside her. She swerved into the shadows then, turned abruptly into the entryway of the hotel, relieved when the door opened to her push. Stanley grunted as it nearly hit him, then caught her arm as she stumbled.

"You are kidding me, right?"

"I'm not."

"Banquet room," the manager ordered while Stanley locked the door, as he had clearly been in the process of doing when she burst in.

The last sight Katherine had of the lobby was of Stanley unlocking the door once more as a dark shape filled the entryway. In the banquet room, she stuffed her bag and jacket under the nearest clothed table and cut in line at the salad bar.

"Shh, quiet," she whispered to Julian, who saw her terror and handed her his plate. The manager entered flustered, ahead of a black-clothed soldier with his gun at the ready. Much as Katherine did not want to, she turned with everyone else and tried to look surprised. The soldier swept the room with cold eyes and Katherine shrunk back with everyone else.

"Violating curfew is a criminal offense. We are authorized to shoot on sight. Your friend is dead. You survived this mistake. Don't make another one."

The soldier then left the banquet room, leaving the manager trembling. Katherine set down the plate as her teeth began to chatter violently. Julian put a comforting hand on her back.

"You had no way of knowing," he assured her.

"My god, the world has gone mad," someone said. "Where is the government in all this?"

There's a question, Katherine thought. *More importantly, where are my husband and father-in-law in all this? And how do I get to where they are without getting myself killed?*

Who would have thought that going for a sauna at the gym could end so badly?

She turned to pick up the plate, the china clattering against the table as her hand shook with adrenaline. Julian put a hand over her hand.

"You go sit down. I'll do this for you. Order a bottle of wine. I think you could use a drink."

Accept the Things We Cannot Change

Emmaus Listening Post

We *probably need kindling.*

Grant chuckled to himself as a thin strip of bark tumbled off into the grass. He hadn't chopped wood in decades. His shoulders were beginning to feel it, but there was something about the physical activity of bringing an axe down into a round of wood that just settled the mind and calmed the spirit. So far, he'd chopped five rounds, creating 20 bits of kindling and five good sized logs. Okay, so they were going to freeze to death this winter if he didn't get better at aiming, but he had time.

I hope I have time.

Whoa, that blow had landed exactly in the middle. Good show. The second blow landed in the same spot and the log split. He bent to pick up one of the halves to quarter it, then paused as Dylan came out of the house.

"Oh, good. You can run the wheelbarrow."

"I'll send the girls out," Dylan shot back. "I just intercepted an encrypted message from the Chinese Consulate in New York to the IMF."

Grant gauged his next blow. It split with one hit and the two quarters tumbled off the chopping block.

"Go on," he said, reaching for that last half.

"The Chinese are asking the IMF to broker a call on the US loans."

Grant let the axe fall and watched with satisfaction as the two quarters rolled off into the grass.

"Did you hear me?" Dylan asked.

"I did. Is there a reply from the IMF yet?"

"No. Won't that cripple the government?"

"Hmm, it probably would have before this, but no. Assuming the IMF wants to look cruel at a time like this, whoever is in charge right now will probably just refuse and blame it on the emergency. Nothing changes ... for now."

"And if that isn't what happens?"

"Well, then things will be interesting from our vantage point. We're data crunchers with guns, Dylan. We have plenty of food and a safe location to sit out the mess. There's no need to panic and nothing we could do about even if we were inclined. Did you think someone could nuke 15 American cities and not make the Chinese worry about their investments?"

Dylan sighed.

"You kept saying the world would not be the same. I didn't really believe you."

"Now you do?"

"I think so. How does the government recover from this without resources? I'll send out the girls and get back to the screening room."

"Nope. We have a record function for a reason. Grab some gloves and start filling the wheelbarrow. Have you ever chopped wood?"

"You're kidding?"

"I'm not. We need to look like folks who are just trying to make it through the disaster. That means you need to chop wood. Besides, it will be good for you to get away from those screens for a while. The world doesn't need you to watch it go to hell in a handbasket. It can do that all by itself."

"Have you been listening to Grandpa a lot lately?"

"Jim may be wearing off on me. I don't think I can chop any faster than you can pick up. Let's see if I'm wrong."

Oh, my! Can I hold us together when the reality of this situation hits all of us? Without the government there will be no trucks of food or fuel rolling down what is left of the interstates. We can survive this winter while our neighbors stave and freeze, but what happens next year if things don't normalize? My god! This is a nightmare!

Discrimination

Emmaus, Huffman Market

Jos recorded the amount of money and credit card information in the ledger as Huffy packed Vin Barrett's bag. They had decided to open for a limited number of hours to sell what they could before things started melting in the freezers.

"When the Internet turns back on, we'll run your credit card," Jos explained. "That'll probably be Monday when the bank reopens."

"Well, thank you kindly, folks." Vin hefted two 50 lb. bags on one shoulder. "I can't believe we were nearly out of dog food."

He went to the door where Alice let him out. They allowed five people in at a time in order to keep control of the situation here at the market. When Alice tried to close the door, a long strong arm pushed her out of the way as Mace Kettridge entered. Huffy had last seen him trying to break in the front window on Thursday morning.

"Mace, go away," she ordered. "I won't sell groceries to you."

"You'd let my family go hungry?" he demanded.

Darn the man. Of course, I wouldn't.

"You need to leave." Jos stood up. "If Granmae doesn't want you here, then you can't be here."

"What are you going to do, boy? Scold me?" Mace taunted as he walked back toward the shelves. Huffy ran around the counter to stop him, but he brushed her off.

"My kids need food, Huffy. You can't play favorites here."

"Actually, she can." Andrew Bennett was armed. He was always armed, even before the bombs, but now she was actually glad to see the gun he usually kept concealed. "This is her private property."

"It's a public store," Mace complained. "Public buildings can't discriminate."

Despite that gun under his arm, Andrew was a diplomatic guy, not a hothead. He held up a hand to keep Mace from overwhelming Huffy.

"How about you give me your list and I'll get the items for you. Jos can come out and have you sign the ledger when we're done. That okay with you, Miss Mae?"

"Yes. I don't want anybody going hungry. I just don't want Mace causing any more trouble for me."

"You got no call closing a public business during times of crisis."

"This is not a public business," Andrew reasoned. "it's privately owned."

"It's a business open to the public. She can't discriminate and this is discrimination."

"Thursday was not discrimination," Jos responded. "We weren't open for anyone."

"But now you're open for everyone but me."

Huffy sighed. She really didn't like seeing herself through Mace's eyes.

"We're open for anyone who stands politely in line and waits their turn," Huffy explained. "People who didn't break our windows or threaten us. Mace, you brought this on yourself." He blushed. "Now, I don't want your family going hungry and I don't want to embarrass you, so let's go get the items you're looking for and then we cannot see each other for a few days until we're not angry anymore. Do you have cash?"

"No, Mae, I don't. Like everyone else I have credit cards that right now aren't working with the Internet down, but I have never stiffed you on a payment. I pay my bills on time, paid off every month. I just got hot headed the other day because I was afraid my family would go hungry."

"There's no need to be angry with me, Mace. I'm a businesswoman. I can't have my stock walking out the door without due compensation or a promise to pay. Jos has a ledger. He'll take your information and we'll record the costs of your items."

Mace breathed deeply and let it out, the color fading from his face.

"That's fine. Mae, I apologize for the other day and I'll pay for the window as soon as the bank reopens. I'll even pay to fix the door to make up for scaring you the other day."

"All right then. Let's just get your items. There's still a long line out there, so best be moving smartly."

Huffy glanced at Jos who shrugged. Andrew gave her a friendly nod. Someone else came up to the counter to purchase their supplies. Huffy had put the meat on sale since some of it was at its sell-by date. It was moving nicely. They shouldn't lose any money on it.

"I'm sorry that I couldn't stop him," Alice told her.

"No, there's nothing to be sorry for. You're not big enough to stand against a man that size. Thank you for coming into work today. We suddenly have to do everything the old-fashioned way and it takes a lot longer."

"I'm pleased to do it. About the apartment … Keri Lufgren offered for us to stay on the farm and Mark is thinking about it."

"Well, that's fine, Alice. It hasn't been rented in years and I only offered because you were asking about places to rent. Just let me know when you've decided."

"Thank you for being so understanding."

Huffy smiled. She prided herself on being a hard-headed businesswoman, but she liked to make people happy when she could. She didn't like having to keep her door closed and just let a few people in at a time. Perilous times called for careful measures, but this felt … wrong. Smart, but wrong.

What Mace had said about discrimination bothered her. She didn't consider herself a bigot. *Hadn't Mace noticed that Vin Barrett had been going out when he was coming in?* The locked door had nothing to do with racism and everything to do with controlling the situation. Thursday morning had been frightening. She'd never thought to see her neighbors picking up rocks to break her windows.

Mace came up to have his box of supplies registered and his credit card information taken. He apologized once more and he and Andrew Bennett left together. Huffy stared down the line of townspeople and sighed. They were going to be open late tonight, but at least she wouldn't lose any money on the meat.

Sins of the Past

Delaney House

Jill hadn't appreciated modern appliances and electricity this much in many years. She savored the fresh scent of clean laundry as she pulled clothes out of the dryer. Even when the kids had been little and there'd been mounds of clothes, she'd enjoyed folding laundry. It was warm in her hands and a few deft gestures rendered it tidy and compact, organized by family member. Unlike so much in life, laundry had a definable beginning, middle and end. You knew when you had accomplished the task. Jill left Marnie's scrubs on the laundry room counter and filled the basket to take upstairs.

Jill paused outside Jacob's door with her basket resting on her hip. Normally, he collected his stack of clothes from the counter as he happened through the mudroom when he came home from whatever he was doing, but now she opened his bedroom door and entered his private sanctum.

It wasn't like it was off-limits. Jacob had a sort of open door policy. It was just that she rarely took him up on it. His bedroom seemed private, something she shouldn't just invite herself into. But everybody was busy right now and she needed to keep herself busy so she wouldn't just dissolve into sobbing grief over the friends who had died at City Hall. Putting laundry away seemed as good a distraction as any other.

Jacob and Vi had moved back here about three years ago after Vi had broken her wrist, making cooking difficult for her. It had been good timing. They'd been able to spend a pleasant couple of years here as a family before Vi died. There'd been a time when Jill and Vi had not gotten along or agreed on much. Those last couple of years had been vindication for them both, really. They'd formed a true friendship centered around quilting, cooking and old family tales.

"I'm the last Greyeyes," Vi had told Jill. *"There's no one to pass the stories to."*

"My children are Greyeyes," Jill had responded and volunteered to write them down. She'd filled a couple of spiral bound notebooks and was, occasionally, transcribing them.

The room still bore Vi's mark – muslin curtains, a colorful bed quilt, lap quilt tossed over the back of the wingback side chair, five cross-stitch samplers decorating one wall, framed family photos on top of the dresser. Jill and Rob had offered to give them the master suite, but it had been Vi who had refused.

"We won't be here long and you'd have to move your stuff again. Besides, I like that back bedroom. That master suite would be too big when it's just one."

Jill sighed with memory.

What is the definition of "long" when you're in your 90s? And, how'd she know that one of them was going home before the other?

Jill set the basket down on the neatly made bed and turned to the dresser to put folded shirts and pants in their respective drawers. When she slid the shirt drawer closed, it stuck and she had to jiggle it a little to get it to go in the rest of the way. A paper slid off the dresser top and floated across the floor. Jill closed the drawer and turned to retrieve it.

Shane took a good photograph. Jill recognized the setting – Beulah Cemetery, Vi's grave. She smiled to see her son there. As she moved to put it back on the dresser, she saw the figure behind him – an Indian woman in a prairie dress with a long knife in her left hand. She looked right at Shane with malice.

"Oh, my God!" Jill gasped as memory rushed back like a dam bursting.

"The men of my family are all haunted by her," Vi had explained, showing Jill a line drawing of the figure now visible in the photograph. *"Galina Greyeyes."*

"Haunted?"

"That's what killed EJ." They'd been sitting in the dining room with Vi's photo albums. It had been a cold winter day outside and the chandelier had been on to brighten the room, a fire crackling in the fireplace insert.

"This 'ghost' killed EJ?"

"You're not listening. EJ hung himself because of her."

"How do you know?

"Carl Sullivan told me. I didn't want to believe it. My father had told me the story. He said she showed up to him after the Great War. He knew what she was and he ignored her. EJ didn't know to watch for her. I should have told him."

"Rob's never mentioned this."

"Well, of course not. She doesn't haunt white men. I had two brothers, you know."

Jill stared at the photo. Carl Sullivan had a very distinctive photographic style. She did not doubt the photo came from him. How could he know about Galina? *Why am I thinking seriously about this? Galina was an old woman's grief. Wasn't she?* Jill had seen the sketch, but Vi had assured her there was a photograph in one of the albums. She'd died a week later, so they'd never gotten to it. *I should have sat down and looked through the rest of them. Why didn't I?*

Jill carried the photo down to the home office to burn a copy. After putting the photo back on Jacob's dresser, she walked the few blocks to Carl's house. She walked so she'd be calm when she got there. She wasn't really, even then. Maybe it was the young men shoveling up dead squirrels or maybe she just didn't want to deal with this. Carl was sitting on his front porch, reading a book.

"Hello, Miss Jill," he greeted. "That a photo of your son with an Indian woman standing behind him?"

Despite the afternoon heat, the hair on Jill's arms stood up.

"How'd you do it?"

"I didn't. I told Miss Vi when she was after EJ, but she didn't believe me. I was crazy back then, so you can't blame her. She knew who I meant though. Called her by a name."

"What do you know about her?"

"Nothing more than that."

"Assuming any of this is real, Carl, why would she be following Shane?"

"Why did she follow EJ?"

"EJ was depressed from his war service."

"He came back with a gook bitch riding his shoulder. And, your boy? What's he been doing these last few years? He's got one of this woman wearing one of those berky things following him. That's what I see with my eyes. That Indian squaw just shows up in the photo ... and, no, I don't know why."

Carl pulled himself out of the chair he was sitting in.

"I gotta go. If you want to know more about this, maybe you should talk to Jacob. He knows about it. That's why I gave him the photo."

Carl closed the door and she heard the bolt shoot. She stared at the photo in her hand. *Galina Greyeyes? Middle Eastern women? What did you do, Shane? Oh, God, why am I even listening to Carl Sullivan, about anything?*

Jill set off toward home, her heart pounding. She wanted to find Shane and protect him or at least warn him.

Vi said her father made her back away. How? Could Shane do that?

She paused and looked about. The air was stifling hot with dog-day humidity. She'd turned the wrong way and was now on a side street she rarely came to. Tears blurred her gaze. She was lost in a town she'd lived in for 30 years.

"Hello, Jill, are you all right?" a Southern-honey voice called across the lawn. Jill blinked and glanced around, finally seeing Calla Thomas sitting on her porch. "I've made some lemonade. Would you like to join me?"

Jill couldn't think of anyone more sane and comforting than Calla Thomas, so she joined her on the porch. The heat of the day dropped away as she stepped under the broad overhang where Calla had a rocker, a wicker chair and a table with a pitcher of lemonade and two glasses.

"If you have company ...," Jill started.

"Don't be silly, Jill. I'd not have invited you to join me if I had other engagements. For some reason I felt I should prepare for company. I guess God knew you were coming. Have a seat. Drink some lemonade. Tell me why you're crying in the middle of the day."

"It's not enough that 30 million people died this week or that 100 more died at City Hall?"

Calla looked younger than her years. Her hair was white, but still thick and shiny, pulled up on her head in a Gibson, but with a fringe of bangs across her forehead. She must have been a lot like Shane when she was younger, because her skin was still taut enough to show her high cheekbones. You could almost see the girl she must have been. She was wearing a yellow and blue seersucker dress today.

"I just don't think that's the reason you're crying," Calla asserted, flashing her characteristic wide smile, the warmth of which could melt a glacier on a winter's day. "Of course, you can demand your privacy. But you might like to share that burden with someone."

Calla crossed her ankles, wriggling her toes in her white leather sandals.

"Vi and I were like two peas in a pod from the day I moved to Emmaus. I miss her every day. I'd love to fill what void I can in your life."

Jill remembered that now. Vi had cherished Calla's friendship. *We haven't paid enough attention since she died. Would she have told her about Galina?*

Jill focused intently on a bead of sweat on the side of the lemonade pitcher. This so went against her beliefs.

"Carl Sullivan took a picture of my son at Vi's grave." She set the copy on the table. Calla picked it up and perused it.

"EJ's demon is back, is she?"

Jill looked up in shock and Calla smiled at her.

"Vi told me about her, not long after EJ died. And, frankly -- well, I didn't see her in the same way Carl did, but I sensed her. Every time I saw EJ those last few months, there was ... something. It went beyond shell shock or PTSD. It wasn't even like what Carl was going through. That was creepy, but with EJ .... I always figured it was a demon. Vi told me about her brothers. Some families are haunted by certain demons."

"You seem pretty certain."

"Vi's story bothered me. I needed to prove it to myself. I looked through the Clarion files and found out that the Greyeyes men kill themselves a lot. And I finally found her – Galina. She was a Wyandot. Owned that allotment there east of town. Does Jacob own it now?

Jill shrugged. She didn't know.

"There was a man – he was part Wyandot. He raped her. Someone killed him. Folks around here thought Galina did it, but they couldn't prove it. Maybe this picture does that 150 years late. Anyway, she was pregnant – gave birth to twins. One of them killed himself when he was really young. The other lived to be an old man. Every Greyeyes generation has at least one, from what I could glean."

"My children are Greyeyes."

"Vi insisted Galina only seemed interested in the dark haired men. That might have been her own bigotry talking or her way of explaining why Rob rejected the whole concept. I don't know."

"Did anyone ever resist her?"

"Vi's father said he did. I remember him. He was a deacon of the church and oh, how he could laugh. Hair black as coal when I first moved here. He was an old, old man when EJ died, so I asked him. He said the secret for holding her back was Jesus."

Jill found it difficult to breathe.

"Shane doesn't have that."

Calla laid a knotted hand on hers.

"Shall we pray for him?" she asked.

Meet the New Governor

Wichita Kansas

One of the bedrooms of the penthouse had been turned into an office with some seriously expensive furniture.

I don't live this nice and I'm one of the richest men in the country.

The woman sitting at the desk surprised. Crystal Lewis smiled at him. Her shining blond hair had been swept up in a French twist rather than her characteristic shoulder length layers.

"I thought I'd be seeing Harmon."

"I believe the security officers told you that you were being taken to see the governor."

"Yes."

"I am the governor."

You're the Lt. Governor, young lady. Unless ....

"Harm is dead?"

313

"Probably. He was at a fund-raiser in Kansas City when the bomb went off."

Ren looked around the office. He'd liked Harm, felt he'd had a bright future.

He could have been the next Kennedy.

"I'm sorry to hear that," he said after a moment's thought. "So why are you pretending he's still with us?"

"It's a crisis. People panic when you change horses midstream. When things have settled down, we'll let them know that I've been in charge all along. Unless, of course, you tell them."

That snake has fangs. I think I always knew that.

"Now why would I do that, darling? I gave to your campaign because I thought you'd make a good Lt. Governor. It's assumed that the Lt. Governor will be a heartbeat from the Governor."

"Good. And in exchange for your silence …?"

Ren considered the possibility.

"We can negotiate. You have things I need and I am sure I can provide things you need."

"I agree. Can I count on you remaining here in Wichita for a few days?"

"I have business locally, so long as I am free to leave when I choose."

"Of course."

"Let me just let my friend go back to the airfield and then you and I can discuss things."

"I'll mix you a drink." Ren wasn't fooled. Her warm smile never quite reached her eyes.

Brother by Another Mother

Wichita Kansas

When the rich man came and told Delaney that he should go back to the airfield, Crispin ordered Mike to escort him out. The guy obviously had some training in acting because he wasn't looking nervous, but his scent tasted of fear. In the elevator, Mike didn't waste time when they were alone.

"How are you related to Ric?"

"I – don't feel comfortable giving you information."

"I get that. World's a scary place right now. You want to protect yourself, your family, your town. But I already know your address, right? So listen to what I know. You have the same last name, so I'm thinking you are brothers. I'm Ric's brother by another mother."

"I don't know anyone named Ric?"

317

"Sure you do. His real name is Shane Delaney. We were partners for a long time. I thought he went to Thailand and was surprised when he showed up on the state line shooting National Guardsmen."

A muscle twitched in Delaney's jaw, but he continued to stare at the doors. Despite the light brown hair and blue eyes, Mike could see a resemblance to Ric. His cheeks weren't as high and his skin not as taut as Shane's, but their noses and chins were similar. They could be brothers. They *were* brothers.

"I see where he gets it from. Never met anyone who could hold information so tightly. So, when you see him, just let him know that I'm here and he has ways to get hold of me. I'm there if he calls."

"I don't know anyone named Ric," Delaney repeated.

Mike laughed. The elevator reached the lobby.

"Just tell *Shane* and also tell him that this reminds me a lot of Miristan. He'll know what that means."

The doors opened and the conversation ended. As they walked back to the parking garage, Mike's phone beeped and he looked at it. He scanned through the alerts, stopping at one. The SullCo driver waited beside the truck, smoking a cigarette.

"You need to get him out of here," Mike told the driver. Phil had been military at some point or worked in an unsettled country. The look he gave Mike was weighing. "I don't know what your employer's orders are, but there's an alert with your photo," he told Cai. He showed him a screen shot with Malacai Delaney following Ric out of the ditch on I70. The color drained from Delaney's face. "Whatever Ric was up to there, I've got his back. *Su hermano es mi hermano* -- I have yours too. Get out of here. They've connected your name to this image, but they don't have a location yet. You need to get as far from here as you can and then split up because they are looking for you and they know you're in this truck."

Phil tossed his cigarette aside and jumped into the truck. Delaney followed suit. Mike watched them until they were out of sight.

What are you up to, Ric? Whatever it is, stay safe. I hope your brother makes it.

Looting the Walmart

Emmaus, Willow Run Road

*T*he south-running county road ran parallel with the railroad tracks and accessed mainly corporate fields on one side and Willow Creek on the town side. The other side of the creek were old Metis lots like the Delaney ranch. Since they didn't have to stop for farmers, their progress south went quickly and soon they drove along the edge of the trailer court, Shane noted that people were moving around, dumping water troughs and pools. Shane used Rob's keys to unlock the overpass gate and then closed it up again.

When he got back into the car, the radio on the dashboard crackled.

"Shane, you got your ears on," Rob asked. Shane glared at it, not sure if he wanted to answer. Jazz stared out the window, a muscle bunching in her cheek. Shane sighed and picked up the radio.

"Copy," he said. *Just stick to the facts.*

"Where are you? Over."

"Headed to the Walmart and then we'll go to Beulah. Over."

"Stan Osimowicz went to Beulah already. He's headed back now. I'll give you a report when I have it. Go check the Box Belt." There was a momentary and, to Shane's ears, pregnant pause. "You doing okay? Over."

Like I'm discussing this on the radio with you.

"The Tanks has military vehicles stationed to their northeast. Looks like Bethlehem Township, so I left it be, but through the field glasses, I could see they weren't dressed in fatigues. Over."

Rob paused. Shane waited.

"Copy that. Go check on the Box Belt. Over."

"Roger that. Over and out."

Shane put the radio down.

"I guess he doesn't want to deal with my sociopathic tendencies over the radio."

Jazz' mouth quirked.

"You do remember what war he fought in, right?"

"Yeah and I've seen Tour of Duty. You got a point."

They turned left into the access road to the collection of box stores that had sprung up in recent years. They were on the opposite side of the interstate, in a new part of town.

"Are we even still in the city limits?" Shane asked Jazz.

"Sure. Through the miracle of forced annexation, Emmaus has a new tax base. Is that the military?"

Shane turned forward to see what she meant. The Walmart parking was mostly empty, except for a National Guard APC backed up to the door. Shane slammed on the brakes.

"Shit. It was bound to happen. Get out!"

"What? Why? You're going to need some help. There's six guys."

"Seven. I can't guarantee your safety."

"No. I'll do that for myself." She released the seatbelt and slid over and between the seats so she could access the cargo area. "I claim the AR. My SKS is an excellent longer distance weapon."

Dad will kick my ass for taking a woman into danger.

"I'll take it," Shane agreed, continuing into the parking lot. "Remember, these guys are armored. Go for head shots or limbs. Uh, yeah, go for limbs."

He slammed on the brakes just as the chains wrapped around the door handles were attached to the truck. He opened the door and stepped out with his 9 mm drawn, aware that Jazz was already prepping the SKS.

"Hey! What do you think you're doing?" he asked. He stayed behind the door for cover.

"What business is it of yours?" one of the seven men countered. "We're confiscating goods that no one is guarding."

"Nope. This Walmart belongs to Emmaus, the town here. And you clearly don't have the key."

"Who the hell are you?" These were not soldiers nor mercenaries. Shane assessed them to be from the area, happened upon a National Guard vehicle and taking advantage.

"Deputy sheriff for the City of Emmaus." *Where'd that come from?* Jazz settled the SKS into the driver's seat. Ten shots for seven shooters. *Nah, I need her help.* "Now this ends one of two ways. Either you remove the chains from the door and drive away, go bother someone else, or I shoot you all dead."

Jazz slapped a magazine home on her weapon. As she slid out the far back door, one of the seven started to walk slowly along the wall of the building.

"Shane?" Jazz asked in a hushed voice.

"Yep." At his signal, she popped one round into the pavement a few feet in front of the man. He flinched back.

The one Shane had been talking to got his hands up, but three others reached for their guns. Shane shot one of them in the leg. While he lay screaming on the ground, Shane heard another vehicle approaching. He let Jazz deal with it. He couldn't afford to get distracted.

"Shit, man, you're crazy!" the leader said.

"Could be. I already killed two people today. That I've allowed you to live so far is only because I don't want to clean up the blood."

"Paul, are you on our side or theirs?" Jazz demanded.

"Hell, honey. I'm always on your side."

"Then point your weapons at them," she demanded in a voice Shane found curiously devoid of emotion.

Shane glanced briefly. Four against seven, but with two semi-auto rifles, one with a 30-round mag. Paul had a 9mm too.

"Hey, we can work this out, man," the leader said. "How about you let us have what we can carry and we can go away as friends."

"That sounds fair to me," Paul interjected.

"The building and what's in doesn't belong to me to give it away," Shane corrected. He hefted the SKS, leveled the stock across the top of the door. It felt small, cut for a Chinese soldier. "I'm not negotiating with you."

Unless Paul decides to change sides. But wait ....

Shane aimed for the blinking red light above the front doors, then dropped the aim by about a handbreadth and fired. Four of the looters ducked and then the alarm began pounding everyone's ears.

"Interrupt the AC current to a commercial security system, it flips to DC and it trips the alarm," Shane shouted over the clamor. "With the power back on, the store manager just got a message on his phone saying he needs to head here. If he gets here before you leave, I will have to arrest you. If you go now, no harm, no foul so long as I don't see you again. If I do, I shoot you in the head and we're done with it."

The spokesman started shouting orders to the others who gathered up their injured friend, dropped the chains and loaded into the truck. They were gone before Shane could count to 100. Shane didn't relax until they were out of sight.

Now he turned to look at Paul and his friend. Shane remembered him from high school, but couldn't recall his name.

"Thanks for the backup," he said, but then he noticed that Jazz hadn't lowered her AR. He didn't know how to read the expression on her face, but he was pretty sure he was glad he wasn't Paul. "Something wrong?" he asked her.

She lowered her gun, but it was still at the ready.

A BMW turned into the parking lot and roared toward them. Shane didn't know the man who got out.

"Shane Delaney?" the man asked.

"Yeah. You must have spoken to the mayor."

"I called. He said he'd send someone, but that you were already headed this way. What happened? Did you try to get inside?"

"No, we stopped looters. Do you have a way to shut off that noise?"

"I do. Thank you!" He headed to the door, juggling keys. Shane turned to Paul.

"I think we're done here. You wouldn't happen to know anything about looting at the pharmacy, would you?"

Paul really wasn't very good at being a criminal. His tells spoke volumes.

"My dad just sent us around to check for crap like this. Your dad too, right?"

Seriously? Are you accusing me of looting? I still have a gun in my hand, you idiot!

"More or less." The clanging ceased, though Shane's ears felt like he'd been rocking out at Red Rocks. "Jazz, you ready to go?"

"Not until Paul does," she said in a voice that could cause frostbite.

"Ah, come on! You know I wouldn't hurt you, darling," Paul insisted.

"I know nothing of the sort."

"The chick's mental," Paul said to Shane.

"Sounds like true love. Shove off, man. Oh, look, here comes Joe."

The Emmaus sheriff's Explorer pulled into the lot and Joe got out. Paul signaled to the other guy and they were out of there before Joe could get out of the car.

"Where are the looters? You didn't become friends with them, right?"

"The actual looters went that way. The potential looters are headed back to Mara Wells."

"Two bands of looters?"

"This is our new normal, Joe. Might as well accept it and learn some coping skills."

"Well, bless your tiny little heart for pointing that out," Joe said good-naturedly.

Shane turned to Jazz, who was putting away the rifles.

"You okay?"

"Yeah." Shane gave her an "I don't believe you" stare. "Paul and I dated for a while in high school."

"My condolences. I can see why you might not trust him any further than you can throw him, and might not want to give a random stranger the details." Shane grinned at her. "Thanks for being my backup. I couldn't have done this without you."

"My pleasure," she told him. She ran a hand over her sweaty face. Her cheeks were red and her forearms were touched with sunburn. "You know, it's been three days since I've had a shower and I've been up for some ridiculous amount of time. Any chance you can give me a ride back to downtown?"

"Of course. Joe, you need us here?"

"No. I'm thinking looters don't like witnesses, so they're gone now." A white van appeared on the access road and then turned into the parking lot. Anders McAuliff got out. "You didn't need to come yourself, sir."

"I was the only one available. Looks like it's under control." He addressed his observation to Shane.

"it is," Shane agreed when Joe deferred to him with silence. "But it would probably be good if you hung out with Joe and the manager while they secure the place ... maybe talk better security or an onsite guard. Things are going to get worse before they get better."

"You're not staying?" Joe asked, looking in the direction Shane had indicated the actual looters had gone.

"Jazz and I have been at this all day. Unless you need us, I think we're headed back to the barn."

Joe released them and Anders promised to stick around. The car was quiet while they drove up Mission Road to Main Street. Shane stopped at the far end of the Factory building from the feed store where he knew the stairs led upstairs.

"Thanks for coming with me today," he said again.

"I was up for an adventure. Thanks for not treating me like a girl."

"You are a girl ... with skills," he observed, grinning at her. He opened the trunk for her and she shouldered her bag and slung the 30-06 across her shoulder.

"Maybe we'll do it again sometime." There was a vaguely hopeful sound to her voice. Shane thought her lips looked very kissable. A movement on the edge of his vision proved to be nothing. He sighed.

"Do you need help in?" he asked.

"No, I'm good. Thanks. And, Shane, I didn't mean to judge you."

"I know. The downside to being a realist is that more optimistic people are always shocked by your realism."

She snorted.

"Okay, tough guy. I'll see you around sometime. You could give me a lesson on how not to have your gun taken away."

"Yeah, I probably owe you that." She laughed and moved toward the door, avoiding awkwardness.

He waited for her to close the door behind her and then considered where he wanted to go. It was just before sunset. He wasn't ready to go home and face his mother or go to City Hall and face his father. The Hotel? Alex's house? Or, er ....

Combating Terror

New York City, Casa Blanca Hotel

*K*atherine had finally stopped shaking after drinking a third of a bottle of wine. Julian asked if she wanted more. She shook her head.

"No. Drunk or hung over right now would be a stupid idea. Lillian's dead."

"I liked her too. Seems a pretty stiff penalty for breaking curfew."

Katherine agreed. *How do I get out of this town?*

"Are you thinking what I'm thinking?" Julian asked.

"I don't even try to read my husband's mind. Just tell me."

"I need to get home to Seattle."

"I definitely have Kansas on my mind. I need a few days to gather my resources, but I'm beginning to realize just how hard it would be to get out of this town."

"There's no transportation running, the bridges are blocked. The police are shooting people who stay out after curfew. I'm pretty sure our phones aren't working because of a dampening field."

"I tried the Internet earlier today. The aps work, but actually using the net is impossible."

"Yeah, indicative of a dampening field."

"Why would they do that?"

"To keep control of the population. Wouldn't want us reporting to anyone that they're killing people who are out one minute past curfew."

"My husband knows I'm here at the hotel. He would come looking for me here first."

"If he can get through."

"He's a billionaire. He has resources to make a way."

"Does he? Who is really in charge right now?"

"I'm going to continue to gather resources, but I have no plans this moment. What about you?"

"I don't know. I kind of think we should go sooner rather than later, but not stupidly. It's dangerous out there."

The image on the television screen showed the start of the news broadcast.

"We're live from Times Square where police halted a terrorist attack in progress." The camera showed a body on the sidewalk, covered with a tarp. Siren lights flashed across the reporter's face as she pushed windblown tendrils back from her face. "Police say that an innocent bystander succumbed to a hail of bullets between car bombers and police. This is a breaking story and we'll bring you more in the morning. Amanda?"

"Police are urging people to remain inside as much as possible and to observe the 7 pm curfew," Amanda said, speaking from her nice safe studio desk. "If you see something, report it."

Katherine and Julian exchanged significant glances as everyone who knew the real story erupted into complaints about media manipulation.

"Sooner rather than later," Julian repeated.

Katherine nodded.

Crossing the Delaware

New Jersey-Pennsylvania Border

*T*he bridge was the most dangerous part of his day's journey because there was absolutely nowhere to go if someone challenged him. It was bumper to bumper in one direction, brake lights shining in the dark. At least they were all moving if only at 5 mph. There were mercenaries stationed at intervals along the railings, but their rifles were slung. They were consulting their phones.

Are they employing facial recognition software?

He tongued the plastic inserts that rounded his cheeks and hopefully, with the haircut and shave, would be enough to fool the software. He'd have to change identities in Pennsylvania. Martin Pulgarin had longer hair in the IDs. He had a wig for that. He might have remembered it before he shaved his head, but it had felt so liberating to leave Francis Xavier behind.

The traffic queue ground to a halt. *Shit! We were so close! Don't panic. You're tired and tired people make stupid mistakes. Remember your training. Stay calm.*

A mercenary came down each lane with a gun-like apparatus that he was sure was catching images. He used his tongue to purse his lips out further, hoping that would be enough.

Nothing moved. He scarcely breathed. In his rearview mirror, he saw the mercenary coming back. Should he go for the railing now or wait for them to target him?

Breathe. You don't know yet that you've been caught. Don't look nervous.

The mercenary was looking right at his car as he spoke into his radio. Javi wrapped his hand in the handle of his backpack, ready to flee, to go over the railing.

Now! His left hand closed on the door handle.

The car in front of him started moving. Javi stared at it in astonishment. The car behind him touched his horn lightly. Javi let go of the backpack and the door handle, shifted into drive and quickly caught up the car in front of him. A moment later, he passed into Pennsylvania.

Gridlock

Wichita

Kellogg Street was in gridlock. Phil tried to parallel the traffic jam by taking Orme, but that wasn't moving any faster. Before he could back out and try another direction another car pulled in behind the truck.

Cai glanced to the west where the sun was dropping toward the horizon.

"We're going nowhere fast," Phil explained. "I don't think we're getting to the airfield before the 7 pm curfew."

First things first. What to do? What are the priorities? Try to think like Shane ... without the bloodshed.

Cai checked his cell phone. He had bars, so he dialed Jacob who answered.

"How are things going there, Grandpa?"

"Got the medicine completely packed. We're going to be close to the weight limit, but I got a phone call from Ren saying he isn't going to be able to make it, so we should be fine … close. Don't eat dinner."

"I don't think I'm going to make it. It's almost curfew and we're stuck in traffic. Go ahead to Emmaus. I'll catch a ride back with Ren."

"You sure?"

"Yes. The pharmacy order is the priority. I'll be fine."

A small dark object dropped into the airspace right above the cars a block ahead of them. Cai flipped the visor down, but he doubted that would do any good.

"Okay. I'll be headed back this way on Monday if we don't hear from you by then."

"Yes, sir."

The drone swept along the side of the truck, its camera swiveling. Cai stared at Phil, his heart banging against his ribs.

"We're sitting ducks here," Phil observed.

"And when they come for me, they'll blame you."

"You think so? I agree with you."

"If I walk away, they shouldn't arrest you."

"On foot for the Apocalypse?! You don't lack for guts." Phil unbuckled and stripped off his jacket. "You aren't carrying, are you?"

"No. I figured that wasn't smart going to the governor's office."

"Take this." Phil shrugged out of his shoulder holster. While Cai donned it, Phil texted someone and got a response. "Head to the SullCo HQ. They'll have a vehicle for you." He pulled a windbreaker out of the back seat. "This will hide the gun. Here's some extra ammo. Do you know where you're going?"

Cai looked around at the area and indicated the direction he thought he should go.

"Yes. Take the hat too. Watch for traffic cams, ATMS, cross midblock if you can. You got about two miles. Take the backroads back home. And, here. This should help you."

Phil handed Cai a couple hundred dollars.

"Don't try to use your credit cards."

"Thank you." Cai scanned the area, saw no drones, slipped out of the truck and walked into a parking lot, head down, hands in his pockets.

God, show me how to do this?

He glanced back to the truck just as he rounded a corner of a building. Phil was being forced onto his belly on the ground by men in Army fatigues. Cai hesitated.

Don't be a fool. They'll let him go when they realize that you're not with him. Go!

It sounded like his lovely and usually very wise wife. He continued south toward SullCo, head down, hands in his pockets. It was maybe a half hour before dark. He just needed to get to SullCo and head home. *Head down, hands in your pockets.*

Avoid traffic cams and ATMs and stay away from drones.

Another Loss

Emmaus City Hall

*R*ob could hear the farmers discussing in the Council Chambers as he slipped on his jacket to head for his truck. This had to be the longest and least enjoyable day of his mayoral career. He started as a shadow resolved into Max Albright. He didn't know Max very well. He was one of the newer people in town.

"Mayor Delaney, I was hoping you had some news for me."

"News?" Rob asked.

"I reported my husband Drew missing this morning."

"That's Joe's field. Is that who you placed the report with?"

"It was. I realize that you're very busy, but I'm getting really worried for him."

"Did he come up missing before or after the bombs?"

"Well, I expected him home that evening for our anniversary, but he didn't show up. He'd been gone to Chicago for business, but I'm told that he left there in the early afternoon, well before the bombs. Calculating how fast he drives, he should have been near home."

Rob had a sinking feeling, remembering a call from the railroad about a crash east of town and the photos Shane had shown him.

"What was he driving?"

"A silver sports car."

Oh, no!

Max read his expression.

"What do you know?"

"There was a derailment Wednesday night. The train hit a sports car. There was fire. The single occupant was burned beyond recognition as was any identifying information." Tears began to flow down Max's face. "They towed the car over to the salvage yard. When things settle down, the Beulah County Sheriff's office will investigate VIN numbers and the like to determine who the car belonged to."

"They can't just leave him in a refrigerated drawer for weeks on end."

"There are greater priorities right now, I'm afraid. I am sorry for your loss."

Max's eyes flashed.

"Oh, I'm sure you are not," he snipped.

"Excuse me?"

"You're a deacon in a Baptist church that teaches gays are an abomination."

Rob sighed.

"I know this is hard to understand, because you're right, I wouldn't attend your wedding and I'd go to jail rather than be forced to participate in it. That's based on my belief that I must obey God rather than man's laws. But that doesn't mean I hate you or that I don't understand the pain you're in and wish you didn't have to go through it. I'll see what we can do about burying him ... assuming it's him. I saw the photos of the body and I don't think you'll get any closure from that, but the car might be recognizable. Before you grieve you might want to assure that you're grieving for Drew and not some other poor man."

Max nodded, swallowing audibly.

"I'm sorry. I shouldn't ...."

"It's fine. We all say heated things when we're upset. Come by Monday and I'll take you to the salvage yard to see the car." As they walked out toward the parking lot, a van pulled up and Brad Snow, the pastor at Emmaus Road Baptist Church, rolled down his window.

"People just started showing up at the church about an hour ago so we're holding an impromptu memorial service. I was hoping you'd join and lead the music, Rob. I couldn't get Dick Vance on the phone"

"I'll be there in a few minutes, Brad. Thanks for letting me know."

Rob pulled his truck keys out of his pocket as Brad drove away.

"You know, Max, you're welcome to join us. It might give you some peace to grieve with others who are also grieving. The church is on the left about five blocks down Mission Road."

"We visited a couple of times," Max said, his blush visible even under the street lights of the parking lot.

"Well, then you know you're welcome."

With that Rob climbed into his truck because he knew that you could only offer the Lord to someone, you couldn't bludgeon them over the head with it.

Poor guy! I wish there were more I could do for him, but .... There are a whole lot of hurting people in this town right now. I can be the best mayor I can be, but it still won't bring their loved ones back.

A Modicum of Freedom

Emmaus Medical Center

Marnie walked Mrs. Miller to the door, listening to her complaints with half an ear. It seemed everyone was concerned about this or that symptom and "could it be radiation poisoning?" Most of them were just temporary hypochondriacs. She knew how they felt.

We all feel like our cells are breaking down right now.

"I'm heading home now," Lila told Marnie. "Vin made dinner. Are you headed home or maybe you'd like to come over?"

"No. I'm going to clean up here, see if Cai and Jacob bring the pharmacy order."

"Will you?" Lila asked.

"I haven't decided," Marnie replied.

"He has a right to know."

"This situation is complicated."

Lila nodded.

"Just think about what I said."

The clinic echoed with Marnie's footsteps as she turned from the door. She hadn't gone 10 steps and someone knocked on the door. Thinking it was Lila forgetting something, she turned back, surprised to see Allison Sullivan standing there, leaning on her crutches.

"Hi, what are you doing here?" Marnie asked, pushing the door open. Allison's mother had taken her to better doctors in the big city, so Marnie really didn't know why the girl was wearing a brace and using crutches.

"Can I come in?"

Outside at the curb, a stately Mercedes waited. Someone was behind the wheel. The Sullivans were a mysterious bunch. Ren seemed friendly enough, but Joseph was contemporary with Jason and Maggie, but had never said a friendly word to them since high school graduation.

"Of course. What can I do for you?"

"I had a horse roll on my leg in the spring. Had surgery. This – erg – was supposed to come off on Thursday, but Denver is gone, so ...."

"And you want me to remove it?"

"I do."

"Well, I can't ethically do that without x-rays to make sure everything's knit back together right." Something like disappointment flickered across Allison's delicate features. "I suppose we could do that now and then make a determination in the morning."

"Why can't you do that tonight?"

"Well, I know how to take x-rays, but I've never had to develop them here. I'd need some help from a nurse for that."

"But you think you could do it tomorrow?"

"Let's say Monday since Sunday is a day of rest." Allison sighed, then nodded. "So, come with me and we'll take the films now. Do your parents or grandfather know you're doing this?"

"My mother would never let me come to this clinic," Allison said.

"Too plebian?"

"Oh, god, you're onto us!"

"Yeah, but I don't resent you for it. Just so you know, I did all the same training as the doctors in Denver did, but I haven't taken my boards test yet. I'm a licensed doctor, but I don't have the special State credential. I was studying to take the test in October."

"Right now, I'd settle for anyone who could free me from this thing."

"Okay. Well, let's see if we can do that."

X-rays really didn't take that long. On their way out, Marnie asked Allison where her parents were.

"Mom was in New York. Dad went to get her and Grandpa went to Wichita."

"They should be home any moment."

"Yeah, I hope so. Thanks. I'll be back Monday."

347

Marnie turned out the lights and locked the door. Her car was with Cai, probably out at the airfield. She turned toward home There were no messages on her phone, so the cell phone towers must not be fully active yet. At least there were still crickets. She paused at Mission Road, thinking. She needed guidance. She turned south and picked up her pace.

Meeting Needs

New York City, Javitz Building

I *have to do this. The secret to the Presidency is to meet people's needs. The military doesn't understand that.*

Marshall Ellerby stared out over the dark streets of New York. He supposed it was still early evening in Omaha. He dialed Carson Wilson's phone number and waited through the unusually long wait times between dials.

Of course there was an assistant to get through before Carson picked up the phone. He was one of the wealthiest men in the United States. One did not simply ring him up, unless you were the Secretary of Homeland Security.

"Marshall, what can I do for you today?"

"First, thank you for assigning Knight Industries to help support security in New York."

"I was pleased to do it, Marshall. My country is in crisis and I am above all a patriot."

"Of course. I have a spot of trouble here. New York City has a warehouse of survival foods, but it's already running out and the UN is delaying my request for aid. Is there anyway Bunnell and Wilson could provide food in the interim?"

"Of course there is. We have enormous warehouses full of food that cannot be distributed because the stores have been destroyed. We can re-route the distribution network to assure that areas without easy access to local food are able to receive what they need. It won't be cheap, of course, but I can give you a 25% discount."

"Of course. Thank you so much for your generosity."

"Let's not make believe. I'm a businessman. I love my country, but I am not motivated by altruism."

"I realize that. I accept the strings attached. What's going on in Seattle?"

"What are you talking about?"

"Black-clad mercenaries attacking US Army troops through the city. You don't know anything about that?"

"We were hired by the mayor of Seattle to expel a hostile force that was running rough-shod over the rights of his citizens."

"It was that bad?"

"My god, yes. The military under Rutherford is completely out of control. Go check with your spies. You'll find that wherever we're in control, the community is well organized and peaceful, which is not what is happening in military controlled areas."

"I will look into that. I may have need of the Knights in coming weeks as it does appear that Rutherford is a megalomaniac."

"My thoughts exactly. If we can just work out a cost for services, we would be glad to assist you in bringing the situation under control."

"The food first. I'll get back to you on the deployments."

Carson's smile was almost visible through the phone. Marshal's stomach stopped hurting for the first time in hours. This was going to work. He knew it would.

Stomping at Callahan's

Emmaus, Callahan's Bar

Callahan's lights spilled out the open door like a warm embrace. Shane parked the Jeep and stashed his 9mm under the seat. The band was warming up like it was any other Saturday night. If the crowd was a little light, that made sense given the events of the last few days. Some people reacted with surprise to see him, but there were a lot of friendly faces here. Shane eased up onto a stool and waved at Maggie who was working the bar.

"You wouldn't happen to have any Broadhead, would you?"

"I've got a good Guinness dark in a bottle."

"I'll take it along with a burger."

"Steak fries?"

"Sure. And a dill pickle."

Maggie sashayed off to give the cook his order. The band was talking among themselves. Shane knew them. He'd played in Ray's band off and on through high school and college. Maggie came back and put a glass and bottle beside his elbow. Shane turned around to pour the foamy beer and enjoy the first long suck. It wasn't Broadhead, but Guinness knew how to make a beer.

He shrugged off a hand from his shoulder and turned to see Ray standing behind him.

"I thought that was you. Almost didn't recognize you without your curls. Military?"

"Adjacent," Shane obfuscated. "How are you doing, Ray?"

"My guitarist was at City Hall."

Shane sucked on his beer for a long swallow.

"I'm sorry to hear that."

"Maggie said we didn't have to play, but by God, we're alive through the rain and this is what we do, but it's hard to do good music without a guitarist. So, I was hoping you'd sit in."

Shane took another swallow of beer.

"I haven't played much in the last few years," he explained. Ray nodded, eyes averted. Shane considered his options. "I'll play a song, eat my burger, maybe play a set after. There's no way I can play the whole night. My calluses aren't up to it."

"That's fine. Noel, the bass player, can play a few songs and so can I. It's just that we're limited to what songs we know the chords to and you can play every song you ever heard. If you play a set in the middle, we'll not sound so redundant. I'll even pay your tab."

"I usually stop at one."

"Since when?"

"Since I grew up and realized drinking makes me too bold. So after the burger?"

Ray thanked him profusely and hurried back to the bandstand. Shane turned back to his beer. Anders McAuliff leaned in beside him.

"Thought that might be you, though I was under the impression that Delaneys don't drink."

"Grandpa's been known to have a beer on a hot summer afternoon. Cai too."

"Not your dad."

"Not your business," Shane told him boldly. Anders laughed.

"You're right, of course, not that Rob keeps it a secret." He leaned in to whisper in Maggie's ear. She smiled slyly, placed two glasses on the bar and brought out a bottle of scotch and one of bourbon. No sooner had she set two-fingers of bourbon beside Shane's beer then the cook brought out his burger.

"I can't drink that without something to eat first."

"Of course. You're a Delaney. If you drink, you're responsible doing it."

"You don't know me or Delaneys in general," Shane offered as he squirted mustard on his bun. "So what's this for?"

"An apology for my brother."

"Nothing to apologize for." Shane bit into the burger. Sam the cook made the best burgers on the planet. Well, maybe he had competition from Les in Brady Tanks. Too bad he was sharing a pleasurable meal with Anders McAuliff. He could probably have invited Jazz. *You should leave her alone.*

"That's what he would say, but he's behind bars, so ...."

"I've had five years to contemplate it. I'd walk away from that assignment today."

"How old were you back then?"

"Just barely legal to drink, which is why I'm grateful you're cutting me some slack for helping to make your brother a political prisoner. I was young. I didn't know better."

"You know what he believes, right?"

"Yeah. He's an anarchist."

"You hold with people who want to blow up the world?"

Shane used chewing the burger as an excuse to delay answering.

"No, but I sort of see the point of people like my grandfather. The government screws things up. Sometimes they just do it because they're inept and don't take human nature into account and sometimes they do it for nefarious reasons. Maybe we shouldn't give incompetent evil people so much power."

"You think they're responsible for this now?"

Shane chewed. *That's the question I don't want to ask because the answer might not be what I want to hear.*

"Ultimately, probably. The US government's got its sticky little fingers in a whole lot of volatile pies. Someone was bound to get this fed-up sooner or later."

He ate two steak fries with ketchup and then picked up the glass.

"To no hard feelings," Anders saluted. They tapped glasses. Shane took a swallow. The burn spread warmth throughout his chest. He ate some more fries. "Is your dad up to this?" Anders asked.

"Nobody is up for this," Shane told him. "But he is more than most."

"We need to talk security. It's all well and good to watch the interstate, but there's miles of roads in all directions."

Shane swallowed the second half of the bourbon and chased it with the last mouthful of his beer.

"Got go play music now." He left Anders to decide who to annoy next. Ray saw him coming and riffed out the opening chords of Let's Get This Party Started. Half the bar clapped. The other half probably didn't know who he was. With two fingers of bourbon and a beer in him, Shane was definitely ready to get the party started, he just wasn't exactly sure what they were celebrating.

Beware the Mysterious Visitor

Emmaus City Hall

City Hall had never given him the creeps before. The thought of a hundred people dying in the basement filled him with anxiety. Alex remembered feeling this way after his parents died ... that the house seemed haunted. As he made coffee, he kept expecting Bart Rawlston to come in and ask him when he would be done or Ross Winther to remind him to put away the chairs. That they would never do those things ever again seemed unfathomable.

One by one, farmers filed into the meeting hall and took seats or gathered at the coffee pot to discuss the events of the last few days. Dick Vance slipped in wearing his bolo tie and fancy cowboy hat ... evening attire for him. Andrew Bennett came right to Alex and shook his hand.

"We're probably on the same side, man," he assured him.

"That's good to know, but I know you're going want to hear what I say first. Looks like enough people are here. Can you go flick the lights so everybody knows we're starting?"

If you were a member of the Farmer's Cooperative hereabouts, you knew how to get the attention of Lufgrens. While Andrew was doing the flickering, a man Alex didn't recognize came in and sat down toward the back.

"Welcome," Alex greeted, speaking and signing at the same time. American Sign Language and English were not the same language and Alex was known to slip into a form of spoken pidgin-sign when forced to sign and talk at the same time for more than a few sentences, so Keri broke off her conversation with Hannah Lufgren to come act as interpreter. Alex then stuffed his hands in his pockets. Sign being his first language, he was always more comfortable in it than English, but the majority of the crowd were English speakers. "I called this meeting because we need to discuss the best way to get in the harvest. We're not going to have the same resources as we would normally have."

"I spoke to Donovan's Elevators," Andrew Bennett explained. "They pointed out that they don't have facilities to dry all the corn. I know most of us field-dry it, but they also don't have room to store all of it on-site. They've been shipping it out for decades. Half of their silos aren't functional and they aren't sure how to make them functional. There's an old bunker silo on my farm. I've got my boys cleaning it out now, but that won't be enough. It'll take half of my corn. What about the rest of you?"

Several of the older farmers allowed that they might still have a bunker or an old silo long unused on their property, but it was going to be a lot of work to get them ready to receive a harvest.

"Hot as it is, we ought to be able to start the harvest Monday," Shoenfeld said. "I don't know where we're going to put it all."

"There's more to this whole thing than harvesting," Jeremiah Lufgren signed. "If things are bad, no government, roads broken, we need to think survive this. Fuel, food, sugar, seed for next year."

"Seed? Roundup corn doesn't reseed itself very well," Andrew said. *Why are you reminding us of that? We know that.*

"Then we eat the GMO corn and save the organic," Alex advised.

"And then we starve next year?" Shoenfeld asked. "Corn worms are going to chew up that organic corn."

The stranger cleared his throat and stood up.

"I'm Cole Packard from the USDA. We've got an agricultural station over up at Wendat Lake with storage facilities enough to take all of your corn, soybeans and sorghum."

"We'll have time to work that out," Alex reasoned. "Jeremiah, you mentioned fuel. We know corn can be made into fuel. Anyone here know how?"

Dick Vance laughed and said he did, but Packard also said the agricultural station could help with that. Someone else mentioned they had old recipes at home for making corn sugar, starch, and syrup.

"How about corn liquor?" Dell Conopher asked.

"It's similar to how you make fuel," Dick explained. "My grandfather was a bootlegger back during Prohibition."

"Which ought to tell you something about its safety for consumption," Alex joked. Dick laughed with him. Others frowned.

"We should think about the cows," Keri said. Alex glanced around to see who she was interpreting for and realized she was speaking for herself. "If we eat them, they aren't available to make milk."

"That's a lot of milk," Hiram said.

"We could make cheese," Andrew said. "My wife's been making it just for our family."

"Good thought," Alex agreed. "We have a lot of beeves out there too. Butchering them means storing the meat, but do we have silage to feed them?"

His list was getting longer as these men and women considered survival in ways nobody had needed to think for generations. And then Eleanor Bradway asked what they were going to do with the corn.

"What are we going to do when the town's going hungry and they want us to give our crops away for free?"

"That's something you'll have to decide for yourselves," Andrew remarked.

"Wouldn't it be wrong to let them starve when we have food?"

"That's not for me to decide for you. My family eats my crop. If we have extra, we sell it. If we feel like giving it away, we will, but my family eats first."'

"I'm thinking most people here know there's no such thing as a free lunch," Sharon Laughlin said. "That's okay, right?"

"Of course it is," Alex assured her. "We haven't become Soviet Russia. We still own our crops and can sell them to whomever we want ... or not, if that's our choice."

The USDA guy, Packard, frowned.

"Storing your grain at our facility would take that pressure off you folks. You'd be able to blame us if your neighbors felt they weren't getting their fair share."

Alex didn't think he liked this guy. There was something of the used-car-salesman about him.

"I'm not storing my family's food 30 miles away," Dick Vance said. Dick was known to have opinions and to voice them without fear of insulting anyone. "It's all well and good if the trains start running again, but until I see that happen, I'm not keen to just give away my crops."

"Well, it's not just you. This entire portion of the state could store at our facility and we'd see it distributed fairly."

Jeremiah, who was known as a math god, signed "There's not enough corn to go around. Fair doesn't' look so fair when you grew it, but now you're starving."

"So you'd let your neighbors starve?" Packard asked.

"That's between us and our conscience or our God," Dick explained. "It's my crop. Not yours."

Packard subsided into his seat, scowling furiously. Joe popped his head in the door.

"Alex, I'm going to the memorial service at the Baptist church. You can go out the back door. Could you make sure it locks behind you?"

"I will."

"I think we're done," Andrew said. "I certainly don't have more to say and I just got a text from my wife saying they're going there too."

Others were starting to move toward the door. By loose affirmation, they agreed to start the harvest Monday morning. They'd talk to one another as storage solutions became available. As Alex pulled the back door shut, Packard materialized out of the dusk.

"Hope I didn't startle you."

"No, I'm fine. Did you need something?"

"I realize you farmers are often very independent, but the community is going to need to pool its resources if we're going to get through this thing."

"That's true, but it's not up to me to order anyone around."

"Of course. I'll speak with the mayor. Thank you for your time."

Alex watched the man walk off into the twilight, anxiety clawing at his chest.

What's that saying? The scariest phrase in the English language is "We're from the government and we're here to help you?" Yeah, I need to get to church and praise my God for getting us this far and ask Him how we get beyond this, because I really don't know.

Requiem

Emmaus Road Baptist Church

The church had enough pews for 300 people, but way more than that were leaning against the walls and drawing up folding chairs in the aisles. There were children gathered in the loft and someone had remoted speakers so that the crowd packing out the fellowship hall in the basement could hear the service if not participate. Jill and Keri, stuck in the middle of the pews, were relieved to see Rob mount the stage with Brad. The choir had automatically gone to sit there since the building was overflowing. The ceiling fans were on high, but the heat was rising. Thankfully, most people had been able to shower since the power came back on.

"I can't believe what has happened in the time since we met Wednesday night," Brad began. "So many of us have lost loved ones, while there are others missing. The world has been turned on its head. And it is in times like these that we seek the Lord where He may be found so that He may comfort our souls. I don't have any magic words to bring us all relief tonight. I didn't prepare a sermon and I'm not going to preach. I'm going to ask you folks to lead this service. To the extent that we can, we've compiled a list of the deceased from City Hall. We're going to read that. As we do, I hope at least one person will stand and say something about the deceased or give a song. We all know Rob can sing every song he's ever heard, but it doesn't matter. If you want to sing it and you can lead it, it doesn't matter what your voice sounds like. Chancey has remoted both speakers and microphones into the fellowship hall, so folks down there can participate too. Let's just lift our voices and our supplications to God."

Jill clasped Keri's hand as she looked around the crowd. She didn't see Marnie, Cai, Jacob or Shane. She wasn't surprised not to see Shane, though she couldn't think of anyone who needed to be here more. Remembering what she'd seen in Jacob's photo, she shivered despite the closeness of the crowd. Were Cai and Jacob not back yet? Marnie had awakened and said she was going to the medical center. Had she squeezed into the basement? Gone home? Was there an emergency at the clinic?

Suddenly Rob's clear strong baritone rang out across the crowded sanctuary.

"Amazing grace, how sweet the sound ...."

Everyone joined in. It seemed like a fitting song to begin with. Jill thought about the people whose pulses she'd been unable to find this morning and suddenly tears spilled down her cheeks. *There but for the grace of God, we could all be.*

She realized that a lot of other folks were thinking the same thing. It had been like this after 9-11, when people who had not been to church in years had suddenly shown up and come for a few weeks before deciding to stay home to watch NASCAR. This was that on steroids. And, so many people knew someone who had died at City Hall.

The songs flowed between brief and not so brief testimonies. Sometimes people sat silent when a name was read. Even in a small town like Emmaus, not everyone was real social. Brad or Rob usually knew them then and would say something.

"Pierce Madragon had that pink house, remember?" someone noted. "It wasn't just pink … it was PINK!"

It didn't feel disrespectful to laugh at that. For years, everybody had used that house as a landmark to get to the Heights. When he'd painted it beige after so many years, the entire town had had to stop and think of new ways to give directions.

"Carol Bradford made the best lemon meringue pies, but the secret was that they weren't really home-made. She used lemon pudding and store-bought crusts."

"Billy used to race his car through downtown bold as brass. Bart would chase him home and make me pay the fine. I do hope they're enjoying each other's company tonight."

"This was my husband's favorite song. 'When we all get to heaven, what a day of rejoicing that will be ....'" Of course Rob picked up the tune immediately and soon everyone was singing lustily.

It pushed the darkness back and brought light into their lives if only for the time they were within these walls. Hope grew in the empty place that grief had forged and Jill heard a still small voice saying "Trust Me. I know what you need."

Keri had her hands lifted to heaven, praising God in the highest. Alex had his head bowed. Jill wondered where Daisy was, but a song service didn't make a lot of sense for a deaf girl so she didn't wonder long.

They laughed and cried, prayed and sang ... and felt the spirit of God step down into that place. It was requiem enough for people who had been too soon ripped from their lives by incomprehensible circumstances.

Freedom

Leavenworth Penitentiary

Silence echoed off the concrete cell walls. Dan pressed his face against the bars, trying to look left and right, but nothing was moving out there. He tugged on the bars, but they weren't going anywhere. Had he not learned that lesson over the last five years.

"Hello, is there anyone out there?"

Nothing.

What the hell is going on?

Right after his cell door locked, about an hour ago, he'd heard shouting and seen prisoners struggling with guards. There'd been no shanks visible. He'd seen a prisoner who had gotten hold of a guard's baton hit the guard on the leg with it, but another prisoner had stopped him from bludgeoning the guard.

This has to be my guys ... right? Why did they keep it from me? No, there might be other groups involved here. Why else am I locked up?

Far to the left, he heard the main entry gate activate. It opened and then didn't close. Then he heard his cell door unlock. Sweat sprung up on his forehead. He had no weapons, no way to protect himself. He had a mattress, a book, and a notebook. He could only wait for his fate.

Monahan strolled up to the cell door. They'd known each other since college. They trusted each other ... until today. Dan stared at him, waiting.

"Are you pissed off that we started without you?" he asked.

"How many guards died?"

"None. One has a broken arm which Kletti is setting now. I told you, we had a plan. Come on, let me show you. Bring your stuff. You won't be coming back here."

After gathering his books and notebooks, Dan followed him down the corridor, past empty cells.

"Kletti has been working in the infirmary since he got here, made friends with one of the doctors, who is philosophically in alignment. Patterson has been working with the chaplain, who also agrees with us. Kowalcsky had key prisoners primed for this and he has been in a sexual relationship with one of the turnkeys. And we locked you up because when the opportunity presented itself, we didn't have time to inform you and we wanted you out of harm's way."

"The opportunity?"

"The turnkey agreed to control the gates so we could do this in an orderly fashion. That was two hours ago."

"So where is everyone?"

"We put the problematic ones in the wing they're remodeling along with all the guards. The chaplain has agreed to let the guards out tomorrow morning. We have a narrow opportunity to get away. According to the doctor, radiations levels have dropped to safe levels, but the weather report suggests that they will increase again by morning. There's a van in the garage that we're prepping for the trip. And, we've got great cover here."

"What do you mean?"

"Fifty low-risk prisoners are going to 'escape' and scatter. We've wiped the surveillance tapes so nobody will know who did what. And we can head west and hide in the bunker, stay out of sight for the time being."

"Good. We need to ditch these clothes."

"Not a problem. The guard's locker room is available for us."

It was a surreal experience walking through gates with nobody challenging him. Some blocks, every cell was locked with a prisoner inside. Some of them shouted with anger while others calmly waited for what would come.

After Dan changed his clothes, he gathered with Monahan and the rest of his crew in the garage. Relief flooded over him when he saw that the van was not a DOD vehicle, but a food truck that had been unloading when the bombs hit.

Kowalcsky closed the hood.

"Everything's in good shape. We're loading some food in case the bunker's been cleaned out. Wish we had some weapons, but my love refused to unlock the weapon's locker."

"She coming with us?"

"You mean, he?" *Awkward.* "His cause is not our cause. It was just sex, not love. He's got a wife and kids to get home to. We're ready to go."

"Won't the other guards know he was involved?" Dan asked. He had no desire to see other men put in jail for helping him.

"We've covered our trail as well as we can. He's going to let us out and close the gate and lock himself in a storage locker so it looks like we forced him to help us. We gotta go. There's a window here."

Josh slid into the driver's seat. The others climbed up and sat down on the floor. Dan paused before climbing in. It had been five long years since he'd been last able to breathe freely.

Do I remember what freedom really means?

The overhead garage door opened. Dan sat down on the floor with his crew. Josh slid the truck into gear. As they turned west, Josh was momentarily lit by the setting sun, sending a pulse of fear through Dan, and then they rolled forward into the future coincidence had afforded them.

Cyber Space

INITIATOR: We intercepted communication between Marshall Ellerby and Wilson re food supplies in NYC and use of Knights for wresting civilian control back from the military. Six of one, half dozen of another. How should we proceed?

RESPONSDENT: The eagle must not rise.

Hole in the World

Callahan's Bar

Shane stared at the second beer sweating on the stool beside him as he played The Eagle's tune "There's a Hole in The World."

> There's a hole in the world tonight,
>
> There's a cloud of fear and sorrow.
>
> There's a hole in the world tonight.
>
> Don't let there be a hole in the world tomorrow.

Someone had requested it. People were down with getting rowdy and loud, but the thought of what had happened was not far from their minds. When the song finished, Shane licked his calluses and grabbed the beer which was still cold enough to chill his damp fingertips and ease some of the pain. The bar was hot and smoky and he knew he only had one more good song in him. Ron played something – repeated a song – to give him a break. Rubbing circulation back into his fingertips, Shane considered the song possibilities. He knew hundreds. All he had to do was hear them in his head and he could play them. If his calluses would hold up.

He paused with his fingers over the fret board, thinking for a moment and then the music flowed, not from his hands, but from his voice.

"There are stars in the southern sky ...."

People picked it up with him. Such an iconic acapella song just demanded a sing-along. When he finished, there was hooting and hollering for more, but he knew his calluses couldn't take another song. He promised to come back, though, and it didn't feel like a lie. He squeezed between two patrons and shouted at Maggie that he wanted to pay his tab.

"...Auliff got it."

Someone squeezed in beside him.

"That was a great set," Stan Osimowicz said. "Buy you a drink?"

Shane knew he'd reached the stage where the drinks were taking drinks and he'd better stop, but he agreed to a beer.

"I went to Beulah," Stan said.

"And?" Shane had always hated the bar scenes where you shouted into each other's faces so close you could smell the beer.

"The Army wiped out most of the Kansas National Guard."

"And a whole lot of innocent people who got trapped in the Denver containment zone."

Stan assayed him with a sharp gaze.

"I thought you might know something about that. Gus, I knew him from when I was in the service. He's commanding a rogue National Guard unit. He warned me that we need to look to our own security and not accept the military's help when it comes."

Shane poured the Guinness, relishing the slow building of the head.

"So why are you plying me with liquor instead of talking to my dad?"

"We both know who the realists are, Shane. Rob will catch up, but right now, he's still hoping normality is just around the corner."

"And you aren't?"

"No! We need to look to our own security and I need your help doing it."

Shane took a long, slow swallow.

"There's a rogue unit harrowing our northeast flank. It's a National Guard truck, but the men with it aren't wearing fatigues. I think they're connected to the group I drove off the Walmart."

"Is that connected to the white van that tried to break into Huffy's?"

"I don't know about that, but it's all looting. Any place like Huffman's or the Walmart where there is a stockpile of food is a target."

"We need to secure our borders."

"Yeah? How are you going to secure even Jericho Township? That's a lot of wide open territory. Nothing but corn fields and prairie."

"We'll think about it and meet on Monday." Shane shrugged, swallowing some more beer. *One more and I'll not care if I get drunk.*

"This is a conversation to have with my dad first."

"You don't think he'll listen to you?"

"I don't think he *should* listen to me. I've always been on the side of those who break the china, not the ones who throw up fences to protect people. My inclinations aren't so warm and fuzzy as you might think." Stan laughed. "So what are your inclinations? Are you looking to protect these towns or are you looking to rule them?"

Stan's eyes widened. Shane slid some money under his almost empty glass and excused himself. Outside, the fresh air wafted over him and made him aware of how warm and muzzy he felt. Yeah, not a good idea to drive. He got his jacket and the 9mm and 45 from the car, locked up and headed in the general direction of home. Technically the guns were illegal right now, because he'd been drinking, but leaving them overnight in a parking lot seemed like a stupid idea.

The town was mostly quiet, which gave him time to think as he strolled along. The day had been successful. It had been a mix of Miristan and Kansas. He'd saved some lives. He'd taken two. He'd enjoyed hanging out with Jazz. He'd thoroughly shredded on the guitar tonight. That dark shadow following him moved closer, sucking the joy out of his night. *She* moved closer, her voice audible as it usually was not. *Die, killer, die.* This was why he never drank more than one beer. He'd let the fun of the night and the older men trick him into being stupid. He'd not make that mistake again.

Why was the Emmaus Road Baptist Church open this late on a Saturday night? All the lights were on and music spilled out through the open windows. Musician that he was, he recognized Rob's guitar playing immediately.

Shane sat down on the back steps, which were right outside the window next to the podium and let the music wash over him. His musical ear picked out individual voices he knew. He wondered why Cai wasn't singing. He leaned back against the wall and breathed the cool evening air. He'd always scoffed at what his parents believed, but tonight, slowed by alcohol and exhausted by events, he recognized the message of comfort. He closed his eyes and listened.

Yes I will rise

Out of these ashes rise

From this trouble I have found

And this rubble on the ground

They were apparently singing the favorite songs of the departed, but it was clear they were winding down.

From the earth to the cross from the cross to the sky,
Lord, I lift your name on high

Shane started to doze, thinking about forgiveness and how it seemed to have made life tolerable for Rob and Jacob. And then *she* touched his throat. He jerked awake, pushing against nothing.

I only really want to see you there. 3 Keith Green

Oh, puke. I am not listening to this! Shane pushed himself off the stairs to approach the bushes. He knew one or the other of his parents would be among the last out of the church. If he missed them, he'd just walk home.

They burst into a final powerful singing of "It Is Well with My Soul."

How can it be well with anyone's soul right now? God punished us for whatever and you people praise him like he's done something good. My soul is a dark bottomless well which even light cannot penetrate. My soul is not well. How can yours be?

As people began to disperse, he could hear Rob's deep voice responding to questions and comments. The church had a fringe of bushes at the edge of the parking lot where the light didn't reach. Shane walked around to it to unload the night's beer. While he stood there staring up at the stars, a shadow slowly walked up beside him. He held his breath, afraid to see her again, but then the shadow joined him in his relief.

"It's a good thing we only have one cop and he drove away some minutes ago," Rob joked.

"How long did you know I was here?"

"I saw you outside the window." Rob sniffed. "You've been drinking."

"Am I going to get a lecture?"

"No. You know what you need to know and I've been lecturing you since you were 14 and it hasn't done any good. I just want you to know that I'm available to listen if you ever want to talk about what you had to do today or whatever else it is that you're holding so tight to your chest that makes dozing off so dangerous."

Everybody always says talk about it. Talk ... talk .... And, then what? It doesn't take the memories away.

"Can I get a ride home? I left my car at Callahan's."

"You want me to encourage a wise choice? Of course, It's been a really long day. Let's go."

Alex waved at them from his truck as he exited the parking lot. Shane climbed into Rob's truck, staring at the plaque affixed to the glove box while he buckled up.

You can no more diminish God's glory by not worshiping Him than a lunatic can put out the sun by scribbling the word 'darkness' on a wall. - Stephen Mackay (The Bearded Evangelist)

Everywhere I turn with you people, you're trying to evangelize me! STOP!

"Nice night," Rob observed. "Hard to believe after the last few days. I heard about Walmart. Good work there."

"Yeah. Jazz had my back. That helped."

Rob started to say something, but then thought better of it. *Are you finally figuring it out?* Shane leaned forward to watch a plane landing.

"I think that's probably Ren's plane," he said, reaching for the CB.

"Bastiat's Ghost, you got your ears on?" he asked. He waited a moment. "Bastiat's Ghost, this is Maverick, come back."

"This is Bastiat's Ghost. I barely set down," Jacob said. "You got a truck? Ren came through with an enormous pharmacy order. I can't unload this all myself and I don't think my truck can carry it all. Over."

"Tell him we'll be there in 15." Rob wheeled around in the opposite direction.

"We're coming, Grandpa. Where's Cai? Over."

"Still in Wichita. He couldn't get back from the Governor's office by curfew, when I would have been grounded, so he'll come back with Ren. Over."

Shane and Rob exchanged glances, but when Shane went to speak into the microphone again, Rob waved him off.

"Ask him why he's arriving so late."

"What about Cai?"

"What about him? He's safe with Ren probably eating a nice meal and sleeping on high-count cotton sheets."

"You think Wichita is safe?"

"Why wouldn't it be?"

Shane stared out of the windshield for a long moment, then pulled out his cell phone and began texting.

"What aren't you saying?" Rob asked.

Shane finished and hit SEND.

"I broke Cai out of the Denver containment zone. If I hadn't been on the wrong side of Mission Ridge, I would have argued that he shouldn't go to Wichita. It never occurred to me in the midst of everything that was going on to ask my handler to scrub our images. He probably has a bot assigned to mine, but I'm not counting on him to have thought of Cai."

Rob rubbed his jaw, shooting glances at Shane.

"Who were you texting?" he asked.

"My handler. I'm not sure he'll get it, but I need his help to locate Cai in Wichita and bring him home."

Rob didn't say anything for a moment as the town dropped behind them, but Shane knew he was just formulating how to say whatever it was he meant to say.

"No," he said softly. "Take a deep breath and listen to me. Keep the current objects in view. The town needs you. *I* need you. I've got one cop, mine security guarding the interstate, Stan trying to push me into turning the towns into a prison camp to protect against looters .... I *need* you. Your brother is not stupid and he's with the richest man in Kansas who has enormous resources and is personal friends with the governor. He can get back here on his own. But the town cannot afford to lose anyone who has a clue about securing our borders. For once in your life, take an order and don't abandon us."

Abandon?

Rob turned into the airfield road and soon they were meeting Jacob on the tarmac. The old man needed a shave.

"You okay, Pa?" Rob asked.

"Tired," Jacob said. He glanced at his watch. "I'm way past my bedtime. I haven't had a shower or a shave in three days and I'm not sure I made the right decision with Cai. Nothing a good night's sleep and 30 less years of life won't cure." Then Jacob looked at Shane. "Do you really think drinking right now is a great idea?"

Shane surprised himself by chuckling. *You're lecturing me? He* didn't lecture me."

"He doesn't want to piss you off. I don't have to worry about that. So, can I go home and sleep? Can you two handle this?"

"Yes, go," Rob assured him. "Are there keys to that thing?"

Shane checked an incoming text.

"That's not how planes work. You should at least know that. There's a code for the door and a sequence of switches. I'll text the code to you since it appears we have cells back. Shane's the only one here that I know can fly it. You aren't going chasing after Cai, are you?"

"My handler says he'll make sure nobody is searching for Cai," Shane told Rob. "No. I'll wait. I can't fly right now and neither can you."

"Go home to bed, Pa. Shane and I'll get this order over to the medical center."

Jacob got into his truck. Rob's phone beeped and then Jacob drove away. Shane and Rob set about loading the pharmacy order into the bed of Rob's truck, using 2x4s in the sides braces with strapping to contain it all. His phone beeped while they worked and after reading the text, Shane climbed up into the plane to make sure everything was gone and then turned to Rob.

"Get off. I'm going to Wichita to get Cai."

"The hell you say," Rob replied. "You're not going anywhere until at least tomorrow."

"You're wrong. I'm going now. Cai's life is in danger."

"I said 'no'," Rob insisted.

"You can't exactly stop me. If you aren't getting off, you'd better buckle up and you might want to assign someone to get the pharmacy order."

Shane sat down in the pilot's seat and began punching buttons. He'd never qualified on this particular plane, but he'd flown one in simulator and he'd flown some similar planes. Fuel looked good. He reached to work through the ignition sequence. He never made it. Rob's arm came around his throat, dragging him over the back of the seat. He struggled against it, but his air was cut off and his head was firmly held. The dashboard wavered.

Killing me.

A syringe plunged into the soft tissue above his collar bone. Blessed air returned, but the lights were dimming. As he slid into the dark abyss, his last thought was he couldn't believe he'd been so dumb as to turn his back on a Vietnam vet.

Warnings

I'm working to scrub your brother. Next time, TELL US! G Shane's phone 10:33 pm

Door code 413250 Don't let him do what he's thinking of doing. Don't trust him. Jacob to Rob 10:37 pm

Your brother is running for his life. I can help, but he may need you. Tico Shane's phone 11:08 pm

Flee

Wichita

When Cai left Phil and started out on foot, he'd had 50 minutes to curfew. Now he had 10. His pace had picked up in anticipation of reaching his destination. He wasn't sure what he was supposed to do for the night, but he figured SullCo could put him up in an office, hopefully with a couch.

In the blocks he'd walked, Cai had figured out that he needed to avoid the drones and the military vehicles. He'd gotten pretty good at hiding his face under the bill of the cap and he deviated from course every time he saw an SUV with military markings. The map on his phone said he was still headed in the right direction, but he'd taken a roundabout way to get to SullCo.

He'd nearly reached his destination when he heard the whirr of a drone coming from the right. Before he could duck or turn his face away, he saw a flash. The drone continued on and Cai let out pent-up breath. *False alarm. Just keep walking. Another two blocks and you're headed home.*

A block and a half ahead, a military SUV turned into the street. Cai glanced behind him and saw another military SUV about three blocks back. He was passing a park, so he turned into the pathway. The street lights had already been turned off here, so he slunk into the shadows as he heard the sound of powerful engines moving up fast out on the streets. The darkness covered his movements, but it also made it difficult to see where he was going. He hit the map for a second to refresh his memory. On the far side of the park was Little Arkansas. There were streets north and south. He needed to get to one of them and run.

He could hear shouts and running footsteps behind him. Lights flared in front of him. Stuffing his phone into his pocket, he dodged left around the corner of a concrete building. There were beams coming from the south too. *Now what? Which way?* Instinctively, he moved away from his pursuers.

"Stop!" someone ordered. *What do I do? What would Shane do? He sure wouldn't stop!* Cai ran hard for the deeper darkness. Trees closed in on both sides. He veered right and then left again. Bullets struck the ground where he'd just been. *They're shooting at me? What the hell?* He ran faster. The uneven ground jarred his knees, but he didn't stop. Light passed over him. He veered left again and suddenly the ground dropped out from under his feet. He stumbled, slipped, tripped and spilled into water over his head. There was no up or down, mud filled his mouth and nose. He surfaced, heard shouting, sucked in a deep breath and dove. He let the current carry him along, waiting, hoping that the shouting would drop behind. When he surfaced and the shouting was distant, he rolled over onto his back with just his face above the water and floated with the current. He hadn't gone far, though, when he saw the beams playing across the water.

Drones? Not more drones.

He forced himself vertical in the water so he could see around. A short swim ahead would bring him to a bridge. To the west was a culvert. Every instinct Cai had said to strike out in flailing terror, but he remembered Shane calmly walking up to the roadblock at the Kanorado line. He aimed for the bank, gliding. The edge of the culvert was about two feet above the waterline. He scrambled hard to get into it. Light rimed the entrance just as he crawled deeper into the murky darkness. He froze, scared to breathe. The glow faded. He scrambled deeper. The far end of the culvert blazed. He froze as the entrance lit up again. He tucked his back against the curve of the pipe and held his breath. *Don't move!*

Because of the bank, the drones couldn't use their cameras to look directly into the culvert and Cai had stopped just shy of their reach. A beam passed within an inch of his left hand. He didn't move, feared to breathe. *Please, God! Please, please, please.* A car passed overhead, freaking him out. Cai held his breath, refused to move.

Suddenly complete darkness slammed down around him as the second drone flew off. Cai waited, ears straining at every sound. A car passed overhead. He couldn't hear the drones. Did that mean they'd gone? Or did that mean humans were following them? *Stay? Go? Which?* He crouched there shivering in the dark, afraid to move, while every instinct said he should run. His breathing echoed off the tunnel's walls. And then he heard the putt-putt of a boat on the river. The entrance to the culvert lit once more with light. He heard men's voices. Running wasn't going to work. He'd been caught.

"And what rough beast, its hour come round at last, slouches toward Bethlehem to be born?

William Butler Yeats

The End

A Taste of ...
A Threatening Fragility

Shane walked on the wall. It was the oddest thing. He stepped down from the dresser to the plaster wall, stepped over the photo of a surfer shredding a big Hawaiian wave.

His eyes closed. When he dragged them open again, Vi stood before him, a shushing finger to her lips. Her long grey-streaked black hair was loose, flowing over her shoulders, down past her hips.

"Don't tell them," she whispered.

"Tell them what, Grandma."

Exhaustion dragged his eyelids down. Next time he opened them, *she* danced before him in scarlet silks, a diaphanous veil covering her face and waist length hair. Her lower belly swelled with a baby. *Bang, pop, bang* and blood began to seep down her gown.

Shane snapped awake, sitting up, gripping the edge of the mattress as dizziness do-say-doed round his head.

My bedroom? How'd I get here? He tried to recall it. He'd been playing guitar at Callahans. There'd been beer and bourbon and ... *How much did I drink?*

Outside in the hall, he could hear Rob and Jacob talking in low urgent voices and then something rattled the house from the north.

He wobbled to the door and flung it open.

"What the hell just blew up? Someone bombing us?"

"I can see smoke northeast above Mission Ridge," Jacob reported and he and Rob moved toward Jacob's bedroom. Shane was slower, still dizzy. Curiously, he didn't have a headache and it didn't feel like he'd puked. He usually puked if he drank heavily.

Through Jacob's north-facing window, they could see massive billows of smoke, black and oily.

"You feel up to coming with?" Rob asked.

He was still wearing his jeans and t-shirt.

"Where's my 9?" he asked. Seeing a water bottle on Jacob's night stand, he opened it and drained it.

"I'll get it. Meet you at the truck two seconds from now. Pa, see if you can scare up the fire department. Looks like Brady's Tanks."

Shane donned his shoes while Rob raced up Willow Creek Run.

"Was I rude last night?"

Rob favored him with an odd expression. Far to the southwest, Shane heard the growling siren of a fire engine.

"You black out?"

"Weirdest damn dreams I've ever had," Shane complained. Ahead, the sky over the corn fields boiled with murky black smoke. A malevolent fog swept down to the ground. Shane closed the vents while Rob slowed. Debris lay in the road, in the street of the Tanks. Flames shot high and hot from what was left of the diner. Several other buildings were on fire, flames voraciously consuming their century-old wood. Shane stripped off his t-shirt and began wetting it with Rob's water bottle.

"It looks like the diner blew up," he observed. "Les and Molly lived above it. Oh, god! That's bad!"

Rob slammed on the brakes, swearing. Behind the conflagration of human structures, backlit by the dawn, was a much more frightening sight.

Rob grabbed the CB mic.

"Anyone with their ears on. All hands to Brady Tanks immediately. Bring buckets, hoses, blankets, anything that can transport water. The corn fields are on fire. Repeat, the corn fields are on fire."

The Story Continues

Other Lela Markham Titles

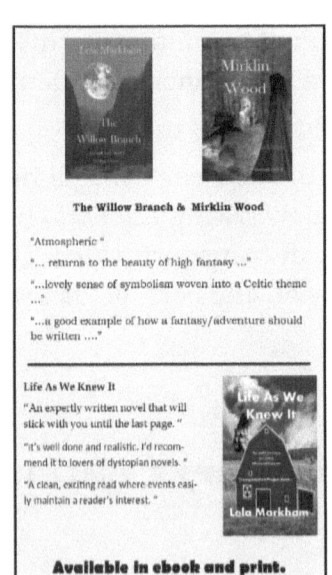

Other Great
Breakwater Harbor Books

Moscow, 2138. With the world only beginning to recover from the complete societal collapse of the late 21st Century, Zoya scrapes by prepping corpses for funerals and dreams of saving enough money to have a child. When her brother forces her to bring him a mysterious package, she witnesses his murder and finds herself on the run from ruthless mobsters. Frantically trying to stay alive and save her loved ones, Zoya opens the package and discovers two unusual data cards, one that allows her to fight back against the mafia and another which may hold the key to everlasting life.

www.breakwaterharborbooks.com

Meet Lela Markham

Hi. I was raised in a house made of books in Alaska and told tales from the time I could talk. A teacher eventually made me write one of them down. I hated the exercise, but it was the spark that ignited a fire that has never gone out.

My daring husband, two fearless offspring and I live the adventure of a lifetime here on the Last Frontier where the midnight sun encourages wandering the wilderness and the long dark winters favor reading, writing and staring at the northern lights … hence the moniker Aurorawatcher.

It's all about the aurora watching!

www.ingramcontent.com/pod-product-compliance
Lightning Source LLC
Chambersburg PA
CBHW051313250626
47155CB00007B/2299